Beat The Brigante

Celtic Fervour Series

Book 5

Nancy Jardine

Ocelot Press

Copyright © 2020 by Nancy Jardine

Cover Artwork: Karen Barrett

Beathan The Brigante
All rights reserved. No part of this book may be stored, shared, copied, transmitted or reproduced in any way without the express written permission from the author, except for brief quotations used for promotion, or in reviews. This is a work of fiction. Names, characters, places, and incidents are used fictitiously.

***First Edition** Nancy Jardine with Ocelot Press 2020*

"The entire series is set firmly among the very best of early Romano British novels."
Helen Hollick Discovering Diamond Reviews.

Find Nancy Jardine online:
http://www.nancyjardineauthor.com/
Join Nancy Jardine on Facebook:
https://www.facebook.com/NancyJardinewrites
Follow Nancy Jardine's blog:
https://nancyjardine.blogspot.com/
Follow Nancy on Twitter: @nansjar

Nancy loves to hear from her readers and can be contacted at nan_jar@btinternet.com or via her blog and website.

Dedication

I've been finalising this story during what has been an incredibly difficult period for the whole globe – that of the Covid 19 pandemic. However, lockdown in my part of Aberdeenshire, Scotland, has not been complete isolation for myself and my husband. Since our older daughter and her family live next door, our isolation has been 'relative'. We have a wraparound garden situation and my grandchildren of 8 and 6 years have grown up playing in my part, as well as in their own.

Though they were unable to visit my house, and vice versa, I would see and hear them playing around and about when I was re-developing my side garden (a lockdown project of mine). Even though I taught primary pupils for more than 25 years, I am still awed by the imagination of children. I'd hear my grandkids acting out some new scenario while I was riddling granite chips to separate the good earth from pernicious weeds. Sometimes they'd come close, though always heartbreakingly aware of social distancing (no hugs allowed at this point in time) and ask me about this, or the other. I'd give them advice, or compliment their dramatic creations. Mostly, I'd just enjoy the energy and imagination they were bringing to their outdoor play.

This novel *Beathan The Brigante* brings my Garrigill Clan tales full circle with the baby of Book 1 taking the lead role in Book 5 – even though he is only a young man of seventeen. I like to think that my Beathan was as imaginative as my grandkids when he was a seven-year-old at the Hillfort of Garrigill, before he became a refugee fleeing from the ravages of Roman invasion. And from the age of eight, I'm sure any role play would have taken Beathan out of what was his current hazardous norm, though I have a hunch that, at some point, he would have been fighting those 'baddie' Roman legionaries!

I dedicate *Beathan The Brigante*, Book 5 of my *Celtic Fervour Saga series*, to my grandchildren Annalise and Riley, whom I love so very dearly. Long may their imaginations soar.

Acknowledgements

I want to send a huge thank you to my fellow authors in the Ocelot Press co-operative – and in particular for this novel to Sue Barnard, Vanessa Couchman, Yvonne Marjot, Stephanie Patterson and Jen Wilson. They give me continuous help and encouragement throughout the whole writing process. They assist with beta reading and editing which is invaluable, and a particular mention goes to Sue this time for some excellent editing suggestions. Lending their expertise and advice comes so naturally to all of my Ocelot colleagues, and it's very much appreciated.

I also give thanks to my cover designer Karen Barrett for designing the wonderful cover for *Beathan The Brigante* which matches the other four books of the series. From my vague idea, she has produced the perfect cover image for the story.

Contents

Characters in Beathan The Brigante
Map of places mentioned in Beathan The Brigante
Map of journey to Rome via Gaul
Chapter One
Chapter Two
Chapter Three
Chapter Four
Chapter Five
Chapter Six
Chapter Seven
Chapter Eight
Chapter Nine
Chapter Ten
Chapter Eleven
Chapter Twelve
Chapter Thirteen
Chapter Fourteen
Chapter Fifteen
Chapter Sixteen
Chapter Seventeen
Chapter Eighteen
Chapter Nineteen
Chapter Twenty
Chapter Twenty-One
Chapter Twenty-Two
Chapter Twenty-Three
Chapter Twenty-Four
Chapter Twenty-Five
Chapter Twenty-Six
Chapter Twenty-Seven
Chapter Twenty-Eight
Chapter Twenty-Nine
Chapter Thirty
Chapter Thirty-One
Chapter Thirty-Two

Chapter Thirty-Three
Chapter Thirty-Four
Chapter Thirty-Five
Chapter Thirty-Six
Chapter Thirty-Seven
Chapter Thirty-Eight
Chapter Thirty-Nine
Chapter Forty
Chapter Forty-One
Map of Tribes in Beathan The Brigante
Glossary
Historical Context
Author's Notes
About the Author
Other Novels by Nancy Jardine
Nominations
Ocelot Press

Beathan The Brigante

Characters in Beathan The Brigante

A – *Agricola (Gnaeus Iulius, General of the legions and Governor of Britannia)*; Aonghas (of Alaunas)

B – *Barrus (Calvus, Centurion at Trimontium)*; *Bassianus (Quintus, Tribune at Pinnata Castra)*; Beathan (of Garrigill, son of Lorcan and Nara); Brennus (of Garrigill, Beathan's uncle)

C – Cailean (of Alaunas); Cathal (hostage); *Crispus (Agricola's secretary)*

D – Derwi (Taexali hostage)

E – Enya (of Garrigill, Beathan's cousin)

F – *Flavinus (Signum of the Turma of Candidus at Corstopitum)*

G – Gillean (Caledon hostage)

L – *Liberalis (Gaius Salvius, Judicial Legate)*; Lorcan (of Garrigill, Beathan's father)

M – Mearna (of Garrigill, Beathan's aunt at Eboracum Fortress)

N – Niamh (of Alaunas); Nith (of Tarras)

S – *Secundus (Attius, Commander at Trimontium Fort)*; Senan (hostage); Seumas (of Alanaus)

T – *Tertius (cook at Trimontium Fort)*; Torquil (of Dunrelugas); Torrin (of Alaunas)

V – *Verecundus (Commander at Vindolanda Fort, also called the Praefectus)*

Please see the glossary section at the end of the book for other characters who are named, though play no dialogue role in the story. The meanings of some of the above character names can also be found at the end of the book.

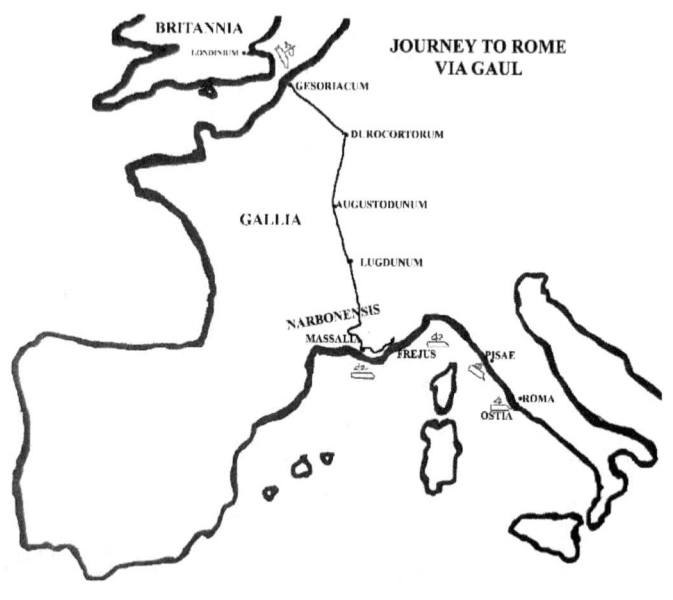

Chapter One

Trimontium Roman Fort AD 85

"Your mother is a Brigante?"

The commander's words were in the tongue of the tribes, but they were hesitant and came slowly.

Beathan stared at the smooth wooden planking beneath his feet and forced himself to stay alert, though could not prevent himself from swaying towards the edge of the wooden table in front of him.

"Answer!"

When the tip of the centurion's vine rod stabbed under his chin, he managed to gather enough strength to raise his head, fully expecting another jaw slap, but it did not come. Weary of the repeated questions, and the pummelling he had already received from the all-too-willing centurion, his answer was faint.

"Nay, I told you already that my mother Nara is the daughter of Callan of Tarras, of the Selgovae."

"Then you are Selgovae."

Commander Secundus was dismissive, as though there could be no other answer.

Too often, during his long journey to this place, he had been gut-wrenchingly repentant over revealing his kinship. He regretted naming his mother and father. He did not even know if they were still alive and he had gone through many moments of self-pity, but those feelings were now replaced by a gnawing resentment.

"Nay. I am a Brigante. I am named as the tribe of my father."

Commander Secundus looked up at him from his seated position. The man's brawny forearms were placed flush with the table-top, and bracketed an open wooden tablet. With difficulty, Beathan focused on the man's grimy right-hand fingernails as they tapped a short rhythm against the smooth surface till the commander finished a calculating, shrewd-eyed inspection.

He had lost count of how many times the senior soldier had asked the same questions.

A swift conversation in Latin followed between Commander Attius Secundus and Centurion Calvus Barrus, only a little of which he understood. They discussed something about the Selgovae tribe though exactly what he could not be sure. Even if he understood all of the words, he was not certain he would know what they referred to anyway.

A fleeting memory of his grandfather's roundhouse came to him. The irascible old Callan's parting words were telling him to never trust the neighbouring Votadini tribe. Callan had never needed to remind him about not trusting the Roman Empire; he knew that from a babe-in-arms.

He focused again on the two men in the room who seemed to be agreeing about something, from the short nods that the centurion was making.

"You say this Callan had a hillfort at Tarras? Where is this place?"

Beathan bit back on the snorted answer he wanted to make, but he was sure the commander would not appreciate any sarcasm. He set his gaze to just above the soldier's head, reluctant to look at the man's penetrating stare.

"I have no idea where I am, just now, so I cannot give you any direction."

The awkward silence lasted too long but, at least, the centurion's nasty stick remained still. He made himself think harder.

"My family trekked northwards to Tarras, when our Brigante Hillfort of Garrigill was in danger of being totally destroyed by…"

An unexpected image of his father lifting a cautionary finger halted his reckless tongue. He paused to lick his chapped lips, suppressing his anxiety about the unknown fate of his father, while he sought some self-control and a better tone. Laying blatant blame on his captors was not the approach that Lorcan of the Brigantes, would ever take. His father was a superior negotiator, as well as a skilled warrior, and would never advocate careless words.

Drawing in a calming breath through his nostrils, he resumed. "To reach Tarras, we journeyed over the high hills that separate the territory of the northernmost Brigantes from the Selgovae."

As before, a soft conversation continued between the two Roman soldiers, though Beathan felt the stare of Commander Secundus even more acutely.

"You have recently been to this Hillfort of Tarras?" the commander prompted.

A deep sigh could not be helped as he righted his tottering balance once more.

"Nay, it was many seasons ago that my Brigante clan were there."

The commander continued to tap his nails against the table.

"Is this stronghold of Tarras the hillfort of the *Ard Righ* of the Selgovae?"

This time Beathan sought the senior soldier's gaze. There was no question of his giving away any important information. Risking yet another stab from the vine rod, he shook his head. "I know nothing of the high chief, or the whereabouts of his hillfort. Callan of Tarras was an important warrior, but he was never the Selgovae High Chief."

On seeing the tiniest of acknowledgements flashing between the commander and the centurion, he just managed to tighten his stomach muscles before the vine rod slashed forward. It missed his chest bones but smacked across his forearms, the clang against the metal wrist band echoing in the small room. Doubling over in sheer agony, he almost did not hear the crowing words of Centurion Barrus.

"The Callan you speak of is long dead and his hillfort is razed to the ground."

From a curled position at the soldier's feet, he suspected an answer was not required. He had heard of his grandfather's death some seasons ago, but that Callan's dwellings were wiped from the landscape was new to him. He sent a silent plea to his mother's goddess *Rhianna*, to give succour to any survivors from Tarras.

"This Brigante will remain here at Trimontium when the slave trader claims his purchases." Commander Secundus' tone continued in a disparaging vein after a swift check of the open wooden tablet. "Find uses for this young Brigante around the fort – tasks that will not kill him – till I receive further orders. Along with the other four hostages from Taexali territory, this one has a significance we have yet to learn about."

While Beathan was hauled to his feet, and bundled out of the room into the icy bite of the night, he forced his muddled head to remember that the fort he was in was named Trimontium, not the Corstopitum supply fort that he thought he was being taken to. Lurching in front of the centurion's prodding weapon, the most significant thing he could think of was that Trimontium was probably in traitorous Votadini territory. And the Votadini tribe, in the pay of the Roman Empire, was as much of an enemy as the Romans were themselves. He needed to remember that if he escaped…

Shoved along a dim walkway, the only illumination in the night-dark being a flickering fire some distance away, he prayed to the goddess *Brigantia* to help him bear the situation he was in. Though, of late, none of his pleas to any of his gods, or goddesses, had given him any encouragement that he was being listened to.

Centurion Barrus' grip at the back of his iron neck collar forced his shackled and shuffling feet around a corner. Only a short way along the path, the man brought him to an abrupt stop in front of a guarded doorway.

Barrus' voice grated at the soldier on duty. "Open up. This one makes the fifth hostage who will remain here at Trimontium."

The guard lost no time in sliding open the huge iron fastener that locked the room from the outside.

Barrus was not done.

"The commander might have singled them out till he receives further orders, but see that this lot get just the same treatment as any of our other fort slaves."

Thrust into the gloom of the tiny room, Beathan's ankle chains tripped him up. His bound hands reached forward to soften his fall, but it was impossible to prevent himself from landing on top of one of the room's shadowy occupants.

Wakened so abruptly, the man's arm lashed at Beathan's face, the solid fist to his nose making his head swim even more than it had been.

"Get off me! *Ròmanach buachar each*!" The man's snarls rang around the room.

Beathan's own oath was muffled around a stream of dripping blood.

When the man below him realised it was another poor unfortunate that had pummelled him, and not an aggressive Roman guard – or even an amorous one – the knowledge hardly made a dent in his displeasure.

"Aye! Those Romans are horse shite right enough, but so will you be if you do not move off into your own place."

Making an awkward attempt to roll free, Beathan's slurred apology was brushed off by a different occupant of the room.

"Save your grumbles till the morning. We need all the sleep we can get."

From the silence around him, Beathan decided that the second man wielded some power over the others. Using the edge of his grubby sleeve, he stopped the flow of fresh blood from slithering into his mouth. Exhausted by all of the recent events, he curled himself into a ball and forced reality away.

But not before he vowed that someday he would kill every Roman soldier in Britannia.

Chapter Two

Pinnata Castra Roman Fortress AD 85

General Gnaeus Iulius Agricola brought his horse to a standstill and surveyed the area, the exhalation of his breath a white puff in the bitter air.

"You have no notion of how I have hungered for this sight."

Alongside him, Gaius Salvius Liberalis – his most senior *judicial legate* in Britannia – pulled up likewise.

Before answering, Gaius held up an arm to halt the long trail which consisted of his mounted guard and Gaius' own, all of whom clopped along behind them. Gaius indicated the *signifer* of the infantry protection should raise his standard, then turned back to him.

"Surely, sir, it is a fortress built to resemble many others?" Gaius' tone was droll.

"That fortress is unparalleled, and you know it!"

He pulled his gaze from the scene to look at his companion, his wide smile an unaccustomed feeling since a taut sober mien was more typical.

"Many times, during this last campaign in Caledonia, I have been so tempted to abandon my objective of reaching the furthermost tip of Britannia. Yet the daily struggle, to find beneficial reasons for remaining in these bleak barbarian lands, has been balanced by the knowledge that this fortress right here, at Pinnata Castra, is the pinnacle of my success."

"That spark of enthusiasm in your eyes, sir, tells me much about your feelings." Gaius' responding smirk was conspiratorial without lessening any of the respect necessary for a senior. "It is a twinkle that has been missing since I joined you here in the north. There is no doubt that this formidable fortress will play its part in the ultimate conquest of Caledonia, even if your successor has yet to know its worth."

"*Jupiter*'s arse licker!" His outburst continued in a pithy vein.

"Definitely someone's." Gaius' chuckle was hearty. "Without doubt."

"And who might my successor be? Has our esteemed Emperor Domitian made up his mind about that in any of your recent correspondence? Information you have withheld from me?" He could not resist the tease. There were few men he really relied on, and in whom he had complete faith. Gaius Salvius Liberalis was definitely one of those.

One of Gaius' eyebrows hitched up a fraction. "My information on the issue of your successor is just as lacking as yours is, sir. This western rim of the empire is very remote from Rome, and the latest information hard to come by."

"You mean gossip is well-dissipated before it reaches us in Caledonia?"

A distant, raucous hollering drew his attention before Gaius could add the rude response he looked ready to make. He swivelled in the saddle to search the river that lay down to his left. A solitary flat-bottomed vessel slowly approached the landing stage, the *gubernator* calling the commands to bring the craft to a halt alongside the small queue of boats that were already moored at the river edge. Ships, he guessed, that lay idle because the day had been too winter-squally for any of them to venture down river, and out into the Mare Germanicum. The weather was hazardous, yet he needed those ships to be constantly on the move, ferrying the necessary provisions to feed his too-often-hungry troops in the north.

He dipped his head and thanked *Tempestas* because she had eventually improved the conditions, though the day was too well-gone for any further fleet movement.

The River Tava provided a perfect transport link for the installations near Pinnata Castra, one of the main reasons that he had chosen this particular site. But plying up river in driving squalls was too much of a challenge for most of his fleet. He also gave thanks to *Neptune* that the small vessel, just tying up, had been well-manned. He could not afford to lose any of his mariners.

"Where do you think that arrival has come from?"

Gaius paused to take a good look at the river before giving him an answer. "Given that the skies only cleared for us a short while ago, when that brutal wind of earlier eased, I cannot imagine it has travelled farther than from the river estuary. Though, no doubt you will make sure to find out soon."

Agricola watched his companion patiently calming his restless mount. They had pushed their horses since daybreak against driving, chilling gusts. It was no surprise the beast was itching to be free of its burden. His own mount was just as weary.

He smiled in answer to Gaius' statement. "I certainly will. Though, given how small that vessel is, there are more likely to be dispatches on it rather than a year's worth of grain!"

Gaius' grunt confirmed the probability. "Maybe a month's worth, if *Fortuna* has been heeding our needs. From its size, I would hazard none at all."

Looking forward to at least gaining new reports from the local area, or even better from further afield, Agricola twisted back to face the impressive view that lay ahead of him.

Situated on the plateau above the floodplain, and close to a tight bend of the River Tava, the fortress was excellently placed for monitoring the surrounding area. In the north-western backdrop were the fringes of the

Caledonian Mountains, and beyond them there were many days' worth of higher peaks, which had the bleakest of terrains most of the year around. Mountainous territory which was still firmly in the keeping of the local Caledon tribes, and of their allies, those tribes who had fled their own lands after his Roman forces had occupied them.

A profound frustration gripped the smile off his face.

"Does the sight of Pinnata Castra displease you now?" Gaius' question sounded confused.

"Not the fortress. I particularly chose this site for its strategic position. The lack of manpower available to carry out my plans is what exasperates me."

"Ah!" Gaius was circumspect, as always.

"You of all people know that with sufficient resources, it will be easy to establish an effective and successful monitoring situation from Pinnata Castra."

He pointed his left index finger towards the north-west, to the hilltops peering just above the tree line, anger mounting in his tone. "Maintaining a controlled flow at each and every entrance to that huge mountain expanse is a formidable challenge I am desperate to tackle…"

Gaius dared to interrupt. "But you are now duty-bound to pass that task on to your replacement, the man who will be the next Governor of Britannia."

"Yes, by *Jupiter*! May he lose his mind, and his eyes be riddled with maggots!" Further, more explicit, curses spilled forth. "That unknown candidate, the person who is no doubt currently, and successfully, courting Emperor Domitian's favours…"

He broke off to curb his temper, though only managed moments. "Even though accepting the post will be a hazardous venture for him given that Domitian is as capricious and mischievous as the god *Mercurius*!"

He suppressed a shiver of apprehension. He was definitely not in Domitian's favour, and his future in Rome was not looking to be an optimistic one. What was positive, though, was the inspiring construction in front of him. He knew, for his own sanity, that he must focus on that.

Drawing in a deep breath of the chilly air, he summoned a smile for his second-in-command in Britannia.

"This fortress is the essential element for subduing and controlling this last stronghold of barbarian rule on the western fringes of the empire. You know it is all within Rome's grasp now. All we need in Caledonia is one more summer campaign."

Gaius' focus was intent on him.

"If it is in my power to continue with your plans, sir, you know I will have them carried out. But you also know, only too well, that my position here is merely tolerated by many of Domitian's associates. My posting to Britannia – an exile in all but name – means less blood on their hands, but that could change in a blink."

Agricola dipped his head and clicked his horse into movement. The topic was over for the moment. Gaius was constantly alert to personal danger and had in place his own first-rate protection.

The inability to personally hand over the reins of Britannic power to his unknown successor badly irritated him but, in the meantime, he was still in control while he wended his way southwards to Londinium.

He could easily have taken passage on a ship from the Taexali coast, berthing only when necessary and bypassing most of Caledonia as he sailed south. Yet, he was determined to enjoy every moment he could spend at this very fortress that he intended to be a pivotal base.

Domitian may have recalled him to Rome; however, his emperor had not specified an arrival date. It was still the winter season, disruption to travel was commonplace, and any traveller reaching Rome safely, and for a particular time, was in the hands of the goddess *Salus*.

While his mount clopped comfortably along the road that had been recently laid with gravel, on the north side of the River Tava – a refreshing change from the mostly beaten-earth tracks that peppered the area – he was pleased to see organized activity in the temporary camps not far from the perimeter walls of the fortress. The bustle of a dismantling process taking place in the nearest encampment was unmistakeable. A file of heavily-stacked low-bedded wagons trundling away from it, all heading towards the eastern gate, was a sure sign of their purpose.

"The interior barrack blocks for the *Legio XX*'s First Cohort must be completed." He could not banish the glow of satisfaction from both words and grin.

"It would appear so," Gaius answered. "Did yesterday's communications not indicate this stage was imminent?"

"They did, and I can see that Quintus Bassianus looks eager to confirm it." He reined in his horse.

The soldier approaching him at a trot brought his mount to a halt before he saluted. "Welcome back to Pinnata Castra, sir. I trust your journey here was uneventful?"

Agricola acknowledged his greeting. "It was. No marauding tribespeople caused us any aggravation, so our progress has been unhindered from the fort at Tameia. In reasonable time, due to that new road laid around the infernal marshes. Was it created by the *Legio XX?*"

Bassianus accepted the unsaid compliment with a dip of his head. "My Fourth Cohort senior centurion is in charge of quarrying the local stone, but the auxiliary vexillation attached to the *Legio II Adiutrix* can claim most of the credit, sir, for the labour involved in the actual gravel laying of the roads close to Pinnata Castra."

Agricola pointed towards the fortress. "Are they also responsible for adding that stone facing to the rampart?"

"Not presently, sir. A half-century from the *Legio XX* are making steady progress on it. When fewer patrols are needed to scour the local forests for the interior wood supplies, more men will become available for the stonework."

Gaius intervened. "When I was last here, you told me there was little urgency about adding the facing. Has that situation changed?"

"No, sir. The Caledon allies seem fairly quiet just now. We have had a few skirmishes lately, some ten miles to the south, but no direct attacks on Pinnata Castra have come from the mountains."

Agricola allowed himself a grin. "Just make sure that the fortress always appears over-manned to the enemy. Let them think you are always working from full-strength."

"Our *speculatores* are doing a grand job of informing us about enemy movements in the area. Sufficient for us to fill the rampart platforms in a blink."

Agricola acknowledged the information then let his gaze span around. "It has been far too long since I was here, Tribune Bassianus, and many changes have taken place that I am eager to inspect." He pointed to the organised removal of goods from the temporary camp. "If I am not to have the pleasure of being billeted in that *Legio XX* camp…" His beam belied any censure in his inquiry. "Where do you suggest?"

Quintus Bassianus, *Tribunus Laticlavius* of the *Legio XX,* maintained a straight face though the twinkle in his eyes was not suppressed. "I am sure the men will turn the wagons around and re-erect the camp, if that is really where you want to be, sir?"

Agricola's chortle startled the horse beneath him and set it to pawing the ground.

"Or, you might prefer the best room in northern Caledonia, which just happens to be available for your use?"

"Legate Liberalis told me that the first of the stone housing was ready some weeks ago, in the temporary officer compound?" Agricola clicked his horse into motion expecting everyone to follow, too eager as he was to see all of the progress on site.

"Three of them are now built, though their interiors are still basic." Bassianus updated more details, his horse keeping pace.

Agricola acknowledged the progress. "Whatever is still lacking cannot be worse than a tent in Taexali territory."

Gaius on his other side was more definite. "I will happily sleep in a tent, so long as I can get into that bathhouse, which was not quite ready when I stopped here on my way north."

The words were really more of a question which Bassianus was happy to answer.

"The furnace was tested yesterday, and all the interiors are being inspected again today. Their finishes are somewhat different from what you would find in the Londinium governor's accommodation, but we are confident our plastering will hold, till a properly tiled bathhouse is built for the fortress. You will be the first to sample the luxury of our first northern Caledonian bathing facility, sir, whether your stay is only a day or a much longer one."

Behind him Agricola heard Gaius' small snort, the man's reaction astute. His second-in-command was most likely going to have to prise him away from the ramparts because a day was not nearly enough time to enjoy being at Pinnata Castra.

He signalled forward his personal guard leader and issued instructions, after which the soldier headed off towards the officers' compound with a small detachment of his men and the baggage wagons.

An immediate use of the bathhouse appealed greatly, but his own comfort would have to wait. His priority was to inspect the progress inside the fortress. Rather than interrupt the flow of wagons entering via the east gate, he nudged his horse towards the main entrance, the *porta principalis,* with Bassianus alongside, Gaius and the remainder of his mounted guard in his wake.

"Look at that, Legate Liberalis." He grinned over his shoulder to where Gaius encouraged his tired mount to keep going.

Gaius stopped patting the horse's neck and looked up, his brows knotting. "What am I looking at?"

Agricola felt more spirited, affected so much by being at Pinnata Castra that his response was an intended tease.

"Think, man! Where else am I going to ride into a legionary fortress with such ease? Name me another one that has such a wide gateway, with no staggered access defences in front of it to slow down entry?"

Gaius eventually understood his humour. "Are you so certain that it will not be invaded by those bothersome Caledonians, in their thousands, while you sleep this night, sir? Even though there are multiple ditches surrounding the fortress on this plateau?"

"Ha!" He was absolutely sure. "They almost wiped out the *Legio IX* some seasons ago, but that will never happen again! Oh, I expect they will make many small attacks, but another pitched battle after our victory at Beinn na Ciche? That will be highly unlikely."

Gaius did not look convinced. One poor consolation was that he would likely be far off in Rome by the time the Caledonian allies mustered up the courage, and more importantly, the numbers to wage another mass attack.

Chapter Three

Pinnata Castra Roman Fortress AD 85

After passing through the main gate entrance, Agricola paused to behold the sight. The fortress was the largest in northern Caledonia. It was almost comparable in size to the legionary fortress of Eboracum, in Brigante territory, which had been first constructed during the governorship of General Quintus Petillius Cerialis. On his own first visit to Eboracum, the headquarters of the *Legio IX,* he had been highly impressed with its location.

The landscape currently around him was nothing like the countryside around Eboracum, but he had remembered the practicality of building close to a strategic river source when he chose his site for Pinnata Castra.

The immense anticipation he was currently experiencing was because his northern fortress would be manned by the *Legio XX*, the Britannic legion he felt most affinity to, and the one he had cut his own legate teeth on.

Unused ground had abounded the last time he had set foot inside Pinnata Castra, but that was no longer the situation. Alongside him, the *intervallum* space that lay just inside the fortress ramparts now had proper drainage channels installed, the earth hard-packed by the troops during drills and manoeuvres. As far as he knew, there had been no reason for the intervallum to be tested in an enemy attack, but the area was typically wide enough to protect his men from any stray weapons that might come over the walls.

Stretching way ahead of him, up the *via praetoria,* small *tabernae* booths lined both sides. Some of the barn-door tops were open, but most of them were closed to keep the biting winds from chilling the contents of the storage rooms.

Agricola gestured to his right-hand side indicating the roof that loomed up behind the row of tabernae. "Was the southern granary built when you were last here, Legate Liberalis?"

Gaius nodded. "The roof was being worked on. And the barrack blocks behind it, to that side, had their walls up but no roofs."

Tribune Bassianus added more. "That granary is now fully complete, General Agricola, though it is not the one we are currently using."

He watched Bassianus turn towards Gaius after his update on the granary, the man preening over the achievements of his soldiers. "The accommodation blocks were checked and passed inspection yesterday. Units of the *Legio XX* are currently moving in."

The tribune's information was unnecessary since he had already noticed the laden baggage carts, but he nodded his approval. "The construction engineers and builders have done a fine job, given that the winter weather in Caledonia has not always been favourable for progress."

Dismounting, he handed his horse over to his personal groom and strode on towards the centre of the fortress with Gaius and Bassianus clicking at his heels.

Acknowledging the many salutes from soldiers he encountered along the route, his questions were endless.

"Yes, sir," said Bassianus, answering yet another. "The supply wagons coming north have re-established a…more regular routine."

"I detect hesitation in that answer. I want the truth. Not what you think I need to hear. So, the attacks on the convoys have not stopped?"

"Not entirely, sir. I have already doubled most of the patrols covering the ground between our small fortlets, but those sneaky Caledons still manage to slip through. There is no way of predicting where they might strike along our roadway."

Agricola heard Gaius' sighs of frustration; the man's tones clipped when he spoke. "Have your native scouts lost their wits as well as their tongues?"

Bassianus bristled. "Legate Liberalis, none of my present scouts have Caledon roots. Neither are they from local Venicones territory. These highlands, forests and marshes are as new to them as they are to us. It takes time for them to infiltrate to the extent that they can send us back reliable information."

"You have had no Caledon chiefs knocking at your gates to pledge their allegiance, recently?" Agricola's words seemed jocular, but they did little to hide the real situation.

He watched his most senior tribune at Pinnata Castra awkwardly swallow before Bassianus spoke.

"I have not, sir. They mostly skulk in the mountains, but like the large wildcats who dwell within their territory, they like to find a new piece of wood to scrape their claws against now and again."

Agricola's reply was determined. "Then we must anticipate more effectively those times when they feel the need to scratch at our installations, especially our smaller guard posts and fortlets. Rome cannot conclude the conquering of those cowardly survivors until we have all of their leaders in chains!"

"Sir." Bassianus' response was automatic, yet his expression mirrored the huge responsibilities involved.

"Have any of the captives that were taken after the battle at Beinn na Ciche ended up here?"

Bassianus' headshake was definite. "No, sir. We have some captives taken during local skirmishes, but none came from the northern pitched battle."

He turned to Gaius. "Have you had word of where the Taexali chiefs are now, Legate Liberalis? Those who were taken hostage in the north?"

The friendly interaction and relaxation of formality with Gaius was over for the time being. He had to ensure that all of the fort commanders they encountered on their journey south would do Gaius' bidding after he left Britannia – at least until the new governor of the province was installed.

"They should be at Trimontium, sir," Gaius answered. "The instructions were to hold the high-ranking hostages there, till further notice."

Agricola nodded approval before turning back to Bassianus, the demands perfectly clear in his tone. "In the future send any captured chiefs, or those you deem important tribespeople, to Trimontium."

Two-thirds of the way along via praetoria he stopped to admire the large building on his right before passing through its entrance doors. Stretching towards the eastern gateway its open courtyard was flanked by various rooms, some double tabernae size.

"How has this courtyard area been used so far?" he asked.

Bassianus cleared his throat. "The senior centurion of the *Legio II Adiutrix* likes this space for drilling his men, sir. Since it presently has no particular designation, I thought it a reasonable use for it."

"There is no lack of space for drilling all of the troops together in this fortress, but if the units of *Legio II Adiutrix* prefer their own space, I have no objections. And it sounds as though the camp prefect has found no reason to disapprove either." Agricola laughed, thinking of the next huge empty space he was likely to encounter. "Is the *Praefectus Castrorum* so busy that he cannot welcome me?"

Bassianus was quick to make excuses. "He is presently haranguing the men who are currently moving into their new accommodation. I have informed him of your arrival."

After a quick poke around the storerooms, Agricola strode ahead of his followers out of the complex. Passing a few more of the typical tabernae doorways, he stopped at the corner to admire what would eventually be a thoroughly busy via praetoria.

An empty space denoted where the *praetorium* would be situated, in good time, but the construction of the commander's living accommodations had no present priority. His eyes instead were drawn to the structure that was proving to be a critical part of the fortress already.

"You are to be congratulated, Tribune Bassianus, for getting the hospital ready in time for that first batch of patients. What has their survival rate been like?"

He watched Bassianus' mouth change from an initial smile of appreciation to one of regret. "The senior *medicus* will give you a full report, sir. Though, generally speaking, about one-third of the original patients are back on duty. Many of the subsequent arrivals are almost back to full strength and will soon resume their posts. Those who died would probably have survived the sickness had they not been so undernourished on arrival, and had their transportation not been hampered by poor weather conditions."

That was not news to him. He had had regular enough reports of the progress of the men who had been deliberately poisoned, the Taexali natives having tampered with the water supply near the Durno temporary camp.

"Would those back to duties have managed that so quickly if they had not been cared for in the *valetudinarium*?"

"Doubtful, sir. Their more spacious accommodations, and the rations issued during recuperation, have been much enhanced as you requested. And, strange though it is to me, being cared for in the hospital wing has encouraged most of them to get back to their own small *contubernium* group as quickly as they were able."

"Something about the hospital they do not find so nice after all?" Agricola smirked having an idea what the cause was.

Gaius intervened. "I heard the sharp tongue and promises made by the senior surgeon when I stayed here on my northward journey. I would say that perhaps the threat of his instruments was an incentive to get better as rapidly as possible, sir. I heard a few of the patients declaring that suffering days of crippling watery stools was preferable to the surgeon's forceps being flashed anywhere near them. The surgeon is widely respected for his skills, though he is not particularly known for his easy-going manner."

On arrival at the valetudinarium, a youthful medical orderly led him to the chief surgeon.

A short while later, Agricola headed back out of the hospital block, his smirk not seen by the chief surgeon who remained by the open door. He was well-satisfied. Any injured and sick soldiers would be competently attended to and sent back to duties without delay after recovery – whether or not the chief surgeon had a full complement of orderlies, or only the few presently assigned to him.

A valetudinarium was not a feature of every fortress he had been associated with, but he was determined that the one at Pinnata Castra would be worth every effort spent to create it and keep it running efficiently.

Striding into one of the new granaries, he gestured Gaius to come closer to him, keeping his tones low. "This should have almost a full year's worth of grain stored in here by now, but look at how meagre the supplies are. If the men further north had been on better than sub-basic rations, they might not have succumbed so easily to the tampering of the water supply in Taexali territory."

Gaius nodded. "I read your reports."

Agricola's growled response was not for Bassianus' ears. "This lack of readiness in Caledonia cannot continue, Gaius. I do not want my legacy to be of empty granaries and starving troops!"

Chapter Four

Trimontium Roman Fort AD 85

"Get a move on with that sack! You shouldered a much heavier one a few days ago."

Beathan lengthened his strides, though not by much, as he passed the hollering soldier on duty at the entrance to the praetorium, on a route he had trodden many times during the last long moon. He did what he had to do to avoid the stab of a *pilum*, and a spiteful tongue lashing, but enthusiasm never played a part.

Investigating the sudden commotion, Tertius' sweat-glistened bald head popped out of the doorway of the kitchen at the far end of the portico. "In here, you lazy Brigante, and be quick about it."

Beathan resisted the urge to shout back as he slapped his feet down the wooden walkway, passing door after door along the edge of the courtyard which lay at the heart of the fort commander's spacious living quarters. Being called a Brigante was never a problem, but being named lazy always jarred. He was at the beck and call of almost every soldier in Trimontium, and they all wanted him to complete tasks instantly, whether in snow or shine.

On his entry into the kitchen, just the smell of food made his stomach protest loudly. Ignoring the noisy rumble, the cook pointed to a corner of the small room where wooden shelves were fixed to the roughly-daubed and whitened wall. An assortment of clay pitchers sat alongside wooden bowls and woven baskets on the flat surfaces, some of them precariously balanced since they were wider-based than the timber slats. The table beneath the shelving held variously-sized *amphorae* which Beathan now knew to be filled with wine, vinegars and oils. Smaller earthenware bowls squeezed in between them held herbs that the cook added to his concoctions. Some were familiar to him – herbs that his mother had used, for cooking and for healing purposes – but many had been unfamiliar till Tertius made demands for him to fetch more.

He was surprised to see the large, wicker egg-basket was still full, since Tertius tended to use eggs faster than the fort hens could lay them. Eggs that he was often sent to fetch. And that was no simple task. The fort hens were as mischievous as the Roman god *Mercurius* was said to be, laying them in secretive hidden spots, according to the soldier in charge of them.

Beathan held back a grunt. Earlier that day, the cook had been insistent that more eggs than usual were needed to create food that Beathan had never heard of. But now it seemed as though making something else had taken priority.

Appreciating the instant warmth of the room, he glanced around, unable to hold back a reluctant fascination. Every day there was something new to learn, Tertius' cooking methods so different from the way that the women of his Brigante tribe cooked over the central fire in a roundhouse.

"Spill any of that emmer wheat and you will pick up every single morsel." Tertius menaced a flour-daubed finger at him.

No matter how precisely Beathan slipped down a grain sack from his shoulder, the brusque response always seemed to be the same. Though he imagined he would snap just as much – and smell just as rank – if he was the one who had to labour in such an over-warm room all day long, the space being no more than six paces in any direction.

He smothered a grin. Here he was thinking it would be too hot to work here, yet most of the day he spent shivering and complaining to himself that he would never again be properly warm. He probably smelled even worse than the cook who stood shoulder to shoulder with him. The soldiers of the fort worked him like a draft animal, but opportunities to wash away his grime and sweat came rarely.

He set down his burden and methodically picked up the few specks that had slipped free. After popping them in the open top of the sack, he then looked to the cook for further instructions…though hopefully not a dismissal. Labouring for Tertius was usually a much less arduous task than doing the jobs for other soldiers of the fort.

Using his sticky fingertips, Tertius scraped out a soft floury mass from a large wooden bowl and plopped it onto the surface of the large central table.

"See to the fire, Brigante!" Tertius' instructions always came at a shout.

Using the heels of both hands to work the dough around the flour-dusted middle of the table, the cook grumbled in the language that was common to most of the tribes of Britannia.

"I am supposed to provide them with more bread than usual, today? That centurion issues orders as though I am a slave like you."

Beathan felt the glower track him when he crossed the room towards the door, his irritation seething. He was not a slave. He was a hostage, though there seemed to be little difference.

There was a deep burr to the cook's words that was unlike the speech of the northern tribes which meant he had to listen more carefully, to catch the mutters.

"Do you know that I willingly volunteered to join this vexillation? That day seems just like yesterday, yet I have served over half of my term already." Tertius slapped a dusty salute to his chest.

"I suppose other warriors of your tribe also joined when you did, Tertius."

By risking an occasional interested remark, though never an initiated question, he was slowly learning about Tertius' Durotriges tribe from southern Britannia. However, the very notion that any tribal warrior had willingly volunteered to join the Roman Army was unfathomable to him.

A brief nod came Beathan's way, the tiniest of smirks stretching the cook's cheeks as he brandished his sticky palms, fingers widespread and flashed them four times. "More than a half-century, but I doubt they are all still hale and hearty. Less than ten of them journeyed north to Eboracum with me. The rest are probably scattered across the empire, two of my brothers included. I have heard nothing of their whereabouts for these last fifteen years."

Beathan could not appreciate Tertius' seeming lack of concern. He had spent many nights, since the disastrous battlegrounds at Beinn na Ciche, worrying about the fate of his own kin.

"I told you to get that fire built up, Brigante! Double the quantity of this olive bread will be needed today, but you can tell Centurion Barrus that he will only get a share, if I see his coin first."

Beathan had no intention of going near Centurion Barrus. Unless given a direct order, he avoided the brute whenever possible.

Lifting armfuls of split logs from the stack just outside the doorway, he set them down near the fire. Then, before doing anything further, he raised his gaze to the roof trusses above him and made sure that the chain of the large cauldron, which sat suspended above the flames, was firmly attached to the large beam-hook. The cautionary tale of a previous slave's arm being burned to the bone when the hook failed to remain in place was never likely to be forgotten. He had endured plenty of instances of viciousness in the fort, but accidental maiming seemed an even worse prospect – although he could not be sure the cook's story held even a grain of truth.

A sidelong glance at Tertius gave him no new answers, the man pounding away at yet another round of dough, locked into his own exasperation. The cook's duties were many, and feeding Commander Secundus, he had learned, seemed to be only one of them.

So far, he had not quite worked it out but Tertius also appeared to make food at certain times for some of the centurions. He knew that feeding the latter gave Tertius more coin, but he still had no real understanding of how the exchange happened in the fort. He had never seen the metal discs he knew to be coins actually being transferred to the cook.

How they were accounted for was just one of the many unexplained events that regularly happened around him. He had heard a mention that there was a special centurion who kept tallies for every single soldier, though how could one man do that when there were nearly a thousand barracked at Trimontium?

Watch and learn – his Uncle Brennus had advised that strategy many a time. He remembered some of the things that Brennus had told him about the huge legionary fortress named Eboracum, in Brigantia. His uncle had traded with the Romans outside the fortress walls, excellent cover for his Brigante spying activities.

Beathan felt a gratified grin sneak through.

He remembered Brennus saying that he had been so chuffed when he had eventually gained entry inside Eboracum Fortress, just the once, because the Romans tended to be very careful about barring entry to local civilians. Brennus had sent really useful information down the spy line, about the inside workings of the fortress, after that visit.

His experience of Trimontium was so different.

The fleeting smile faded.

He had already learned about the workings of a very different kind of fort from the inside, though he would much rather have not gained the knowledge as one of the fort's general slaves.

"Stop dawdling, you idle Brigante! Do you think I only have this bread to bake, today?"

One by one, Beathan carefully added logs to the still-burning glow, sneaking them in between the searing-hot iron bars of the grille that held them in place, while avoiding a scorching from the underside of the large cauldron suspended just above the flames. Sniffing the aroma of a simmering fowl was compulsive as he fed in the last of the logs, though it was also agonising since he was rarely fed anything other than a weak oatmeal brose and chunks of dry bread.

He stepped back and dusted off the bark shavings from his fingers on his filthy tunic, glad at least that the one he was wearing now was a whole garment. Which dead warrior the checked tunic and woollen braccae had come from was something he would never know, but he surely was grateful that the man had been a good bit larger than he was. It meant more warmth was to be had from the folded material that he tucked beneath the frayed and knotted rope that served him for a belt.

"Replenish that outside log pile and be quick about it!" Tertius grumbled as he set aside the balls of dough onto a different table, one that sat closer to the raised fire area. Beathan had already watched the cook leaving them there for a while before baking them, though he could not work out why.

"What are you staring at? Fetch the wood."

Beathan drew his gaze away from the fascination of Tertius' cooking area. Unlike the bending his mother did to stir the contents of a cooking pot over the central hearth-fire of a roundhouse, everything Tertius cooked was at waist height. A baking slab was built adjacent to the flames. The heat for the baking process was fed from below, channelled along to it from the heat of the fire. That process was not so different from his mother laying her flatbread on the hearth stones to slow-bake but, when cooked, Roman bread tasted nothing like the flat oaten – or barley – bread of the tribes.

Slipping past the cook, to avoid the worst of the harassed slap at his shoulders, he nipped out of the room. Glancing alongside the door, he sighed with sheer relief. He had fetched wood so often that he knew the rules. Use the small two-wheeled cart, if it was there. If not – bear the load himself. He knew which situation he preferred though, in truth, his arms ended up aching either way.

Sliding himself in between the shafts, he gripped them firmly and padded out of the praetorium, the guard at the gateway ushering him through without comment, Tertius' orders loud enough for the whole fort to likely hear them.

Out of sight, Beathan beamed. Going this direction was the easy bit, the wicker-sided cart light enough to run with. Though if he ever dared to go too fast, he would no doubt have a pilum fired at him, the guards thinking he was attempting an escape. The very thought of trying something wayward kept him grinning as he judged just what speed would keep him clear of injury.

The woodpile stocks were a good haul away, close to the outer wall by the east gate. Eyes followed his progress as he turned the corner and headed down past the workshops to *via quintana,* the pathway which ran behind all the central administration buildings. At the junction, the guard posted there ensured the purpose of him having the cart before he was allowed continue. It was always the same.

Glad to be no longer in chains, he had learned that his survival presently depended on him acquiescing to the many orders issued to him. Soldiers were posted at regular intervals; escape not something he could work out how to manage. However, that did not mean he would never try, if a situation meant he could flee successfully.

His keen eyes assessed all, and he tried to remember when anything seemed to be different. Presently, there seemed to be an even greater buzz of activity. More soldiers than usual were scurrying to and fro, completing all sorts of duties in the middle of the fort.

Though once onto *via decumana*, the road that led to the east gate, the opposite was the case. Fewer than usual of the infantry were lounging outside the first row of barrack blocks, the pillared walkways relatively empty. Any men who were clustered outside looked to be having intense conversations, after which some were darting off. He had a feeling their reasons were not to do with the usual disagreements over games and wagers gone wrong.

It was cold and windy, but that did not usually stop the men from sitting outside playing knucklebones, or the other games they played with small stones at the doorways when not on duty. Someday, he might like to learn how to play the Roman pastimes but so far, he could only see them from a distance.

Picking up the pace a little, he passed the last row of infantry accommodation and watched a similar hum of conversation.

"Hey, Brigante! You pay attention to where you are going!"

Skidding to an abrupt halt Beathan just missed barrelling into the auxiliary who led his horse out from the additional cavalry quarters, on the other side of the street.

Muttering an apology, he waited for the cavalryman to precede him down to the intervallum area where the horses were walked when not outside the fort on active duty.

Trimontium, he had soon learned after his arrival, was different to some of the other forts in Caledonia. Primarily garrisoned by mounted soldiers, the legionary infantry quartered at Trimontium was only a small detachment, and there for general fort maintenance. The need to shelter more horses meant the design of Trimontium differed from forts which housed infantry legions. Beathan now knew that an individual barrack room at Trimontium was built to accommodate a man and his horse.

Each of the long cavalry barrack blocks, that he now trudged past, led down to the intervallum. And down the length of each row, soldiers of the *turma* were sweeping out the rooms with great gusto, cleaning the living and sleeping spaces. To the sounds of raucous singing and noisy chatter, spent straw and dung flew out into the dip at the centre of the earthen pathway. Other men were hard at work forking up the deposited muck onto a low bedded cart. The stench of manure, and the vinegary paste that was used for cleaning leather, vied with the stink of human sweat, the west wind blowing the entire whiff in Beathan's direction as he negotiated his way past the workers to reach the wood stocks at the far end.

"Who is that delivery for?" The shout came from the guard nearest the log store after Beathan began to load up the cart.

"Tertius, the commander's cook."

When no further information was required of him, he systematically loaded up. After a check to ensure the stacks were well-balanced and securely roped, he grabbed hold of the shafts, took a deep breath and heaved the two-wheeled cart into motion. Ensuring the way ahead was clear, he only managed a couple of steps before the Roman legionary's raised hand halted him.

Bending down, the soldier hefted a few more logs and chucked them on to the already well-piled cart. "You tell Tertius that I have given him more than usual and that Rubrius, of *Cohort IV*, expects a return. Now stop dawdling and make sure to bring me something next time you come back."

Beathan stifled a grin till he was well out of the sight of the guard. From what he had learned of Tertius, any favours received had to be worth more than a couple of bits of firewood before the cook parted with his precious food.

Struggling to make sure the cart did not tip over, he made his way along the empty intervallum and turned up towards the north gate, taking a much longer route than he had come. The vacant ground, between the fort walls and the rows of wooden cavalry accommodation, was out of spear range from attack. It was often used for drilling men and mounts, though not presently. The beaten earth beneath his tattered leather boots was rutted and slippery, ice glistening in what had been uneven shallow puddles the previous day.

When he was almost opposite the north gate, he stopped awhile to draw breath. Slumping one shoulder and arm against the wooden cladding of one of the granary buildings, he let the wall bear some of the weight, not daring to lay down the shafts in case the logs tipped out. Keeping an eye on the nearby guard, he wondered how many moments it would take before he was chivvied on.

"Hey! That is no latrine, Brigante. Get back to work."

Beathan smothered an oath and pressed against the wall to surge back into motion, all the while detesting being ordered about. His curiosity was piqued, though, when he tottered around the corner and onto the *via principalis*.

Chapter Five

Trimontium Roman Fort AD 85

Up ahead, the entrance to the *principia* was blocked. A flow of troops in and out of the fort administration block was fairly normal. But the low four-wheeled wagon, heavily laden with something bulky, that was stopped at the doorway was unusual.

Approaching him was Gillean. The man was the only person he could call a friend, though chances for them to talk were rare. Their allocated bed spaces were now in different sections of the fort, yet they seemed to be sharing the same fate. Gillean, a Caledon chief, was another hostage used as a general fort-slave – at least until Commander Secundus declared differently. The Caledon was presently yanking forward a reluctant and very vocal mule.

"Is there something odd happening down there, Gillean?"

"It is going into their *aedes*," Gillean answered while gently stroking the mule's muzzle, a failed attempt to placate since it snapped and brayed at his fingers. The Caledon's laugh was almost as loud while he sidled back from the bared teeth. "Stupid animal. It does not realise that, unlike its mate, it has been freed from hauling a great weight. The mules were protesting so much at the entrance that one auxiliary had his foot stomped on." Gillean laughed even more heartily. "So, while he is hobbling off to the medicus, I now have the job of hauling this troublemaker back to its pen."

Beathan shared Gillean's humour though his curiosity was piqued even more. "Is the aedes the central square of the principia?"

Gillean grunted over his shoulder, the animal refusing to budge. "Nay. The aedes is the place for worshipping their gods. The niches lie at the far end of the complex."

The defiant braying of the mule was drowned out by hollering from soldiers near the wagon who were now with shoulders down, and were heaving the vehicle through the entrance.

Gillean chortled, his thumb indicating what was happening behind him. "I would rather take this misbehaving mule away than have that job!"

Beathan grinned agreement. "I feel a bustle today around the fort that seems different. Do you know why?"

"Aye." Gillean yanked again at the mule tether. "An important arrival is imminent. I have heard no name but think it must be…"

"Hey! Take that animal back to its pen, Caledon!"

Beathan groaned as he watched the soldier hastening towards him. Centurion Barrus seemed to appear everywhere. Gillean shared a moment of sympathy when he passed by, the mule still intent on being awkward.

"I suppose those logs are for Tertius?" As always, the self-important derision made the centurion's upper lip curl.

Beathan nodded just once, taking care not to unbalance the cart, though from experience it was more likely to be the vine rod that flicked in front of him that was responsible.

"Tell him I need you back here immediately, to the principia, when you have delivered those logs."

Strutting off, displaying the conceit that Barrus believed was his due, the senior centurion of the *Legio XX* vexillation disappeared through the now-cleared entrance into the administration area, his low words to the legionary on guard too soft for Beathan to hear.

Moving at a fair clip, an excitement gripped him that he had not felt for some time. For so long, he had wondered what the inside of the headquarters building was like. He had been in every other area of the fort but had never been given a reason to enter the principia.

He stacked the new logs, back at Tertius' domain, careful to be as quick as possible.

Tossing a half-plucked fowl down on the table, Tertius came out to confront him. The cook slapped his feathery palms onto the cloth that hung from his belt, setting a flurry of dusty fluff aloft. "So, Brigante! What have you done to make you so popular a garrison slave that everyone and their cur can claim your services, immediately?"

Beathan did not appreciate the snide grin on the cook's face. Nor did he like the words used. It had taken some cunning to steer well-clear of various predatory soldiers that he had to fulfil orders for. A well-aimed punch that broke the nose of a soldier who tried to use him as a whore had earned him a useful reputation. Neither that particular soldier, nor any other, had since tried to compromise him.

He had not noticed anyone striding ahead to inform Tertius of his latest command, though no doubt that was because hauling the stacked cart had taken up all of his concentration.

"Nothing special."

"Well, you tell Centurion Barrus he will get some of today's food, but only if he sends you back as soon as he is done with you. I need your hands on that quern stone or our esteemed…" A slight hissing noise interrupted the flow of the cook's tirade. The contents of one of his pots was boiling over the brim. "By all the putrid gore of *Pluto's* boiling pits! You have added too much wood! Get out of here."

Beathan stumbled away from the kitchen, the clout at his shoulder having been sound enough to knock him to his knees.

Hastening along to the principia, he wondered who was important enough to have the place all of a flutter. The pilum tipping sideward to bar the headquarters building entrance was expected. The guard leaning forward to thrust his face right at his chin was not.

"It seems your curiosity just might be satisfied, today, slave. I have seen your interest in our principia." The stench of the man's breath made him gag, the pink to the guard's eyes an indication there may have been too much of something stale available to the man the previous night. After an over-long glare, the guard pulled back and allowed him through the gateway.

There was a central courtyard in front of him, but this one had nothing adorning it, no benches for relaxation set out in the sunlight for the officers as in the praetorium. It was a larger empty space of beaten earth flanked all the way around by an oak-pillared roofed walkway which sheltered the doorways to many different rooms. The wooden doors were tight-shut against the nipping gusts, so it was disappointing not to learn something of their purpose. Straight ahead, another guard stood ready at the entrance into a second part of the building complex. Centurion Barrus was nowhere to be seen, but he could hear him hollering somewhere beyond, a general hubbub of noise indicating that many more were involved in whatever was happening.

The sentry's nod was brief, but the lack of questioning was unusual enough to make him step warily through into the fully-roofed room of the second area. The empty space in the middle would hold a sizable number of men if congregated there: a far more comfortable spot in poor weather than in the outside courtyard. A glance took in a raised wooden platform in one corner though most of the hustle and bustle was concentrated around the central doorway that led into yet another section of the principia.

The second mule had been released from the traces and was tethered nearby. Wedges were being placed under the wheels of the wagon to keep it in a stationary position at the entrance, and a couple of legionaries were securing a wooden ramp. Others were laying a pathway of short logs from it into the interior.

"About time you got here, Brigante!" Barrus barked at him. "We need another pair of hands to get that stone altar off this cart." He drew breath to indicate with a pointing thumb the soldiers ranged around him. "One of this clumsy lot managed to get his foot broken! I want no more useless workers around here."

The bindings securing the covered block to the wagon were loosened and, when tow ropes were all secured, he was prodded into position by the centurion's nasty stick. He was certain the group could have managed the dragging without Barrus bellowing out a beat right at his ear, but the men seemed oblivious. Slowly and surely, the waist-height stone was hauled down the ramp slope and onto the track of logs, after which it slid along with a bit less effort into the building until a corner needed to be turned.

It took concerted determination to pull the block round using a different set of ropes after which they got it on to a new log row. During the pauses in this procedure, he was able to examine the partition that faced the doorway. His gaze widened, reluctant amazement forming.

There were so many different poles with carved icons on them that were carried by the special standard bearers of the units when they paraded around. He had been sent to fetch the sandy grit that was used to polish the shiny metal discs, but he had no idea that there were handfuls of different poles balanced against the walls. He would have liked to look at the images more closely, but Barrus barked at him to get hold of a rope.

"Set the altar, right there!" Centurion Barrus pointed to a spot at the back of the next partition, areas for worship that were separated by wicker hurdles to head height. "But turn it on the logs first. Make sure the white mark on that covering faces forwards. The dedication and focus lip must face the devotee."

Beathan had no idea what part the focus was and judged it best to wait till instructions came his way. After much rope-hauling, and physical manoeuvring, the stone was turned around, off the logs and in the position required.

Barrus then proceeded to uncover the stone.

He couldn't stifle the gasp quickly enough. The stone was newly painted: bright white vying with blood red, yellow and blue markings.

He had never seen anything like it.

Barrus tossed the rope and sacking to the nearest auxiliaries. With impatient hand flaps, the centurion indicated they clear the logs away to the entrance so that one last check could be made. "And get this floor cleaned up!"

While the men scurried around doing the bidding, he watched the centurion run a finger along the finished edges of the block, ensuring that it had not been chipped.

After a huge exhalation, which Beathan thought could have been one of relief, or perhaps plumped-up pride, Barrus turned back to them. After a quick check of the floor, more orders flowed.

"Brigante! You wait right around that corner." The centurion pointed to the access corridor beyond the screening before he addressed the *decanus*. "Your men can get that log mess cleared away from the principia, and be quick about it."

Beathan reckoned that from the speed the legionaries scurried out of the room, they liked their centurion about as much as he did.

While the legionaries efficiently set to the task, not seeing what Barrus was doing proved too tempting. Sneaking his head around the partition opening, he saw the centurion delve into a skin pouch that dangled from his waist belt. Having withdrawn something, he watched the man place it into the carved dip on the top of the wide altar stone. The man then murmured some fervent vows, only a little of which he understood.

He pulled himself back just in time, and avoided being caught watching. Though the centurion's next bark made him wonder.

"Follow me, Brigante! Help me get this cover off." The centurion pointed to a bulky object at the side of the partition which housed the tall emblem poles.

When the cloth was almost pulled free, he leapt back in surprise. Someone highly skilled had carved the outspread wings and body of an eagle. The fine details of each and every feather were visible, the wingspan much wider than his own outstretched arms would be. The curved beak and grasping talons that clutched a gnarled branch were picked out in a creamy yellow colour, the rest of the bird in varying shades of brown apart from the beady eyes which were a startling green-streaked purple. Though unsettling it was a majestic sight. The eagle was primed and ready to soar off into freedom – unlike he could.

"You have deep thoughts, Brigante," Barrus grunted while pointing to the wooden eagle. "Your gods, I am told, live in the woods and the streams, and in the sky, but have no face as ours do. Would your god *Tarani*s be of a similar look to this?"

Beathan stared at the object. He had no answer for the man. How could he know such a thing?

"Help move the standards to the side for now. I need that wall to be clear." Barrus began to lift the poles away from the end wall. "Not there, you fool! We need that wooden block over there moved into the space when it is clear. Put them all to this side."

More grunts and orders followed, with him saying and doing nothing till he knew exactly what Barrus wanted. The centurion was always tetchy, yet some different emotion drove him now. If he had known the man better, he might have said Barrus was excited, Yet, the centurion also appeared nervous about what he was doing.

After some hefty shunting, and plentiful curses from Barrus about him being a Brigante weakling, they rocked the heavy wooden block from edge to edge into exactly the place nominated. The front of it was smooth and shone with some sort of oily substance, though the back was not so well-finished, the marks of the paring tools still there to see.

"Stop gawping! I need to get our eagle on top, now."

Barrus' impatient gestures indicated he should take hold of the base of the carving. The wooden eagle was much heavier than he expected, clearly made from a very dense wood. Even Barrus was breathless by the time they raised it high enough to get it close to the top of the pedestal.

The centurion's grunts were worse when more orders escaped through gritted teeth. "We need it further back!"

He shuffled one foot closer to the wall and edged the carving back a bit further. Without warning Barrus yanked away his hands.

"By *Taranis*!" Beathan howled, the tips of his fingers well and truly trapped under the full weight.

One hand earned some serious grazes from the wooden plinth when he forced his fingers free.

Chapter Six

Trimontium Roman Fort AD 85

"Salve, General Agricola! Welcome back to Trimontium." Commander Secundus' smile was a fleeting one.

Agricola acknowledged the formal greeting before he dismounted, just inside the defensive offset gates at Trimontium. Unusual in a fort, he directly faced the blank end of a granary, a fort design he still had to be convinced was practical. He was eager to stretch his legs although the ride from the fortlet in northern Votadini territory – the site where oxen were reared as draft animals for the Caledonian convoys – had actually been the most enjoyable for some days.

Tempestas was resting and the sky was a cloudless blue. It had made meandering through the numerous valleys and hills on the route south a pleasure, a short spell when he could temporarily forget the reason for his southern travel. There had been little sight of any natives. Those he did glimpse were undertaking mundane daily tasks and the occasional sightings of unhurried Roman cavalry patrols confirmed a settled environment.

Handing the reins to his cavalryman, he strode forward just a step ahead of Gaius, keen to see any changes. It had been quite a while since he had been at Trimontium.

Commander Secundus awaited his orders.

"What new developments are there for me to see?" The question was optimistic since he had approved no new building, and no major changes to be made at

Trimontium for some months. To his surprise there was the tiniest twinkle to Secundus' eyes.

"There is one very new aspect in the principia which I hope will meet with your approval, sir."

He looked at Gaius whose shoulders hitched the tiniest bit, his expression curious.

Secundus' outstretched arm indicated they turn the nearby corner and head up the via principalis, the man's expression not giving any hint of what it might be.

He was intrigued, even slightly amused, since Gaius had stopped at Trimontium on his way north and had mentioned nothing new at the cavalry fort. Turning the corner alongside the commander, he issued his first instruction.

"See that the three hostages I brought are quartered along with any others that you still have here. One of those with me is a Taexali chief." He stopped for a moment to confirm, ensuring Secundus' attention. "You do still have other high-ranking captives here in the fort?"

"Yes, sir. Three await further instructions from you regarding future action, but they currently sleep in different areas of the fort." Secundus' scorn was clear when he added, "Two of the weaker hostages did not survive."

Agricola paused. He chose not to question why that had occurred, though decided he might save the inquiry for later. It rankled that treatment meted out at Trimontium may have hastened the warriors' deaths. Especially if they were of treaty-making status – though that was doubtful. In sending high-valued warriors south, his expectation had been to make them useful to him at a later date, since he had made no formal treaties with the Caledon allies after the pitched-battle confrontation with them. Corpses were no use to him.

His response was cool, sarcasm unveiled. "All those of high rank – still alive in the morning – will journey south with me when I leave tomorrow."

The slight hitch to the commander's stride probably meant his barb had not gone amiss, though he did not know the soldier well enough to be sure.

Having arrived at the principia, Secundus ushered him through the inner courtyard and headed for the aedes, his manner more obsequious than before. "I requested something recently which I now expect to be in situ, sir."

Agricola acknowledged the man's eagerness with a slight nod at the same moment as a squeal rent the air.

"*Taranis*?" he inquired, looking aside for Gaius to confirm. "Is that what I just heard?"

Worship of many different gods was commonplace in the aedes of any Roman fort, but praising the god in a screeching howl was highly unusual.

Once into the partition where the noise came from, the scene was not what he expected, and probably not what Commander Secundus expected either judging by the oaths that issued from behind him. An impressive carving dominated the back wall, but the whole effect was marred by the two people hopping around in front of it.

"Stop fussing, Brigante, and get out of here!" The fierce hiss came from a centurion wildly flailing his vine rod.

In response, a young native sucking at fingers that dripped blood onto the floor, was ducking the punishment as he made for the door.

Agricola stared at the native. A little taller than himself, he watched a flicker of recognition cross the young warrior's gaze. "Brigante?" he asked.

When no answer came quickly enough, the centurion whacked at the youth's spine.

"Aye." The mumble was barely discernible but the warrior's head rose the tiniest bit, profound resentment pursing the lad's lips.

"I remember you at our Durno encampment." He leaned towards him. "Though, I can see that you have still not learned to school that defiant expression."

His next words were for the centurion. "Why is this Brigante hostage in the aedes?"

He could not miss the tiniest straining at the centurion's neck. The man was clearly not at all pleased with the timing of the incident. "He was helping me to raise the eagle onto its plinth, sir."

"Centurion Barrus. Get that Brigante out of here!" Commander Secundus ordered.

Secundus was furious, though Agricola had yet to work out why. He held up his palm to countermand the order. "Wait! Not before this – Brigante – learns how to properly praise our emblem. This hostage also needs to learn how to give appropriate praise to his own supreme god *Taranis,* in this sanctuary."

He turned to the young warrior, his words in the language of the tribes. "This is a place of quiet worship. You, on the other hand, were not observing that. Explain!"

The Brigante youth faced him, though a response was lacking. The set to the jaw was even more pronounced. Something stirred inside him, something about the arrogance and stupidity of youth, since the young warrior knew exactly who he was. Though, perhaps the Brigante was so inured to his situation that he had reached a stage where he cared no longer about what his fate might be?

The blood flow from the hostage's fingers was less than before, but the drips continued to mar the clean floor beneath him. Yet, however painful, the Brigante allowed no sign of the injuries to show across his features.

Addressing the centurion, he indicated the damaged hand. "How did that occur?"

"He trapped his fingers under the carving, sir."

A flicker of protest flashed across the Brigante's countenance, though the youth said nothing.

He turned to Commander Secundus. "Have this Brigante assigned to my personal staff. The obedience of a household slave will be drilled into him."

He noted that Secundus spent little effort in the dismissal before turning back to him, the man still clearly bent on explaining something else.

"I brought you to the aedes to see something new in the next niche, sir, which I hope will meet with your approval?"

Secundus' outstretched hand invited him to move on to the next partition.

One new aspect in the aedes was impressive in itself, but another?

He stepped around the wattled-wall into the adjacent area wondering what the fort commander might be referring to. Once there, he drew in a satisfied breath, his head dipping in response.

The stone altar that took pride of place near the rear of the niche gave a permanence to the fort that had previously been lacking. The functional written dedication was fitting. The scrollwork carved at the top – which included a few tiny images picked out in various colours – drew his attention. However, compared to the detail of the eagle carving in the next-door niche, the altar was simple work.

He took a moment to think of a diplomatic answer before turning back to Secundus.

"Indeed, your new altar definitely meets my approval, Commander Secundus. *Jupiter Optimus Maximus* will be much better praised now. This is a highly worthy dedication that you have erected, and it will be appreciated by all of *Jupiter's* followers."

"Thank you, sir." Secundus preened.

He bent down to read more of the altar's details.

"Did a different soldier work this exceptionally neat inscription for you?" He pointed out the abbreviations at the ends of some of the lines on the stone altar as he read the full dedication. "Here…and here. The lettering and the images above are well done."

"Thank you, sir. I am pleased with his work."

"You may send him my congratulations. And you may also tell your wood carver, who created the eagle next door, that his work is also much appreciated."

He felt that Secundus sounded strained, the answer coming from behind a degree of awkward throat clearing.

"The woodcarver has recently been garrisoned at Trimontium, sir."

"Then Centurion Barrus personally organised the eagle carving? To enhance the status of the garrison?"

Secundus' nod was confirmation of his opinion. "I am only now aware of its existence, sir. But, no doubt, his legionary vexillation will be pleased."

An afterthought tripped on quickly. "As will the whole of the fort."

Agricola acknowledged that slight adjustments often needed to be made between legionary and auxiliary vexillations inhabiting the same fort. "You may tell the woodcarver that his detail rivals the best I have seen in Rome itself."

Gaius's words from behind him soothed any awkwardness. "I am sure that Centurion Barrus became aware that the woodcarver's skills are worthy of far more than just dressing wooden pillars on the walkways of the via quintana."

The unsaid compliment was acknowledged by Secundus. "Yes, Legate Liberalis. That unseasoned wood, that batch that was used during the initial fort-building, has been replaced."

Agricola could see that Secundus was preparing himself to relate more fort business, but he was not quite ready to hear it. There were other priorities.

"I will appreciate a full update, in due course, Commander Secundus. Though not quite yet."

"Sir."

"My first sight of your splendid new addition in the aedes is clearly not what you planned for me, but both *Jupiter Optimus Maximus,* and the eagle of *Mars* next door, must be well praised. With your leave, I will do that immediately?"

Secundus was highly unlikely to refuse, but he knew it was important that he should be the first to use the altar. Secundus would then be able to boast that the Governor of Britannia and Commander of the Legions inaugurated it. The story would be trotted out for an airing at many officer meals for years to come.

Realising there were far too many bodies in the aedes, Agricola waved everyone out.

Chapter Seven

Trimontium Roman Fort AD 85

When Agricola went closer to the altar to add something to the focus, he realised that someone had already been there before him. A small pile of barley hugged the central dip. A smile broke free. Whoever had put the grain there could have been importuning *Jupiter Optimus Maximus* to ensure that he was well fed. Or, more entertainingly, it could have been a plea that the bearer was spared the need to eat the generally detested barley rations. Something he felt sure of, was that Secundus was not the first supplicant.

He raked around in one of the pouches attached to his belt. He had intended to add a coin, a newly minted gold aureus. The deity deserved it, and so did Secundus for organising the altar, but now he needed to add something else. Clearing out the barley grains was unthinkable, since they had already been given to the deity, however, the dried berries that he had not finished from the day before would be perfect.

He added what was left of them and the gold aureus, mouthing some earnest bargains of his own.

Stopping at the niche with the standards, he spent a few moments alone admiring *Mars,* and then strode outside where Secundus awaited him. Legate Liberalis and everyone else had disappeared.

"First the bathhouse, for me, and then food. Unless you have any other new developments for me to see, Commander Secundus?"

Secundus signalled the nearest legionary and issued instructions before he led the way back out of the fort gates.

"What can you tell me about that Brigante hostage? I see no chains, or restrictions, placed on his movements." Agricola asked.

His question seemed to baffle the commander. "He has been here for some months, sir. When we were sure he would not attempt any further futile escapes, we freed his chains. He is well aware that to get any food he has to work for it."

They were on the slope down to the small, though adequate, bathhouse. His response was doubtful. "Captives will always attempt an escape."

"That is true, sir. Two of the hostages did try to sneak out at night, after the lad had made his own useless attempts."

Commander Secundus was not as prudent as he should have been. Agricola halted for a moment, just short of the bathhouse entrance. "You mean the two who did not survive?"

Secundus failed to look him properly in the eye. "They died some days after we caught them and dragged them back to the fort."

The inference was enough for him to know that the hostages were most likely beaten and starved to death. He determined to find out about any other captives sent from Taexali territory, those held in forts and not yet sold to the slavers.

"When food is brought to me later, we will talk further about this."

He did not need to ask whether, or not, he would be quartered in Secundus' own living area. As during his previous visit, it was expected he would use the fort commander's accommodation, since the *mansio* that was being built in stone for the official travellers of the Empire was still not yet ready.

Not long after, he was helping himself to more of the olive bread and cooked meats from the platter in front of him. He answered Gaius before popping a piece of pickled pork into his mouth. "Yes, that is my plan. I do not intend to sail south from Segedunum, and I will not leave Britannia's shores without first visiting Eboracum, Lindum and Londinium."

Gaius plucked an olive stone from his mouth and set it at the side of his plate before reaching for more food, a cheery smile bracketing his mouth. "If your journey is going to be that long, you should take this cook with you. He makes a fine feast from what is generally ordinary ingredients."

"Ha!" Agricola smiled round a mouthful of honey cake. "I would no doubt have to take his full kitchen and fireside with us. Cooks like this one are happiest in their own little space."

Gaius helped himself to a chunk of smoked ham. "Did you know that the cook, Tertius, is not happy with you, sir?"

He made his eyebrows rise, an amused question hovering. Many soldiers around the fort were not keen on some of his latest orders. "Now why would that be?"

Gaius smirked. "It seems that, in assigning the young Brigante to your personal staff, you have stolen Tertius' best kitchen assistant. That same slave who has just delivered your food, and is being schooled right now in his duties by your household supervisor."

Agricola thought on the Brigante's hollow cheek bones and thin, gangly frame. "Well, I will hazard a guess that he has not managed to steal food from Tertius, or he would have a lot more flesh on him."

Gaius nodded before chewing off the last of the meat from a roasted bird-bone. "The Brigante is only beginning his thirteenth year. If he lives, he will be an even taller and stronger warrior. Many of his Brigante clan have those characteristics."

"How do you know his age?" Agricola had had enough food but wanted more information.

Gaius wiped off his mouth before dipping his hands into a water-filled bowl. After using a drying cloth, he signalled the domestic slaves to clear away the empty dishes. "I questioned him when you moved into the *frigidarium*."

"So that is why you took so long!"

Gaius smirked. "The hostage does not divulge information readily, but he is quick to learn. I would wager he has never been in any kind of bathhouse, or seen anyone cleaned off with a *strigil* before, but when prompted he was quick to fetch what my personal slave needed. The youth bears a cavernous rancour at this fate, but he also has an intense innate curiosity, even if he does not realise it."

Agricola rose up and went to the table at the side of the room, the surface almost completely obliterated with opened out tablets and scrolls.

"His background intrigues me, Gaius. Why was a Brigante youth so far from his own area when he engaged with our troops near our Durno encampment on Taexali territory? I can see that the tribes would deem him already able to wield a weapon, but why was he on his own? We did not take any other Brigante captives from that confrontation in the far north…" He broke off speaking because something was eluding him. "I had a particular reason for not sending him to the main slave lines at our Durno encampment. Though right now, I cannot quite remember why."

"Hmm…" Gaius debated only a moment before adding, "I was told that many Brigantes fled to Caledonia."

"I was with the *Legio XX*, in Brigantia, during the early part of Emperor Vespasian's rule. Treaties were made with Brigantes who had initially resisted General Cerialis' invasion. But it was when I began my tenure as

Governor of Britannia, years later, that some of them abandoned their Brigante hillforts."

Gaius dared a laugh. "So, they fled to Caledonia to avoid you?"

"Most likely. They were well aware that I had no intentions of calling a halt to our Roman Empire expansion into the far north."

Gaius made a short bow, in acknowledgement of his achievements. "And, indeed, you did not."

Agricola looked at the over-full tabletop. "I intend to question the stripling later. But for now, come over here and read these legal dispatches from Javolenus Priscus."

Gaius finished the dregs of wine in his goblet before he rose from the couch to take the scroll from him and then read it quickly. "That will be an interesting case for you to give an opinion on, though Priscus will already have decided on the outcome of the trial."

His snort was loud enough to be heard outside the room. "Ah! That is so very true, Gaius. But the man is good at his work and tends to pass judgement in similar vein to myself. He has had a number of cases to rule on lately, but you must already have knowledge of this particular one in Londinium." He flashed a particular scroll in the air. "Here is a man of business who wants to spend as little of his own finances as possible. He will part with monies for the empire when obliged to do so. But he is unwilling to pay for the misdeeds of others who renege on their obligations and blame someone else for their ineptitude."

Gaius made a quick read of the scroll. "Ah, the temple near the forum. I do know of this dispute. It has been ongoing for some months. I am not surprised to see that Priscus has ruled that it must be built just west of the forum. The question has always been who would gain access to the temple. It has been that aspect that the sponsor balked at, when asked to add more funds for the building of it."

He looked at his second-in-command. "You are likely to need to deal with this, and others like it, for some time to come."

Gaius nod was sufficient. The circumstances would be dealt with, though he would be long gone by then and who knew to where?

After they completed the correspondence that needed the attention of both of them, Gaius headed for the door. "Do you intend to leave at first light? If so, I will ensure the arrangements."

Steeped in correspondence from Eboracum, he managed a nod. There was nothing urgent that required him to stay longer at Trimontium, and no personal urge to enjoy it for longer as had been the case at Pinnata Castra. Knowing that Gaius was perfectly capable of ensuring their escort and baggage was all in order, he called for his secretary to organise the necessary responses to the pile in front of him.

A good while later, he stretched his arms above his head, exhaled loudly, and got up to wander the room. "That should do till tomorrow, Crispus."

Crispus acknowledged the instruction with his usual silent nod then swiftly tidied the contents strewn across the table. But before leaving the room, the secretary indicated one of the piles. "Lentulus and I can finish this tonight."

Agricola smiled. It was typical of his skilled secretary to ask a question while actually making a statement. His arm wave gave the permission, though he knew Crispus was probably as weary as he now felt. "If you choose to, but first find that Brigante hostage and send him here."

The door opened after only a few moments and Gaius re-entered, the Brigante youth at his heels.

He beckoned the hostage to stand in front of him and studied him closely. Though the lad faced him, it was interesting to note the young warrior's lack of fear. For some reason, he was unsure why that should be.

Going behind the table, he sat down on the stool and relaxed his forearms onto the carved wooden rests.

"How many Brigantes had assembled together, to be under the leadership of the Caledon, Calgacus, at Beinn na Ciche?"

The question, in Latin, caused the tiniest flicker to cross the young Brigante's expression, though no answer was attempted.

Alongside the table, Gaius repeated the question using the common language of the tribes, and then repeated it again even more slowly.

The Brigante's answer seemed sensible when it eventually came. "How could I know how many Brigantes were there? There were thousands of warriors rallying to Calgach's call, and I only spoke with a small number of them."

Agricola kept his many questions wide-ranging about the lad's whereabouts before arriving at Calgacus' mustering point in Taexali territory. Most were asked in the language of the tribes but some were in Latin, on purpose, with Gaius translating where necessary. The lad's answers were cautious, as though the questions were oddly random, but they were exactly what he needed to know. The young Brigante probably had a limited knowledge of Latin but was quite skilled at guarding his tongue.

Eventually the cat and mouse game no longer appealed. He wanted to sleep. He lifted a stack of wooden tablets from the table and searched through them till he found one he particularly wanted. Though bone weary, he felt the beginnings of a smile. He knew there had been something special about the youth.

"How many Selgovae warriors did you speak to at the campfires of Calgacus?" His question alarmed the hostage, exactly as he had intended.

The Brigante's hands clenched into fists at his sides, though he would not raise his head to meet his gaze.

Gaius' repetition of the question right at the boy's ear eventually gleaned a response.

"I met no Selgovae warriors around the campfires at Beinn na Ciche."

The youth's claim was infuriating, even though he expected it.

He got up and pushed the tablet under the Brigante's nose, confident that reading it was unlikely. He allowed a darker edge to creep into his tone.

"Your mother, Nara, is Selgovae."

The boy's momentary flicker was sufficient, but he decided that further interrogation could be left till another day. He looked over at Gaius. "Take him out of my sight."

Gaius' fist grabbed the back of the lad's tunic. Agricola watched him manhandle the Brigante to the door. Opening it with one hand, the roar at the nearest guard to fetch Commander Secundus made Agricola smile. It was a waste of breath since he could already see Secundus in the courtyard, beyond the opened doorway. The man had probably been snooping outside what was normally his own living quarters. The officer was quick to respond to Gaius.

"Lock him up for the night. Somewhere close to here."

Agricola watched Gaius' deliberate shake that rattled the lad's very bones before he pushed the Brigante out of sight. Gaius was taller than the hostage, and Agricola knew from experience that his friend was much stronger than he appeared.

Chapter Eight

South of Trimontium Roman Fort AD 85

The iron collar ripped at Beathan's neck, but the greater hurt that gripped him now was on the inside, not the blood leaks which seeped down the neck of his tunic. Resentment was bottomless and would probably never be erased. For many of his previous days at Trimontium, he had been released from the indignity of being chained, and he wanted that freedom back again, albeit it was not true liberty from the tyranny of Rome.

Before he could properly open his eyes that morning, he had been dragged outside the storage room he had been dumped in. His hands had been chained in front of him, a hinged collar was clamped around his neck, and he had been led like a protesting mule down the via principalis towards the southern gate of the fort.

The whole intervallum area swarmed with soldiers from General Agricola's Gallia Narbonensis guard. Horses were being brought forward by their cavalrymen and wagons were being checked to ensure the contents were secure. Like an extra draft animal, he was tethered to one of Agricola's wagons.

It was really no consolation that his friend Gillean, the Caledon, was chained to another.

The pleas he sent to *Taranis* to send retribution went unheard, but when he opened his eyes, the sight of three other natives being dragged out of one of the workshop doors startled him. He ogled when the men were hauled down to share the same discomfort as he was in.

Derwi?

One of the men definitely looked like the Taexali friend that he feared dead.

When the three captives were halted near him, he was too scared to make it obvious that he knew one of them. He made cautious eye contact. Typical of his erstwhile friend, when Derwi judged none of the guards were looking, his wink was pronounced. Unable to use his hands without the chains clanking, Beathan watched Derwi clamp his lips together after which he gave the tiniest head shake to indicate they should save any talk for later.

The cheeriest thought he had had for ages came to him. Perhaps in a very strange way *Taranis* was listening to him?

His earlier rancour abated slightly when Derwi was chained to the opposite side of his wagon. It was only when they were eventually in motion, and journeying down the Roman road, that they were able to share their stories, the noise of the wagon muffling their voices.

"I regained my senses the day after that mess on the road. By then I did not know where I was, or where you all were. You can imagine how many of my pestering questions were answered."

Beathan could only raise a weak smile, rather than receive any of the friendly shoulder nudging that he had become used to from Derwi on their journey south from the Durno Roman Camp, after the bloody battlegrounds of Beinn na Ciche. The Taexali chief was so good at encouraging him to think of better things. He was heartily glad to find that Derwi's attitude was little changed and that his outward appearance still hid the man's determination to survive, and to somehow free himself.

"I thought that some of the other injured captives were with you when your cart turned off the Roman road. I mean at the junction where the lot I was with carried on?" he asked.

Derwi had to increase his volume since one of the oxen pulling the wagon was kicking up a stushie, causing his handler to bawl at it. "Aye, they were. At first there were four of us, but one warrior had already moved on to the otherworld before we arrived at the fortlet. I was favoured by the goddess *Andarta*. The lump on my head healed much quicker than the broken leg bones of the other two survivors, the ones who are tethered to that cart behind us."

"Were you kept in chains?"

"In the beginning, we were. The fortlet we were taken to is very isolated. And later on, the other two were only fit to hobble around, so they removed our leg shackles. The garrison used us as farm slaves till that *Ceigan Ròmanach* Agricola arrived."

He found that information surprising. "Why would Agricola visit such a small fortlet?"

"Only one century garrisons it, but it has a specific function. Oxen, like the ones pulling this wagon, are reared and trained at that fortlet – its name means 'place of the many oxen'. One of my tasks was to keep the bulls separated from those already castrated."

He chortled. "Because they had learned you are a very tough warrior?"

Derwi's laugh rang much louder. "Nay, lad. It was because some of their auxiliaries had already been trampled by belligerent bulls, and my life was much less important."

"You two, stop talking!" The command came from one of Agricola's personal guards.

The soldier glared at him as he moved past the wagons that were in the middle of the convoy, and then headed towards Agricola who led at the front.

Most of the mounted forces back at Trimontium wore chainmail armour, and their shields and swords were a good length for attack when riding, but the guard who had just ridden past wore the segmented armour he had seen the legionaries wear. Some of those special security forces rode at the front near Agricola and others were in the rear. He was not in a position to count them, but guessed they numbered around a quarter-century.

When the guard was well past, he lowered his voice though refused to obey the order. "Was Agricola inspecting that fortlet to assess how good the oxen stocks were?"

Derwi's expression displayed his amusement. "Agricola wants to know about every single thing that happens in Britannia, but it was more that the fort housed more than draft animals. The simple answer is that he came to collect his hostages, me included."

"Why?"

"Collateral. We are all tribal chiefs, even though our clans are small. He will use us to bargain with."

"Then why does he take me?" He stumbled over his words, his thoughts racing. "I am no chief!"

Derwi lowered his voice just enough for Beathan to interpret. "You are the first-born of your parents who were both much more important chiefs than any of us chained to these wagons. Do not doubt it, Beathan, you are Agricola's most important hostage. And though this may seem an impossible vow, by *Taranis,* I will see you free before they will break your spirit, or bond you to an impossible Romanised fate."

His insides were in turmoil. The other captives around him were grown men. How could he possibly be more important? Though it was true that his parents had been held in high regard in Derwi's Taexali territory.

An unbidden lump lodged at the back of his throat, his eyes stinging. He had no idea if Nara and Lorcan, or any of his family still lived!

Derwi peered at him. "So, young Brigante, while I was dodging cattle shite and bone-breaking hooves, what easy jobs were you given at the fort of the three hills?"

"The three hills?

Derwi chuckled. "Did you learn nothing? Trimontium means three hills. You must have seen the hills behind the fort? The lowering orb of *Lugh* behind them was an impressive sight when we arrived, last night."

He preferred to forget about his own arrival to Trimontium in the night dark. And, mostly, he wanted to erase the brutal welcome to Trimontium that he had been given by Centurion Barrus.

The sudden smile that flashed across to Derwi was one of triumph. "That Roman shite back in Trimontium – Centurion Barrus – is really going to miss me!"

Derwi's peal of laughter showed he understood the sarcasm, but there was some concern in the next words. "And what in particular will he be missing?"

"Using that vicious vine rod on me, for a start."

Derwi's furious expression drew his full focus. "And that was the only thing he used on you? Assuming you were an unwilling participant?"

The memory that came to him was not a particularly good one, though he knew the incident had been inevitable in a fort of hundreds of soldiers. The young and weak would always be the prey of stronger men desperate for sexual release.

"Nay, Barrus never bent me over to use like that, and the one soldier who did try got a broken nose from me."

The trudge southward to the next fort was long, and it afforded plenty of time for Beathan to share his own recent experience. His walking pace was determined by the speed of the oxen pull, since the chain from his collar was short, though he tried not to mind it. Instead, finding positive things to talk about, he summoned up a smile, relieved that Derwi was within talking distance.

Derwi was the next best thing to the Garrigill kin that he missed so much.

Four day-long trudges later Beathan looked up ahead, chained as every other day, to one of the wagons, though not always by the neck. This time the man on the opposite side was one of those who had spent time with Derwi at the fort of the oxen. Senan's shattered leg bones had not healed well and had the man not been able to clutch the side of the laden wagon, Senan would have been dragged along. Their Roman captors were not known for issuing sympathy.

It seemed to be a newly-built fort that they were approaching, but it was still too far off for him to estimate its size. Though how big it was hardly mattered. During the trek southwards, he was only released after they entered the fort that Agricola had chosen to spend the night in.

"Look," he hissed, gaining the exhausted warrior's attention. "Stay strong. We are almost at the next fort."

Senan's eyes struggled to open.

Beathan could almost taste the man's pain but knew encouragement was needed for a little bit longer.

"Rest is coming, *mo charaid*. Think of the fine food we will be offered and the soft bed that awaits us.

The brief respite that came after the convoy abruptly came to a halt gave his companion time to catch his breath.

"Aye, you are a good friend, indeed." The voice was weak, but a certain amount of humour was forced through. "It is high time we feasted, young Beathan. Are you bard enough to entertain us with fine tales, and sing some of the songs of our ancient triumphs?"

Beathan laughed. "A rusty sword would sing better than I can. Uncle Brennus is the bard in my Garrigill clan. His voice is true as a lark, though he is a giant of a man. But from him, I can spin a tale for you right now…"

His story lasted till they passed through the gates of the fort, though he had asked some questions to ensure Senan would appear alert on arrival. He was not convinced that showing any weakness was a good strategy for his new friend.

"What kind of fort is this?" Beathan hissed at Derwi a short while later as they passed each other along a pillared corridor. His arms strained under the weight of a large platter full of food he would never get a taste of, the meal destined for Agricola and Liberalis.

Derwi's head shook the tiniest bit. "We will talk later."

Guards were posted at almost every door in what seemed to be a building that served mainly as a headquarters block, but which also had sleeping rooms. Agricola and Liberalis had been allocated space in them, their personal possessions having been delivered there.

At every fort they had stayed in, Agricola had demanded that he fetch and carry for him, Derwi having been chosen to play a similar role for Liberalis. Since both of the Romans had their own staff, he knew it was unnecessary to use them like that. Derwi was right in that it was a deliberate ploy to undermine their self-worth. Forced into demeaning servitude would drain the reserves of the best of men and yet, in some ways, he also found it liberating.

It was better to be worn down with work tasks than to be chained up in a dank store-room and left from dusk till dawn.

What seemed like ages later, Beathan was in one of those tiny store rooms, weak torchlight from outside the door doing a poor job of lighting the interior. He attacked the brose and clumps of dry bread from the wooden platter that had been dumped on the floor. Food that was shared out amongst the hostages who encircled it.

Derwi slurped from his wooden bowl, unwilling to lose a single drop, his words kept low since there were two guards posted right outside the door. "Aye, this fort is definitely different."

Gillean tossed down his empty bowl and rooted around in the growing darkness seeking crumbs from the shared bread platter, his leg shackles clanking on the hard-packed floor. "Some wear different tunics. And those returning through the fort gates are the only ones I have seen wearing any armour."

Derwi agreed. "I saw cavalry units but others look like legionary infantry."

One of Beathan's orders that evening had been to find the *optio* in charge of Agricola's wagons. It had been a pointless task, though, since he was escorted by a reluctant junior scribe who could easily have done the job by himself. He could not yet work out why Agricola personally issued such tasks to him, knowing that he would have a shadow follow him the whole way. At such times his leg shackles had been removed, but the collar remained. With that round his neck, he could never pass anywhere unnoticed.

Only some of the goods deemed necessary for Agricola and Liberalis were removed at night from the vehicles. The wagons were then parked near the southern gate, ready for departure the next morning.

The optio of Agricola's private guard was responsible for the general's wagons during the southerly trek and the man was efficient, since the leather satchel only took a short while to locate.

Beathan regretted not having enough time to understand more of the fort operations, but he had managed to make some observations.

"The cavalry is from the *Ala Petriana*. I heard guards on the ramparts mocking about how the mounted soldiers like to lord it over his infantry unit." He sucked his bread slowly to make it last as long as possible.

"How did you manage to understand that?" Gillean asked, reaching around their circle to locate his arm before passing the one and only, now empty, wooden beaker.

He knelt forward and located the bucket of what was meant to be fresh water, though it tasted stale after he filled the beaker and glugged some down. "The two guards were speaking a tongue similar to ours."

Derwi clucked like a hen, his wide smile only seen by his white teeth illuminated by the torchlight. "Now that is interesting. Let us see what we can find out, before we leave tomorrow. We need to share as much as we can about who does what at all these places we are dragged to. Someday, it may be of use to us."

"This place is called Coria." Senan rubbed constantly at his lower leg. "Though, right now, all I care for is that I never carry another water bucket again. They know full-well that my lurching gait means a half-empty bucket by the time I reach my destination."

Beathan could just make out Derwi patting the man's shoulder in sympathy.

Derwi's words encouraged, as always. "The tasks they choose for us are meant to demean. Do not let them win."

Gillean brought them back to the discussion of the fort. "Why do the granaries and storehouses outnumber those newly-built barrack blocks at this fort?"

"And did any of you notice the other Roman road that went towards the west?" Cathal, another of the hostages, was finding the best position to lie down in.

Beathan had not noticed either of those things, but they worked out that only the captives who had been walking towards the fort on the opposite side from Beathan would have been placed to see them.

The entry of one of their guards, who remained under the doorway lintel, halted the conversation. "Bring them!" The soldier remained there, pilum at the ready

Beathan got to his feet, knowing he was in better shape than most of the others to collect the bowls, beakers and metal pot. In silence, he piled them up and hobbled over as fast as the shackles allowed. It was the same routine no matter the fort they slept in. The sentry would point outside and expect the bowls to be deposited there. There was never an opportunity to overpower because there were always other armed soldiers out on the wooden walkway.

After the door bolt had clanged back into place, their conversation resumed though little was added, the yawns and shuffles increasing as they all found the most comfortable way to settle on the bare earthen floor.

When he closed his eyes to sleep, Beathan willed himself to remember that the fort of Coria was probably a supply fort that Agricola had recently had built. It was definitely big enough to be important. The smell of newly seasoned wood was still evident in many of the buildings, including the row of storerooms where he was bedded down in, though what was housed in the other small rooms along the pillared walkway was unknown.

He should probably remember that a meeting point of two Roman roads also needed to be remembered.

Hatred of all of the Roman shite resurfaced, General Agricola most of all…

The snoring around him ceased to be noticed.

Chapter Nine

Corstopitum Roman Fort AD 85

Agricola chewed the last of his bread before wiping his fingers free of the oil from the olives. He had already done an early inspection of the fort, with Gaius at his heels, though always enjoyed a second opinion.

"What role should Corstopitum play now?" Gaius was finishing a small pile of hazelnuts, his tongue licking between teeth and gums. After smacking his lips, he added, "Are you wondering if your successor, as Governor of Britannia, will choose to operate it with the same garrison strength?"

As usual, Gaius understood his concern.

"It is already undermanned," Agricola said, pushing his plate aside.

"True, but threat from local tribes does not seem imminent." Gaius went to the door to order the remains of the meal to be removed.

"Gaius." His tone was heavy with sarcasm. "Do you really believe that situation will last for long if our presence in the area is reduced?" He stopped speaking when he realised that the young Brigante hostage had entered, followed by one of his servants who prodded and pushed the lad towards the low table.

The hostage looked wan, more than before, a brand-new bruise to his cheek obvious against a grey pastiness. He wondered what had merited that. The iron collar around the youth's neck bones shifted forward when he bent to collect the dishes.

The tiniest twitch at the Brigante's lips, as he lifted the translucent-green glass cup nearest to him, indicated that a spark of defiance still lurked there. It intrigued him that the young hostage was not cowed in his presence, though it was true that the treatment meted out may have been caused by more than the indignity of wearing a slave collar. There would be plenty of time to question the hostage further when they reached Eboracum. Till then, he would make sure that the Brigante was kept occupied by his own servants.

Once youth and servant had gone, he turned to Gaius. "Did I tell you that I may have met that Brigante's father?"

As anticipated, it stopped Gaius in his reading of one of the wooden tablets on the heavily-laden table. "What makes you say that?"

"Till more questions are answered, I cannot be sure. Commander Secundus, at Trimontium, said the boy claimed his father to be Lorcan of Garrigill. More than a decade ago, when I was in command of *Legio XX,* one of the main representatives who signed the treaties between the northern Brigantes and General Cerialis was named Lorcan of Garrigill. I was not directly involved in the treaty signing, but I was visiting the new fortress at Eboracum at that time, ready to receive new orders from Petillius Cerialis."

"If you are correct, then that youth is a worthwhile hostage and must be kept alive."

Agricola laughed, though it was hollow. "I see you did not miss his latest mistreatment. Yes, he must be alive to be of use, but a surly slave will not find favour with our men. Our training does not encourage a soft touch."

He watched Gaius' shrewd expression. "You have been using the boy as a general servant these past nights to keep a better eye on him? Even though his father is probably long dead, and current treaties with any Brigante tribes are very different from during the time of Cerialis?"

He nodded. "Yes, to all of that, but it is also to gauge the boy's character. If I think it worthwhile, I will drag that Brigante youth all the way to Rome and educate him in the ways of our culture."

Gaius snorted. "But you are realistic. You know that it will take a lot more than some petty high-ranking nobles to make our Emperor Domitian think it worthwhile to focus money, and men, on a renewed Caledonian campaign."

"What else do I take back to Rome? Answer me that? Do I have Calgacus, and a sack full of signed scrolls, to prove what has been achieved in Caledonia?" He stomped to the door and called for his armour. There was no more to say on the sensitive subject of success, or failure, in Caledonia.

"You might want to hear about this, General Agricola, before we head south," Gaius declared only a short while after.

Gaius was back to formality, having approached him at speed from the direction of the principia, after going there to discuss the details of a newly arrived dispatch the fort commander had just received. Behind Gaius was a small trail of bloody and bedraggled cavalrymen, some with armour more tattered than whole and all nursing some form of wound. He was in the intervallum surrounded by his personal guard, the wagons packed and ready, the hostages neck chains being secured. The sorry state of the cavalrymen told a tale of its own. "Who will speak for you?" he asked, since he could see no obvious leader amongst them.

After a swift look at the others, one man stepped forward. His battered, out-of-shape helmet was in one hand and blood dripped freely from a substantial gash at his temple.

"Name?" he asked.

"Flavinus of the Turma of Candidus, sir!"

The young cavalryman's clothes were filthy and his chain mail blood-splashed in more than one place, indicating numerous small wounds in addition to the head wound. Underneath the crimson streaks, the soldier had the corn-coloured hair of the Germanic tribes and a long nose.

"Why are you all in this disreputable state?"

"Sir."

The cavalryman visibly swallowed down his humiliation though could not erase it from his eyes while Agricola waited for an explanation.

"We were out on a routine patrol after dawn, a little to the north. Our orders were to inspect the area between here and the nearest signal station. It has been very quiet of late regarding the natives, so we were…" There was an awkward pause. "Taken unawares when we were ambushed."

"Fatalities?" Agricola asked.

"Sir, three men and a few others badly injured."

Agricola looked at the state of those in front of him and wondered what constituted minor injuries. "But you made it back here?"

Flavinus nodded. "There were a lot more of them but once the men rallied round me, we gained ground." The cavalryman looked momentarily stunned by what he had said before he continued. "I mean, we held our ground, sir. We identified their Brigante leader – or maybe they were some other tribe, I am not sure – but once he was killed, the surviving cowards fled."

The sound of rattling metal coming from one of the wagons distracted Flavinus.

Agricola looked behind to see what was happening. One of his personal guards was nudging his horse towards the young Brigante hostage. The hostile expression on the young Brigante's face was unmistakeable.

He turned back to Flavinus. "You said that the men rallied around you?"

Flavinus looked unsure of what to say next. Another of the bedraggled soldiers indicated he would like to speak, one who was some years older than Flavinus.

After permission was granted, Agricola's suspicions were clarified.

"Sir. Our patrol leader was their first target. We were approaching the end of a small gorge riding single file, because of the tight gap that we had to go through, when the first spear was thrown at us." The soldier momentarily dropped his gaze, clearly ashamed of his conduct. "It happened so fast. Some of those who were hit lost control of their horses and caused panic along the line. It was young Flavinus who bawled some orders and got us back into position to first defend ourselves, and then go on the attack."

He reflected on the information, then addressed Flavinus. "Had no scouts been sent to check the passage?"

"Yes, sir. They reckoned it was clear but those *Brittunculi*…paltry little Britons…must have had hiding places we have not yet found."

A stream of low oaths came from his Brigante hostage. When he turned back to him, he could not miss the intent stare. Though, he was not the focus of the boy's attention. The hawking spit that came out of the boy's mouth was intended for Flavinus.

Agricola did not know whether to praise the boy for his courage when completely surrounded by so many of his enemies, or punish him for the foolishness of the protest. But either way it did not matter, because the young Brigante's head was almost whacked off by the blow from his nearby guardsman.

He turned to the Praefectus Castrorum who had accompanied Legate Liberalis. "See that this never happens again in the Corstopitum area." Deliberately lowering his voice, he continued, "You cannot afford to lose one single soldier from this fort."

Chapter Ten

Cataractonium Roman Fort AD 85

"Did you find out what this place is named?" Derwi whispered.

Beathan was going in with the last of the empty dishes and Derwi was going out of yet another commander's kitchen. They had been trekking back and forth to the living accommodation with food and drink many times. Though it was their usual slave tasks of an evening, they were even busier since Agricola had invited the senior soldiers of the fort to dine with him.

"Hurry up there, you lazy Taexali!"

Derwi's mumble about killing the *Ceigan Ròmanach* thankfully went unchallenged as they passed each other.

The door guard's hassling meant no time for conversation, though he was desperate to share what he knew. He had heard someone name the place as Cataractonium and that there were only a couple more forts to stop at on the Roman road, before they would reach Eboracum Fortress.

The trek southwards had been predictable as far as he was concerned. They plodded all day long alongside the wagons, collar-connected, till they reached the next fort. The only breaks came when the horses were rested. At such times, the chains were connected to each other so that they could sit on the ground. Water was dished out to them, but food only came later. Escape was constantly in Beathan's thoughts, and it was no doubt the same for the others, but Agricola's guard was a quarter-century of well-armed soldiers alert to every movement across the landscape.

The Roman road had been almost barren of natives. Any they did encounter stepped back from it as soon as they noticed the Roman convoy. There was definitely no sign of confrontation as had happened near Corstopitum.

Gillean began the discussion as they all bedded down for the night, their meagre broth having been a definite change from the usual watery brose.

"Who knows what?"

Beathan was slightly miffed when Cathal was first to share the name of the fort. He was not sure of what else he could contribute.

"I was sent to the stabling where the mounts of visitors are sheltered over-night." Cathal continued with information that washed over his tired head until the man talked of the river they had forded earlier that day, prior to reaching the fort. From a lying position, he sat up so abruptly that his head was spinning.

"Are you sure they said it was the River Swale?" he asked.

"Definitely. Does the name mean something to you?"

He did not know whether to be glad, or sad, about being reminded of the name. Memories flooded him, thoughts of his family almost ripping him apart. He let his head drop and forced the emotions to abate. Eventually, when he realised the pause was too long, he gathered sufficient composure to speak.

"Before I was born, my father's clan from Garrigill Hillfort joined King Venutius' forces at Whorl. There was a huge battle against General Cerialis' legions which devastated the Brigantes. Agricola was also there as commander of the *Legio XX*."

Derwi's reaction was explosive. "Yet another reason for killing that Roman turd!

The ripples around the room gave him a moment to think of what was important to share. "Most of my family survived, thanks be given to *Araun* who did not call them to the otherworld, but some paid a heavy price in life-changing injuries. My mother was wounded in a skirmish with marauding Romans when she went to search for my father who was missing after the battle."

A tentative question came from Gillean. "That sounds like a different tale to be told, but did you not say this battle was at Whorl?"

Beathan dipped his head, though it was unlikely to be seen much in the dim room. "Aye."

"Ah, I believe I understand." Derwi prodded gently. "Was that battle near the River Swale?"

"Nay. I think Whorl is a good trek west of it. It was Roman units from the fort by the River Swale who were first to form ranks at Whorl, before more Roman troops from southern forts swelled their numbers." Beathan summoned his hatred of the invading Roman scum, rather than wallow in an unknown dread about his family.

Gillean's growl rang around the small storeroom. "You think that those bastards came from this very garrison?"

The men around added their own venom. He was asked more questions about his family and of how he eventually ended up in Taexali Territory. As he slipped into sleep, he thought of Gillean's last words.

"Beathan, I have only been involved in that one huge confrontation at Beinn na Ciche. It humbles me to know that your Garrigill clan have been fighting the Roman invaders for all of your young life. Their struggles have been endless, but though you fear for their survival, I would guess that the goddess *Andraste* has kept them alive to thwart the Romans for many more seasons to come."

He prayed to *Andraste,* and to *Brigantia,* and *Taranis,* and *Araun,* and every other deity he knew of, to keep his family safe. Eventually, he slipped into a troubled sleep. His mother and father, younger siblings, cousins and their parents, wove around him. Some were alive, though others were barely recognisable and seemed to come to him from the otherworld.

With no suitable fort to spend the night in, a hastily constructed encampment was the shelter the following night. He and the other hostages were not required to do any menial tasks but were chained together to a post set outside Agricola's tent. The few ragged bits of blankets thrown at them would not have covered even the largest warrior amongst them. The best they had was their own shared heat in the bitterly cold night where a thousand twinkling stars shed some light around them.

"The Roman shite will pay for this someday. I vow I will make their lives as miserable as this."

His curses were beginning to equal those of Derwi.

Chapter Eleven

Eboracum Roman Fortress AD 85

"Was the settlement as busy as this when you came north, Gaius? There looks to be a lot more activity over there than during my last visit."

Agricola was savouring the last opportunities of being informal with Gaius as they approached the west gate of Eboracum Fortress. A huddle of roughly-built huts and tents had spread as far as the south-western corner. From a distance, the shops and houses looked far too close to the corner guard-tower, but he would reserve judgement till he was able to see properly. The far side of the river now had some buildings on it which blocked the long-distance view down the vale.

He remembered the permission given for that development, but seeing it was not the same as agreeing on a papyrus scroll.

Acknowledging that Eboracum was thriving, a civilian settlement around it was inevitable. However, what he was seeing needed some thought because Eboracum was only a short march away from Isurium Brigantum. Isurium was where he had envisaged that the main civilian settlement would flourish, since that location was already meaningful to the local Brigantes. Effective civic control by the currently ruling Brigantes was essential. Rome demanded that the area be settled and prosperous, but in the proper place and circumstances.

Realising Gaius had answered, and his own thoughts had wandered, he faced him.

Seeing his raised eyebrows, Gaius repeated.

"I see nothing different, though I had never visited Eboracum before going north to meet you." The force of Gaius' gaze reached him. "Though you must have seen many changes here during your years in Britannia?"

"Indeed." Agricola dipped his head. "The outside settlement to the south of the walls was established soon after the initial fortress was built by Cerialis, though for years it only straddled the Porta Praetoria. It has gradually spread along the walls, and like the initial wall timbers there has been a renewal of many of those booths as well."

He sighed. His tenure in Britannia had been an unusually long one and, reluctant to admit it, perhaps it really was time he went home. Though, he would not stay long in Rome itself. He could not countenance that while Domitian was emperor.

If a suitable posting elsewhere across the Empire did not transpire, the thought of enjoying some relaxation at his estates in Gallia Narbonensis was an increasingly appealing one.

Though circumspect, Gaius was as usual astute to his mood.

"The Britannia you will depart from will not be anything like it was when you took up the reins of governorship."

He laughed, knowing there were few who had the same estimation of his achievements as Gaius had. "Tell me what you regard as successful?"

Gaius continued. "The civic policies you put in place at Isurium are bearing fruit already, under the oversight of Commander Longus. The trading booths are operating profitably and the native mood is settled."

Again, he chortled. "As long as we maintain the troop compliment to ensure that."

He slowed his horse down on approach to the gates, the signifer of his personal guard having just raised his standard to halt the column.

Gaius looked across at him even more keenly, his words – as ever – being carefully chosen. "Our legionary presence in southern Britannia is maintaining the peace. It does not nearly have the same strength as a decade ago, but it does it not need that now. The population favours the adoption of Roman customs in the ways you have nurtured."

His smile was wry. "You have done a very good job in Londinium for me, Gaius. But during your trek north to collect me, you have seen how volatile the natives can be, at the whim of a capable leader."

Gaius's expression clouded. "Do you fear an insurrection after you leave?"

"Not what I mean!" He was quick to clarify. "Certainly, my successor must keep as good a grip on any native unrest, as I have. What I fear, if anything, is that our legions will rebel if we stretch their resources even further than at present. Domitian tarries over nominating my successor. He may not even do that till after I return to Rome, which means that you and your staff must maintain control even more rigorously. Without a strong commander, the province will run to seed."

Chapter Twelve

Eboracum Roman Fortress AD 85

"You!"

When the guard pointed his pilum, Beathan knew he was the chosen one but whether that was good, or not, was debatable. From the expressions on the faces of his fellow hostages, they did not think so.

Scrambling to his feet, he shuffled to the doorway where a second legionary knelt down to undo his leg shackles. The former was impatient enough to stab at him with the spear tip, though not hard enough to go skin-deep.

"Get out, and go along to the fuller!"

He stared at the soldier not knowing which way to turn until the pilum jabbed to the right.

He had been at Eboracum for three days, most of which had been spent in a dank room, one of the empty tabernae that lay opposite the principia entrance. Along with his fellow hostages he was fed and watered, though barely, just sufficient to prevent starvation from settling in.

Their tempers were frayed having nothing to do. Nevertheless, each man tried hard to avoid confrontation with the others. They had long since all told their life stories, had run out of conversation, and had descended into their own thoughts.

He knew he was more fortunate than the rest of them, since Agricola had again had him used in menial service in the late afternoons. It had not been fetching and carrying food but had, at least, got him out of the tiny room.

The mule stalls had been much cleaner when he had mucked them out, and the central gutter between two rows of infantry barracks was free-flowing, rather than blocked with hay-strands and horse-dung.

Even worse was when he had had to crawl into a hole under the wall fortification, under the southern corner guard-tower, where he had to spread-thin the muck and human turds that were blocking what he could only term a man-made burn that was meant to flow right outside the fort. He had never seen the likes of it before. The iron bars that separated outside from inside naturally prevented his escape, though he had tried to squeeze through them anyway.

He stank so much that Derwi had banished him to lie as close to the draught of the door as possible.

This call to labour was different, though, and more worrying, since it was hardly past dawn.

"Stop!" The guard had no need to bawl in his ear, yet he did.

He was at the end of the main street called the via principalis and was opposite the eastern entrance. Before he could take a deep breath of fresh air, his collar had a chain attached and he was yanked across the hard-packed dirt towards the sentries at the gate. Panic set in, resistance following on its heels, but the soldier pulling the tether was much stronger than he was.

"Where are you taking him?"

He recognised the voice before he even caught sight of Agricola exiting from their bathing area which lay opposite the commander's personal quarters in the extensive praetoria, much bigger than the one at Trimontium with buildings in addition to sleeping quarters.

After saluting the general, his guard cleared his throat. "Order to take him to the fuller, sir."

Beathan noted Agricola's reaction. His insides rebelled even more than the indignity of the neck tether. The general was not even hiding the short-lived smirk.

"On whose orders?" Agricola asked.

"Legate Liberalis, sir." His hauler was good at giving the briefest of information.

Agricola turned to the few soldiers who were his current personal guard and pointed to one in particular. "Go with them. Two may not be enough for this task."

When Agricola's hand waved them out of the fortress, he looked on with dread. He did want to be outside, but he wanted to be free when it happened! Once he was through the gate, he stopped protesting so much. His back had taken as much of a pummelling and prodding from the second legionary, as his neck was getting from the one leading by the chain. Agricola's personal guard, on the other hand, maintained a distance that was quite obvious.

The fortress had bustled with activity, but beyond the staggered gate ramparts there was a huge commotion in the direction of the river. Loaded carts and wagons were turning off the road that led to the east gate and were heading down a narrower track towards the south corner of the fortress. They were going closer to the riverside and towards the biggest settlement he had ever seen.

There was none of the orderly building of barrack blocks as inside the fortress. Wooden houses and temporary tents were all different heights and widths, with people scurrying to and fro along narrow paths that ran between them. The noises got even louder when he was dragged closer. People shouted in many different tongues: others argued in huddles. Even more were cursing and berating the children, and feral creatures, that ran amok. They all threatened to trip him up as the guards constantly changed direction to negotiate a pathway through the narrow, crowded streets.

He was so busy absorbing what was going on around him that he almost forgot about his slave collar till a gaggle of young children pointed to it. Their exaggerated snorting and gesturing, as they darted past, were a slap in the face.

Almost right on the riverside, he was halted at one of the many tented booths created from multiple hides sewn together. Though the tent itself was lengthy, the entrance was narrow, its edges almost blocked by upturned wooden tubs, bigger than Beathan had ever seen used by any of his kin.

A hefty nudge at his shoulder propelled him inside the dim enclosure, the only daylight seeping in through thinner areas of the leather roof, or where the seams were unevenly sewn. He had been inside Agricola's leather tent at the Moran Dhuirn Roman encampment, but this shelter was nothing like as well-made.

The noises inside were even more deafening than outside and the smell breath-catching. The reek of tanned leather was overpowering. It was mixed with many other stenches he could not identify and others he did not want to. A slushing and sloshing of water vied with the splashing and dull stamping of feet, which in turn was drowned out by what was not particularly tuneful singing.

And there were similar noises coming from sections beyond which he could not see, since the interior was partitioned by stout cloth walls.

His hauler shouted over the stramash. "Fuller! This Brigante is for you!"

"Bring him over here."

On hearing the command, the singing stopped. So did the water dins.

The wiry man who issued the order sounded wearied with everything. Beathan realised the man's gestures indicated that the legionaries should attach his chain link to a post that was set in front of a row of young boys. Youngsters who stood inside large-based, iron-banded wooden tubs, similar to the ones he had seen at the doorway.

"What are you gaping at? Get back to work!" The fuller bawled at the boys.

The foot stomping began, but not the singing which Beathan belatedly appreciated had been in his native Brigantian tongue.

He swallowed down the craving. He had not heard the sounds of his birthplace being spoken for so long. Though the words were common throughout a vast area, the speech rhythms and cadences of the Brigantes differed from those of the northern Caledons and Taexali.

"Wait!" The man shouted, even though relative quiet reigned around him. "Strip off that stinking tunic and the braccae before you attach the chain."

His legionaries had a good chuckle while they wrestled off his tattered boots and manky clothes, his protests doing no good at all.

Naked, he was chained to the post by the neck collar, after which his wrists were manacled together behind his back. One of the guards smirked in a manner he did not like at all. "He is now in your hands, Fuller, until midday, when we will return for him."

The second guard was more than pleased to add. "Make sure he works for this…pleasure."

Cackling like wild pigs, the legionaries left the tent. Agricola's guard was nowhere to be seen and must have sneaked away unnoticed. Beathan was glad to see all of them go, though his new situation was worrying.

When the soldiers were well out of sight, the booth overseer leaned forward eye-to-eye with him. The fuller spoke the common tongue, but it sounded more like Tertius at Trimontium, who had spoken with a southern lilt. "I am the best buyer of cloth; the best maker of garments and best cleaner of wool at Eboracum. And you, Brigante? You will leave here smelling like the sweetest of flowers."

Beathan reeled under a substantial slap to his jaw before the man went to the front of the tent. Drawing a deep breath to mask the suddenness of the violence, he made yet one more vow to *Taranis* to give him a chance to return every injury meted out to him.

The fuller rolled a vast empty tub towards him which he set down in front of the post, the sides high enough to reach above his knees.

After dumping the manky tunic and trousers into it, the man grunted, "Get in!"

Without waiting to see if he did as bid, the washer man turned away towards the separating curtain and bustled into the next section of the long tent, hollering as he went. "Bring water! Enough to fill to the top of the tub and be quick about it."

It seemed that the launderer was incapable of speaking quietly. A file of young girls followed the man's return, steadily adding pails of water to the tub before retreating.

"I told you to get in, Brigante!" The fuller slapped at his shoulders.

Stepping one leg over the lip, he found it difficult to maintain his balance with his hands tied behind his back. However, his efforts were in vain because the man dunted the rest of him in, making him end up on his buttocks amongst the now-floating clothes. His face almost submerged under the swilling cold water. The shock of it made him squirm around to get onto his knees before surging up to his feet, glad that the chain was long enough to not strangle him. He gasped and shook his head, drips flying all around him. Even though the tub was barely half-full, water had sloshed all over the sides which set the fuller to cursing even more.

"Get on with filling this tub!"

Beathan tried to ignore the snickering laughs of the girls as they cascaded more water over his legs and whispered up to him about him being a well-formed warrior. His tethered situation did nothing to diminish his instinctive appreciation of the first young females he had seen for so long. He had been aware of his growing into manhood for some seasons, but had not the opportunities to do anything about it. This was clearly not an appropriate situation either, but for the first time in a long while he felt more than just a mere hostage of Agricola.

The ribald comments from the boys behind him were also liberating in a very strange way. They wore tunics that were tucked up under their belts, to bare their legs in the water. Their many lewd gestures were designed to snare the attention of the girls.

"Enough of that! Get on with your work!" The laundryman ushered the girls out of the room, tutting like a clucking hen as he followed them. The boys' laughs and jeers settled into sniggering instead.

"Been a while since you saw a girl then, Brigante?" One of them shouted, splashing water on his back.

Beathan turned around to even more points and taunts as his short-lived reaction shrank. It was only then that he noticed the boys were not wearing a slave collar, but the heavy iron bracelet, with a large fastening link that was around each boy's wrist, was not a Brigante armband. The boys were slaves belonging to the fuller.

A different one halted the taunts. "Aye, Brigante! You can see that we are enslaved just like you are, though we were not collected after a morning's work like you will be by General Agricola's personal guard." The boy stomped his feet, the line restarting their own tramping and sloshing. "We only eat, if we clean enough of these shit-infested Roman clothes."

Beathan was noticing how thin they were when a woman entered though the curtain opening. She looked about twenty-five summers, though she could have been much younger since hard toil was etched across her features. Premature grey already streaked the dark tresses that were tied back in a long single plait.

Chapter Thirteen

Eboracum Roman Fortress AD 85

The bucket the woman emptied into his tub was the weirdest stink. The piss-smell was unmistakeable, but there was something gritty that smelled even more pungent.

He was glad that the contents of her bucket dissipated when it mixed in with the river water, though that result could also have been because the woman tipped in something from a small pouch that was tied to her waistbelt.

"Stamp your feet." Her tone was kinder, even sympathetic, but her stance was awkward, since she strained to listen to noises coming from the adjacent section. She, too, wore a slave bracelet which clanked against the bucket handle when she bent forward to hiss at him. "The fuller is coming back. Do whatever he asks you."

He did not think that boded well and attempted to free his feet, which were entangled. The woman reached into the tub and pushed the garments down, giving him a chance to get into the semblance of a stepping rhythm.

"Mearna!" The fuller was in a hurry when he headed for the main entrance door. "Stay in here till I return. Organise that pile of washing over there, and afterwards you can sort him out. And you had better do a good job, or I will not get paid my dues from Legate Liberalis!"

Beathan watched him pointing to one particular pile, though the tent was full of heaps dotted around.

Some mounds were as high as a full-grown man.

"A shipment of raw cloth has arrived and I want to buy it, before anyone else hears of it." Turning to look at the boys, the man hollered. "No food for you, if those tunics are not fully clean by the time I return."

The boys went back to their tuneless singing but were more subdued than before.

"I heard him mutter that you are a Brigante. Is that true?" Mearna asked, peering at him after her owner disappeared out into the street.

She had begun to separate the mound of tunics into different piles according to their faded colours. They looked like ones he had seen worn in the fort, those worn by the men who traipsed in-and-out of the principia. He wondered how much to tell her while he tried to trap cloth that was determined to float. She may be an enslaved tribeswoman, but he had no idea if she could be trusted.

As though she sensed his reticence, she sighed. "I am a northern Brigante. I have been a slave of the fuller for many, many seasons, but I do not forget what my life used to be like."

Beathan could not miss the wretchedness in her wistful expression. Her dark brown eyes reminded him of the hounds that used to trail after his grandfather Callan.

"What part of Brigantia are you from?" she asked.

Before he could even decide if he was going to answer she continued, holding one of the filthy tunics out to inspect the stains. She tutted at the state of it. "I hardly remember the hillfort of my parents. I was bought from the slave market when I was about your age."

He sloshed his feet back and forth, enjoying the feel of the water, though unwilling to do the proper stomping that the other boys managed. He continued in silence while she created a new pile for the most stained garments. With every other tunic sorted, she gazed over at him as though willing him to respond. "Though, I was not snatched from the hillfort of my own clan. I was fostered long before then, and was at a southern Brigante stronghold. This was when battle raged at Whorl."

He gulped and tried to maintain an untroubled expression, though inside he willed the woman to keep talking.

Done with her sorting, she came closer to his tub and regarded him from his head down to the water level. "Mmm…"

Feeling highly vulnerable, he was unable to do more than stare back.

"You first!" she declared, before she bustled over to the section divider. Like the fuller had done, she popped her head though the curtain and called on one of the girls to bring her a small pail, some cloths and two buckets of fresh water.

She trudged back to him after they were passed through to her. "Kneel down."

He stared at her, not sure what she was about to do but ceased his rhythmic sloshing.

"By *Rhianna*! You should see your face." Her change to humour warmed him. "I am going to wash the filth from you, before more of the muck from the clothes makes that impossible.

Her hand at his shoulder helped guide him down to his hunkers.

Dipping the small pail into the water, she lifted it towards his head and repeated the emptying till she was satisfied his hair and upper body were wet enough before she began to scrub at him with a scrunched-up piece of cloth.

He decided that a few questions from him would not give up any secrets. He cleared his mouth of water trickles. "I have heard tales of the Brigantes at Whorl. What can you tell me about it?"

Satisfied with his hair being a bit cleaner, she used fresh water to rinse his long mane before beginning on the back of his neck.

"Whorl? I was not there myself, so cannot speak of the fighting. It was after the Brigante defeat that the Romans tramped everywhere and took many captives. Me included. They dragged me here to Eboracum, to the slave market, and I was sold to the fuller."

Beathan felt her cloth move around to his chest. He squirmed away. It had been a very long time since his mother had bathed him…and though this woman might seem kind, she was not Nara of the Selgovae.

Her voice became a whisper as she dipped her cloth in to rinse it. "I was terrified. They killed my foster-mother in front of my eyes, but I never found out about my foster-father. He was probably killed at Whorl, like many a-thousand other Brigante warriors."

The expression reaching out to him was of profound grief, but also of resignation. Having wrung out the cloth, the woman absently spread it back and forth along the edge of the tub.

"And of my own kin? I can only imagine their fate was exactly the same."

He could no longer stay silent. "Some of my family went to Whorl, though most of them returned to our northern Brigante hillfort."

He felt her smile bathe him. It was wan, yet comforting.

"That was good. Thanks be to *Rhianna* that some survived." She indicated he should stand. "You had better make an attempt with the clothes, young Brigante warrior. Though I do not yet know your story, your body already bears many scars and you want to receive no more as a result of the fuller's wrath."

His hands being shackled made his rise awkward. While water dripped from him, he found himself talking. The boys behind him were probably listening, though their foot-stamping and sloshing muffled some of the conversation. "*Rhianna* is my mother's favourite goddess, though she is not a Brigante."

Mearna's expression was mystified. "But you are a Brigante?"

Naming yourself as the tribe of your mother was usual in the north, so Beathan explained. "My father is a northern Brigante, but my mother is from the Selgovae tribe."

Her brows furrowed. "She is a Selgovae servant?"

Beathan laughed loud enough to make his chest rattle. "My mother would take affront at that description! Nay, she is a chief's daughter."

Mearna's interest was clearly piqued. "Why did he not take a Brigante woman as his official hearth-wife?"

There was sufficient slight in her tone to make him grin again. "That is a long story, too long to tell here." He sobered a little thinking of how to continue. "If you were captured after the battle at Whorl, you may have heard that many of the northern tribes made alliances before the confrontation, so that they could fight against the Roman scourge as a united front."

Mearna nodded, as though trying to remember the circumstances.

"My father's Garrigill clan made an alliance with the Selgovae, with my mother as the bride-price."

She jumped back from him, as though scalded. Her hiss was a terrified one, her eyes flaring.

"You are from Garrigill Hillfort?"

Beathan tried to catch the woman when she sank to her knees and overbalanced, slumping against the tub sides, but his wrist shackles prevented him.

Once again, he slipped to his knees amongst the foul-smelling floating waste and faced the sobbing woman. He nudged her fingers with his ribs "I was born and raised at Garrigill Hillfort till I was seven summers old."

Tear-drenched eyes matched a tremulous smile when she raised her chin. "I, too, was born and bred at Garrigill, till I was about seven summers. Then I was sent south to be fostered at the hillfort of my mother's clan."

Beathan could not work out who she could be. He was sure he had never ever seen her before, though his time at Garrigill was such a long time ago. He made sure to keep his whispers steady. "My father is Lorcan of Garrigill."

Mearna's smile became more pronounced. "And my father is Tully, the chief of Garrigill."

Beathan squeaked. "My Brigante grandfather? I never knew him. He died just after Whorl, but before I was born."

Mearna was horrified. "Did Tully go to battle at Whorl?"

Beathan wanted to pat her hand to reassure her but could only strain forward. "Nay. My mother said he was already dying from a wasting disease. She could not cure him. It was no blade that killed him, but I believe she eased his passing."

Mearna patted his shoulder. "She sounds like a wonderful woman. But tell me of your father, Lorcan. He was my much older brother…" she paused, tears again hovering, as though the recall was difficult. "I had many brothers, of course. At least five, perhaps even six?"

Beathan gulped back his own emotion as they shared their sorrows. "I do not know who amongst them still live. My father, mother, my uncles – Brennus and Gabrond."

He felt Mearna's calloused hands bracket his face, her tremulous smile returned. "Brennus sang like a linnet. Gabrond was always laughing and playing foolish pranks to gain the attention of the young females. Lorcan was already in his own roundhouse with his new hearth-wife when I was fostered." She broke off to stare at him again, obviously confused by her memories.

He hastened to reassure her. "My father's first hearth-wife died during childbirth, as did the child. Lorcan took no permanent woman till he met my mother, many seasons afterwards."

Mearna shook her head as though focusing better. "How is it that you do not know if they are still alive?"

The words spilled out at speed, so fast he amazed even himself. He told her about his clan's trek to Caledonia and about the times when his family had been separated from Uncle Brennus, before they were all reunited again in the encampments of the Caledon leader, Calgach. He skipped the worst of the details of the battlegrounds at Beinn na Ciche, but he felt the tight grip of Mearna's fingers when he mentioned becoming separated from his cousin, Ruoridh.

"Is this Ruoridh you speak of my oldest brother Arian's son?"

"Nay. Arian died before my parents met each other. He had no children named for him, but your brother, Gabrond, has a healthy brood."

He stopped to reflect for a moment, unable to prevent the glisten that came to his eyes which had nothing to do with the herbs that Mearna had put into the water he was steeped in.

"Ruoridh is Gabrond's eldest, followed by Enya. Then there are three younger ones." He summoned a smile for the woman whose own gaze was filled with sorrow, and longing. "Before Beinn na Ciche, Ruoridh was my best friend as well as being kin."

Mearna patted his shoulder. For reassurance, and clearly to encourage him to continue.

"Tell me of Enya? And later, of your own sisters and brothers, if you have any?"

He managed a proper grin. "That would take a long time."

He felt Mearna's palm gently curving around his cheek. "I need to hear everything you can tell me about my lost kin."

"Enya is older than me by a few seasons. She was already warrior trained before the battle led by Calgach. She does not talk much, nor laugh much either, but she can be as fierce, and as skilled, as any warrior I have ever met."

More, and more, of his family members were mentioned. In turn, Mearna told him of her fostering and of what came after she was enslaved.

"Tell me how you came to be captured?"

Beathan sighed. Hindsight was a fine thing. He had asked himself so many times what could he have done differently to avoid being in that bit of the woods behind Beinn na Ciche when the Roman patrol overpowered him and Ruoridh.

"Moran Dhuirn. Many Fists! That is the name we gave to Agricola's encampment. And it was so well-named because there were far too many of those Roman fists. A Roman shield boss knocked me senseless, but it was the strong grip of four fists that dragged me away from Ruoridh."

He could not look at the woman, could only stare vacantly at the tent material when he told her of his last sight of Ruoridh. That Roman sword held high above his cousin's body, poised and ready to plunge still came to him in the night-dark.

Mearna rose up to pace around, her fingertips pressed against her forehead. "So, after they questioned you at their Moran Dhuirn camp, they learned that you are the son of a Brigante Chief? Agricola knows this, too?"

He nodded but could say no more since their dip into the past was interrupted by the noisy return of the fuller who was organising people outside. It gave Beathan just time to surge to his feet to restart his awkward sloshing and for Mearna to hasten to the farthermost pile of clothing, well away from him.

She managed to speak to him a couple of times more during that long morning, sharing memories of her brothers and of the hillfort at Garrigill. By then, he had no doubt she was who she claimed to be.

It seemed unbelievable that he had just met his father's younger sister. He had no idea which goddess had favoured him, but one of them had!

By the time he was dragged back to his fellow-hostages he was much cleaner, even if his clothes were still damp. The flailing of the cloth that he had seen the other boys undertake was impossible for him when chains bound him.

He felt more wrung-out than his garments had been, especially since he had not managed to say a proper farewell to Mearna.

She had been sent off to do something away from the area by her owner who had not even noticed any reluctance on her part, nor the lingering look of pity she sent his way.

Chapter Fourteen

Londinium Fort AD 85

Gaius strode into the room Agricola had appropriated as a work space, in the Governor's Palace in Londinium. He had ordered that his correspondence be delivered there, rather than to the Basilica where official documentation was generally sent.

"Another one for you, sir." Gaius held forward a scroll.

He looked up from his seated position behind the desk and heaved a huge sigh, but not one of relief. The reports coming his way had been flowing as freely as ever since they left Eboracum, his stay there longer than he had anticipated. But, till a change was made by Emperor Domitian, all the decisions regarding Britannia still rested on his shoulders.

"Add it to that pile." He indicated the largest heap of scrolls on the desk which was also littered with wooden boards and wax tablets.

"Sir. I believe you may want to read this one right away."

Gaius' humour-laced prompt had him look up from his reading, to raise his eyebrows in enquiry.

Gaius chuckled as he handed the scroll across to him. "No, I have not been taking a sneaky look. I believe I may have been sent a similar piece of information."

Since Gaius was rarely wrong about such things, Agricola broke the seal. "Maybe this is just a ruse, and your curiosity is getting the better of you?"

"Ah, perhaps you are right, sir, and I am completely mistaken."

He unrolled what proved to be a short and fairly curt communication. He looked up to see Gaius smirking, and then he re-read it. "I am to have a statue created in my honour?"

Gaius' expression made him snigger, an incredulous laughter building up which almost got out of control before he sobered up.

"I should consider that a great honour, if it happens, though my letter does not say where the statue will be erected. Does yours?"

Gaius' smile slipped away. "Unfortunately, sir, it does not. Though I have to assume somewhere around the Forum in Rome."

He pointed the re-rolled scroll at Gaius, his expression full of mock reprimand even though the message was serious. "The Forum? More likely a back street! Have you learned nothing? Never trust a thing our esteemed Emperor Domitian decides upon. Nor those of the Senate who merely do his bidding."

He watched Gaius reach into a pouch that dangled from his tunic belt and then the man offered him the correspondence that had been in it.

"You can read here that I have some other instructions, though my missive contains nothing about any further additional honours that should be conferred upon you."

Agricola waved the scroll away, not needing such reassurance. "Just tell me anything I need to know about it, while I am still here in Britannia."

Gaius bent over the desk, the scroll still in his hand. "Do you wish to leave Britannia sooner? I mean, to reach Rome even more quickly than you had intended, now you have this new information?"

He tapped his fingertips on a clear bit of the wooden desk surface, his lips narrowing. "No. My plans remain the same. I will set sail four days from now, which is just long enough to enjoy these well-executed mosaics." He tapped his feet on the floor. "This scroll does not change a thing since, yet again, Domitian has sent no word of my replacement as Governor of Britannia."

Gaius cleared his throat. "Ah, that brings me to the rest of my letter that you do need to hear about, if not read yourself."

Resignation flooded him at Gaius' rueful expression. "Pull the seat up close, Gaius."

"As you well know, when it comes to Domitian's disfavour, I am as vulnerable as you are, sir."

He could not help but make an exaggerated cough. Gaius' disgruntled expression was as he expected.

The sigh from Gaius was bile laced. "Future promotion for me is currently out of the question but my…"

Agricola heard a distinct hesitation before his friend's next words.

"My 'banishment' to Britannia looks set to remain unchanged for now. That has a disadvantage in that I will not be returning to Rome soon, and will not be able to accompany you there. The more positive thought is that by remaining here I should escape the swingeing sword, that Domitian brandishes, for a bit longer. It will come as no surprise to you that remaining in Britannia seems a healthier choice, though my personal guard will continue to be chosen very wisely."

Agricola knew there was nothing he could add to change those circumstances, so he merely nodded before Gaius continued.

"Information comes to me that Javolenus Priscus is gaining more favour in Roman circles."

Agricola nodded again. "The man may never be a friend of mine, but he is efficient. Your news does not surprise me."

It was Gaius' turn to affirm with nods of his own. "He may well become the next Consul of Britannia, though I doubt Domitian will give him command of the Britannic forces."

Agricola could not dispute any of what Gaius had just stated. "What of Sallustius Lucullus? Domitia sends rumours that he is, perhaps, gaining even better favour, and my wife is generally correct with her suspicions."

There was a quirk to Gaius' mouth that was almost more positive. "It could well be. Lucullus' current consulship ends soon."

A silence descended as he pondered the possible successors, Gaius equally reflective. It was a grave pity that the Senate did not have the same regard for Gaius as he had. The man had made no worse an error of judgement than many others had, but they had not ended up being shunned and exiled to the furthest reaches of the empire.

He got up, opened the door and addressed the guard. "Summon Crispus."

"Sir!" The soldier was already moving along the corridor, his boots clicking against the recently-laid wooden flooring of the corridor. In due time it would be tiled, but the main rooms of the Governor's Palace had current decorative priority. He savoured the fresh air for a few moments and gained some inner peace from the gentle lapping as water spouted from the goddess *Juturna's* cornucopia into the central pool of the courtyard. It was an oasis of Rome in its westernmost province.

It had been a whimsical notion, at an early point of his long tenure, to organise the province of Britannia from behind a desk such as the one he had just left, in surroundings similar to his present ones. The reality had been different, of course. He always gained satisfaction from his successful civic reforms, though military subjugation of the barbarians of the north held an even greater lure.

But now?

Ordered back to Rome ignominiously, tail between legs and head cowed. Oh, a statue in his honour was a fitting and very fine thing…the maximum ostentatious symbol that anyone who was not an emperor could ever have. Many thousands across the empire would probably see it as a gesture of advancement…but in his own heart, he had failed to capture all that he wanted for Rome.

Seeing the approach of his secretary, Crispus, he forced himself to deal with the present.

The next while was spent with Gaius, assessing the many communications that begged attention, since Gaius would need to continue processes, and ensure completion for the foreseeable future.

Crispus, with stylus in hand, was taking copious notes and the piles on his desk gradually receded. Crispus' table, set against the wall, naturally displayed the opposite situation. The mounds for him to make responses to grew and grew.

Agricola got up to pace around the room, stretching the crick out of his back. Pausing by Gaius, he gestured towards Crispus who worked in silence – an almost invisible presence. "Are you as confident with your own, regarding discretion?"

There were still many sensitive situations in Britannia which were soon to be in Gaius' total control, even if only very temporary.

An assured nod was sufficient before he went on to discuss a still thorny subject. Instead of sitting behind his desk, he sat down on one of the many low couches dotted around the room and indicated Gaius should join him. "What state are the hostages in?"

"Not exactly healthy." Gaius cleared his throat before sitting down on a nearby couch. "But neither are they near death. I checked on them this morning."

Agricola leaned his forearms on his thighs and exhaled towards the mosaic floor. The scene depicted an idyllic, bucolic one with *Bacchus* in full splendour. "If only those cowardly Caledonian allies had signed treaties!" He lowered his voice to a growled whisper. "May the fate of putrid gore befall Domitian! I could have subdued this whole island, if I had had sufficient men. And, even now, he demands that more of the *Legio II Adiutrix* withdraw from the north."

"The Vacomagi captives, who have already reached the slave markets of Rome, are proof of your Caledonian conquest."

"Paltry evidence of my subjugation." He thumped his fist against his thigh. "They are just slave bodies among the thousands who will be bought and sold many times till they are useless to their owners. Whoever purchases those Vacomagi, in Rome, will use them no differently from captives taken from any other part of the empire."

He swivelled his legs, stretched himself the full length of the couch and folded his arms behind his head. Staring at the ceiling, he breathed in and out in a regular rhythm. "My clutch of higher-ranking hostages ought to be more useful to me than that."

Gaius lounged back, mimicking the attempt at relaxation. "Do you see them as important bargain material in Rome?"

Stretching out was doing him no good at all, so he sat up again. Gaius, however, looked far too comfortable. The hostages he had were not nearly important enough for him to use as proper leverage with the Senate, yet he needed to return with something tangible.

"Dragging all of them to Rome may prove a useless gesture but I will take a few, and find a suitable use for them. Who are the most compliant?"

Gaius jerked upwards. The snort intended. "Compliant? None of them. Your young Brigante is not the only rebellious one."

Agricola absently scratched at itchy leg hairs. "I truly believe he is the best of the hostages. Though, without his parents, Domitian will discard him as a useless youth –

not worth the time and effort to mould him into an ally of Rome."

Gaius' head dips showed agreement. "His parents would both have been more useful to you. Definitely better than the two who had broken bones. Making them walk any distance will be a liability."

"There lies your next task, Gaius! Return to Taexali Territory and flush out his Brigante father and Selgovae mother. Send them to me, and I will see that parents and son all become dependent on the benefits of Rome."

Gaius chuckled. "Or, I could just keep the boy as my house-slave. And in a few years, when I eventually regain my own favour, I can bring all three to Rome. They could be my triumphal bargaining material, though I do not anticipate anything at all in the way of honours from Domitian."

Agricola pondered the idea, a resigned laugh escaping. "You have many wonderful suggestions, Gaius. I will think on it. But bear in mind, that young Brigante is a very quick study. Even though we only spent a few extra days in Eboracum, my evening conversations with the youth were informative."

"Conversations?" Gaius sounded intrigued.

"When not trying to slay me with hastily veiled looks of antipathy, he answered my questions about Caledonia. He detests his enslavement. There is no doubt about that, yet he displays a pragmatism that I find admirable. He makes the best of his situation, knowing that escape is not realistic. His knowledge of Latin is also more than I first thought, and he picks up new words easily."

Gaius' chortles were loud. "So, while you two were rehearsing for a performance at the Roman Forum, I was dodging the Taexali chief's attempts to acquire a knife to stab me in the back. Allow any of those hostages to thieve a weapon, and it will be to our detriment. They presently exist only to kill their captors. And that means you and I are first in their queue!"

"Do you really think the Brigante lad is primed for such revenge? Given a situation were to occur?"

The look Gaius sent his way allowed only one interpretation.

He mostly agreed, yet there was something about the young Brigante warrior that set him aside. He had a feeling that the Brigante's father must have had good reason to be proud of the way the lad was maturing.

Memories of the early deaths of his own sons brought sorrow bubbling to the surface. If the first son born to him and Domitia had survived, and if the *cursus honorum* usual career route had been undertaken, his son might already have completed his tribune training and be a *quaestor*. The loss of possibility was deep and even more acute when he thought of the second son born to him. It was barely two years since the baby died, and Domitia had still not recovered properly from the event.

Was the profound grief over losing his own sons the reason he was drawn to the Brigante?

Many times, he had lamented that *Mana Genita* had claimed his sons. He had no desire for infant mortality to grieve other parents, but fervently wished that the severity of the goddess had fallen elsewhere.

Chapter Fifteen

Londinium Fort AD 85

"Get up!"

The order was abrupt in the pre-dawn gloom of the tiny cell, the guards having burst in and disturbed Beathan's restless sleep. While one gave him a vicious kick in the stomach, another wasted no time in unlocking his ankle shackles. He wondered what retribution was about to happen next but, after so many days of being chained up, he was relieved to be bundled outside.

When Derwi and Gillean barrelled into him, having been shoved out of the door after him, it took all of his resilience to keep his balance. The task was even more difficult since his hands were being manacled in front of him and a pull-chain attached. That indignity was only slightly better than the chain being attached to his slave collar.

"Bear up, young Brigante!" Derwi dared a heartening whisper even though the three of them were vastly outnumbered by a contubernium of eight legionaries.

It was soon apparent that the other hostages were not joining them when the heavy wooden door was slammed shut and the iron bolt drawn across the outside.

He once again found himself at the front of the line when he was dragged along and out of the eastern gate of the fort.

"Have you ever seen the like?" Gillean's comments were many and plentiful from behind him as they stumbled along the middle of the street in the growing blue. Lugh's ball of fire was creeping up and dispelling the many shadows of the night. Building after building lay to his left with little or no space between them. They were rectangular like the barrack blocks of the forts, though not all were the same size or even the same height.

"Is that also a house?" he asked, indicating the long wall of stark wooden boards on his sword-arm side, no doors breaking the unending regularity of the timber.

Derwi, at the end of their linked-line, posed his own questions after the legionary yanked him around a corner. "Where are the fields? And the livestock? How do all of these people around here feed themselves?"

Though barely light, there were already carts and wagons on the streets, pulled along by mules and oxen. Horses had been a-plenty inside the fort but none were in sight now, and no domestic fowl were pecking around

Conversation was halted when he reached the end of the long wall and looked on to the next section. Gillean's sudden halt wrenched the chain so hard that Beathan thought his arm had been pulled off at the shoulder, the force enough to have made him make a half-turn

"Move on!" The legionary alongside his Caledon friend was impatient, his pilum flashing out first at Gillean's thigh, and then he stretched it forwards to prod at his arm.

"Roman turd!" Gillean's further curses included pleas to *Araun* to lavish some divine and fatal retribution on his enemies.

"Keep going, Beathan," Derwi urged him. "Do not give the Roman shite any reason to hurt you."

When Gillean picked up his pace, to relax the tension on his pull-chain, Beathan marvelled at the next building that was set back a few steps from the street.

"Why would any chief build a roundhouse as huge as that, but put no roof on it?"

When he darted a look behind him, the others were too busy ogling the sight to answer.

He trudged passed the strange circular walls, four or five times as high as the largest roundhouse he had ever seen. The timbers were worn, some had even been repaired in places, so he guessed it was not newly built. It was only on passing the wide double-arched doorway, at least double the width of a Roman wagon, that he could see it teemed with people inside. A line of slaves raked the dusty ground, others following in behind to add fresh sand to level the surface. Before his guard hauled him past, he caught glimpses of the shafts of a metal-sided Roman chariot propped against wooden doors at the far end. Above that a man shouted instructions from a position far above the ground level. He had seen stairs leading to the top of the guard towers in the forts he had been in, but nothing compared to the rows and rows of wide steps that went around the inside of the building.

"What is that place for?"

Behind him Derwi mocked as he passed the opening. "A round chariot race?"

What Beathan had seen was nothing like the Celtic chariots his grandfather Callan had had at his Hillfort of Tarras, chariots that were raced across huge tracts of flat land.

Beathan smiled for the first time in ages. "No horsemanship skills are needed in there. Are you any good with horses, Derwi? Or just with oxen?"

The jest did not get a chance to mature because the nearest pilum jabbed towards him. Conversation was obviously not welcome in the hostage line.

Turning another corner, it got much busier. People bustled around as though they had already been up for ages, carrying all manner of goods from place to place. Some were stacked in their arms, but others were hauled along inside small two-wheeled carts. Many of the people he could see wore slave bands around their wrists.

Gillean's whisper was venomous. "The *Ceigan Ròmanach* are taking us to a different fort!"

Beathan looked at the long wooden wall that stretched way ahead down the street, even longer than those of the fort they had been imprisoned in.

Derwi dared a low comment. "It cannot be a fort wall. It has a roof!"

A few more steps took him around the front of the huge building where a colonnaded walkway was dotted here and there with tables groaning with produce. He was dragged past tempting food smells, newly-baked breads and even some meaty aromas, though he had no idea of what the animal source was.

Pulled through the arched entrance and into an interior courtyard, his ears rang with confusing heckles from even more people trading goods from some of the tiny one-room booths that were set along three sides of the courtyard.

The tongues spoken around him were many and varied.

All sorts of things were displayed on the tables: bolts of cloth; tunics; leather boots and belts; small knives and other iron ware.

"I have a feeling that someone very important lives down there."

He could not doubt Derwi's whistled comment.

The building he was dragged towards at the far end of the courtyard was the grandest he had ever seen. The front part was the height of one room, but in behind it was at least double that. A pillared walkway sheltered door accesses to many ground-floor rooms.

A sentry waved his line through a wide opening into the next section which was yet another gathering space – though a roofed one, the far wall leading into further chambers. The basic structure reminded him of the headquarters at Trimontium fort.

Gillean thought so, too. "It looks important, like the principia. But why is it outside the fort and amongst all these houses and warehouses?"

"Legate Liberalis wants them in there!" Thumb pointing backwards, the guard on duty indicated the room behind him.

Still chained together, Beathan was rough-handled to stand in front of the table with Gillean and Derwi alongside him, then their escort patrol was ordered to wait outside.

The legate began to speak in Latin, his words interspersed and translated into the tongue of the tribes by the man who stood at his side with a stylus and wax tablet at the ready. Beathan was immediately suspicious. He had already heard the legate speak his Brigante tongue well enough.

"My intention was to send you all to the slave trader who embarks for Rome today, but it seems that General Agricola has other intentions for you three."

It had been so long since his capture after the battle at Beinn na Ciche, that the prospect of slavery had been less of a priority than willing himself to live through another day. He had proof of mistreatment all over his body, yet Beathan knew that genuine slavery would be much worse, and for far longer. Perhaps even his lifetime.

He watched the legate shuffle through a pile of boards before he selected one. Looking up after reading it, Gillean was Liberalis' first target, questions coming at speed. Derwi, like Gillean, gave reluctant answers as insisted on when it was his turn, to confirm the details Liberalis already had of their tribe and status within.

When Legate Liberalis addressed him, he was surprised to be asked fewer questions – though it was much tougher to answer when the legate asked if he had seen his mother, or father, perish on the battlefield at Beinn na Ciche. It was too painful to answer and impossible to pretend indifference. Whatever, his silence did not seem to rile the legate. An over-long stare from the officer only served to make him suppress his yearnings even more.

Turning to the details on a new wax tablet, passed to him by the secretary, the legate added something to the bottom after which he made for the door to instruct the escort patrol.

"Remove this contamination from the Basilica! General Agricola awaits them."

When Beathan passed by the legate, the dismissive tones were a threat. "If you want to reach true manhood, I suggest you control your tendency to disrespect, Brigante."

More streets were trudged along, though this time he was at the rear of their file. On turning a new corner, the long-range view changed to one of distant water with ships on it, but the smells that came to him were not of the salty sea. On one side of the street, warehouse after warehouse swarmed with people going in and out of openings that were much higher and wider than normal doors. Carts filled with numerous goods spilled forth from the entrances, and sometimes empty wagons trundled in. Newly tanned leather smells mingled with those of smoked meats and fish. Some carts passed him going down to the waterside while others headed back to the basilica, where he had been questioned by Legate Liberalis.

The other side of the street was entirely different. Through the gates of the building, it was similar to the praetorium at Trimontium, though much grander.

Beathan was soon to find that although General Agricola lived in luxury in the Governor's Palace, that was not quite the case for him. He spent the night stuffed into a grubby little storeroom with the other two but, surprisingly, the food dished out to them was the best Beathan had had for many moons.

The following day Derwi cursed and groaned, in between heaving up the better food they had been served the previous evening.

"May the wrath of *Araun* be upon Agricola and every single Roman soldier."

He fared only a little better than either of his companions. His vomiting had been violent enough to completely empty his innards in one bout.

"We Caledons are mountain men! We are not born to sail the waters of *Manaan*." Gillean also vowed vengeance on General Agricola for dragging them into the vessel that was bobbing them up and down and carrying them off to unknown lands.

Chapter Sixteen

Southern Gaul AD 85

"We are definitely escaping!"

Gillean's vow, in between bouts of a racking cough, was one that Beathan agreed with.

Though how?

"I gather you have a plan, my Caledon friend?" Derwi sounded unimpressed, but that was fairly usual, given their circumstances. In some form, or other, they had had the same conversation many times since the *liburna* had tied up on the shores of Gaul, near Gesoriacum.

Having listened intently to Agricola's Gallia Narbonensis soldiers, as often as possible, meant Beathan had gleaned useful information, the names of the many Roman forts they passed through being only one of the results.

The quarter-century of mounted and infantry legionaries, who had made up Agricola's private guard from Britannia, was topped up by another twenty from local infantry troops. Though, he could not work out why they were needed. The Roman road they travelled south on was busy with travellers moving in both directions, yet it did not seem in any way threatening. But from fort to fort, the infantry compliment changed.

He understood more Latin words every day, blatantly eavesdropping the conversations when the soldiers walked alongside the three-vehicle baggage train. And, depending on which of the troops he trod next to, he learned even more about what was happening since some of them spoke a language that was similar enough to his own.

Mostly he was forced to walk, attached to the wagon-side. But occasionally, as now, he and the other two had been dumped inside one.

He wondered if it was because some of Agricola's personal escort had complained about the noise Gillean was making alongside them, but that did not sound realistic. That smacked too much of Agricola showing some concern, which was highly unlikely.

Some of Agricola's personal guard were delighted to be on the way to Rome. Others spoke of returning to the place of their upbringing for a short time with mixed feelings, some having been soldiers for so long that they talked of being unsure of how they would fit in with their old life. He had heard others moan that they had not been granted leave, but they were eager to see the heart of the Roman Empire for the first time.

His curiosity increased with every step that got nearer to Rome. He could not imagine anywhere bigger than the Londinium they had sailed away from. However, the knowledge that his fate lay in the hands of General Agricola adversely dulled any prospect of seeing the city of Rome.

It was inexplicable, but Agricola did not seem in a tearing hurry to get there. Beathan had limited experience of travelling on Roman roads, but it seemed to him that the daily distance covered across Gaul was steady, at best.

Setting aside his musings, he listened to the current conversation and joined in. "Even if we could get out of these chains, Gillean – which would surprise me greatly – how would we get back to Caledonia?"

Derwi's mock heave from his sprawling position on the cart bed sounded surprisingly realistic. "I am not ready to have another sail quite yet, *mo chàirdean*. I am thinking that I might just get to know this road to Rome for a little while longer."

He laughed heartily. They were presently fettered onto a baggage wagon that jounced along a stone paved road with almost as much of a sway as there had been on the liburna.

The countryside around them was unlike any he had ever seen in Britannia. The relatively-flat land they traversed now had none of the rain-enriched greens of Caledonia. It was pale-brown and parched, withered like spent hay. The season seemed to be much progressed, even compared to the countryside near Londinium, but he had been on the move so long he had lost count of how many days had come and gone. He had a notion that two full moons had passed, since they had landed on dry land, but could not quite remember.

He imagined the feast time of Beltane must have already been celebrated, though he had no way of finding out. In the middle of the day, the searing warmth from *Lugh* was overpowering. Avid prayers to make it a bit less hot had gone unanswered, and he was now as brown as a hazelnut. In contrast to him, Gillean's reddish-fair colouring had suffered badly. Livid-red weals, and peeling skin, were depleting the Caledon's strength almost as much as the persistent bark that the man could not get rid of.

The amount of daylight being short also confused him. In Caledonia, it was never usual to have short days that were extremely hot, and long dark nights which were also stifling.

"Remind me of your latest time spent with the very friendly general, Beathan?" Derwi's question sounded sleepy.

He let the rhythm of the wagon take him back to the previous evening. "I will tell you, but only if you stay awake."

Every evening, the convoy stopped at a *mansio* – a comfortable overnight stop for Agricola though much less comfortable for him. He knew that for sure, since it was

Agricola's habit to call for him to serve the food and wine that had been made ready in the mansio's kitchen.

"Agricola's room was not as spacious as some he has slept in," he said.

In response, Derwi groaned. "I do not want to hear of his soft bed!"

Beathan watched Gillean's nudge of Derwi's arm, the accompanying chortle a tease. "If you start to talk of that, young Beathan, we will toss you out of this wagon."

The warm smile he felt inside was reassuring. His two friends had no need to worry that Agricola had been using him for more than fetching and carrying food. After the first occasion that he had spent ages in Agricola's company, Derwi and Gillean had been ready to strangle the general with their chains – till he reassured them that he was never used for unwanted sexual purposes.

"Last night, Agricola talked of the Roman Forum."

Gillean scratched at peeling skin. "There was one of those back in Londinium."

"Ah, but nowhere is supposed to be better than the one in Rome." He told his friends all he could remember of the differences.

"Just tell us the most important words for us to learn." Derwi was nearly as interested in speaking Latin as he was, but Gillean liked to hear more about the places.

Agricola talking to him about the city of Rome and the wider Roman Empire had been confusing, at first. The general mostly dined alone, unless there was a fellow traveller who was of similar status to join him, though those events had been rare.

When he was alone with the general in the usually well-appointed rooms, Agricola maintained a formality – master to servant as far as he could tell – which was adhered to. He had learned to tolerate standing nearby while Agricola ate, sometimes lounged on a couch and at other times seated. The general rarely expected him to speak, but when he did, his reluctance kept it brief.

He bitterly resented being thrust into the role of a slave, but if Agricola ever noticed that, it was never acknowledged. Slaves, he had heard, were ill-treated by their masters, though he could never claim that of Agricola. If the man wanted him to do something new, then he was given precise instructions, and he was never beaten if he got it wrong first time.

Those nights were filled with him battling high emotions. He hated Agricola, yet he wanted to learn from him. He wanted to know what emotions drove Agricola but almost never glimpsed anything that clarified the man's true personality.

Mostly one-sided, almost dispassionate, conversations often began with 'Did you know…?' which developed into Agricola giving long explanations in Latin, interspersed with translation into the common tribal language to be sure he understood. Agricola often ordered him to repeat a Latin word, or a phrase, the man seemingly eager for him to learn. He never minded doing that, since it took no effort and made the time pass quickly, though he tried to mask any eagerness. However, it also made him wary that the man was using knowledge as a way to diffuse his hatred.

The general mentioned the Senate in Rome and how they were a powerful group of men. Emperor Domitian was another topic. There was an edge to Agricola's tone when he spoke of Domitian and some of the Senators that Beathan could not quite work out. He could not call it bitterness, or even real dislike, yet it was never complimentary.

"Enough of why they go to talk in the Forum. Tell me about Agricola's food last night."

He sniggered. Derwi almost always brought the conversation round to food, even though it made them disgruntled.

"He ate *Dulcia Piperata*." He said the words again to be sure they sounded right.

"Is that good, or bad?" Gillean rubbed his growling stomach.

He chortled at the distrust on his Caledon friend's face. "Good, I would say. They are like little rounds of bread, yet are not bread. They are made with some of the spices I have mentioned before, and with nuts – like hazelnuts."

"Would that not be too gritty to eat?" Derwi also looked doubtful.

"I am thinking the honey and wine added to them must solve that problem."

"You did not get a chance to taste them?" Derwi pretended that the previous night had to be different from before.

It was a full-blown laugh that came next. "Never. Agricola only likes me to learn about what goes into his food."

Items on the table, that were imported to Rome from across the empire, were explained – details he could not help but find fascinating, even if he never tasted them. A hunger grew as the journey progressed. One not for food, but to learn about the lands of the empire that were all so different.

It was not all good, though. He did not want to hear about the thousands of slaves who pandered to the nobility and rich in Rome. He had to calm his rising temper and wipe expressions of disgust and rage from his face. Hatred was abundant that Agricola could be so detached about the Roman process of acquiring those slaves. Yet, seeing the buildings the rich patricians lived in, along with those multiple slaves, definitely appealed.

Answering questions about Caledonia happened occasionally, since that was sometimes the subject of Agricola's conversation. It was difficult to prevent regret for all that he had lost from bubbling over into violence. Yet, although at such times when it was himself and Agricola in the room, there were always at least two of his guards on duty, just outside the door, and within calling distance. He had quickly worked out that even if he attacked Agricola in any way, he would not get out of the room and escape.

When the evening was over, and he was no longer needed by Agricola, sore feet from standing in one position became expected, but it was a small price to pay for what he gained. He was then escorted to wherever the other two hostages were and ordered to get some sleep.

Derwi and Gillean, sometimes made to do chores around the mansio while he served Agricola, often bemoaned being used for labour, but they were always keen to talk about things they had learned before bedding down for the night.

Before drifting off, the evenings with Agricola reminded him of times when he was much younger and was being instructed in the ways of a Garrigill warrior, sometimes schooled by his father and at others by his uncles. His father would tell him of ways to think through issues that could be potentially dangerous ones for the tribe, even deadly. Brennus would tell him about spying for Venutius, King of the Brigantes, or would teach him song-stories of past victories and of famous warrior-kings. Gabrond would teach him how to ride, or train horses to accept the drag of a chariot with driver and spearman aboard. He had so loved those times at the feet of his kin. Warm memories of them made him more determined that one day he would return to them.

When he was not so tired…

Chapter Seventeen

Southern Gaul AD 85

The stars were his only shelter much of the time. Being bundled into a stable when the rain teemed down was an indulgence. He was sure that those inside stays were only ordered by Agricola to avoid them being so drenched they would be unable to totter along the next stretch of road without drowning the mules.

"Take heart my friends, I believe we are stopping again." Derwi's declaration accompanied braying from the mules who were always vocal about being slowed down too harshly by their driver.

At the front of the wagon, he guessed the beasts could at least see when a halt was more likely, though they were probably too stupid to work that out.

The prospect of being chained, yet again, to a roadside post held no appeal when the wheels came to a rest. In the midst of the usual noises of orders being issued, he closed his eyes and listened carefully. The manager of each mansio always sounded so enthusiastic about the quality available to their esteemed guest, and this present one did not disappoint.

"Salve, General Agricola! Welcome again. Here you will find that I have prepared nothing but the best for you."

More useful to him was Agricola's reply.

"Any mansio in the Province of Narbonensis is closer to home for me, so I am sure to be well-pleased with whatever you offer me this time."

Beathan could not prevent a smile at the less than complimentary response from Agricola. The informative soldiers had mentioned the previous evening that Agricola had not been enthused during his last visit to this particular mansio, though the admission was that had been some time ago, Agricola not having been in Rome for several years.

The iron-work rattling at his ear prevented him from overhearing any further.

"Out!"

With the usual bad grace, and lots of oaths being uttered, as though a wearisome duty for the legionary, the end ring of his wrist shackles was detached from the huge iron clamp attached to the wagon and he was unceremoniously hauled off the end boards. Fleeing was never possible at this point of the process, since there was always a convenient post outside the mansio entrance to attach beasts, or hostages to.

Alongside the other two, he slipped to the ground and sat against the wall of the now-cooling building, preparing himself for another endless wait. The burnt-orange orb was low in the sky and the intense heat of the day softened to a pleasant warmth, the wall-stones behind him soothing his back after the vigorous jarring of the wagon.

Only after the general was ensconced in whatever accommodation was found for him, and only well-after Agricola's Gallia Narbonensis troops had been fed, was it ever his turn. And there had been times when he did not get his food finished before he was called upon to serve Agricola.

"*Seall*! Here come our hosts. Have my prayers to *Brighid* been answered this time? Do we have a pleasant hearthside and plentiful food coming our way? If so, my friends, I will be having your share as well as mine since I am most senior here!" Gillean still had the strength to joke, one of the few ways they had found to pass the time while their echoing innards threatened to make the ground rumble like the stampede of cattle at a Beltane purifying ceremony.

Derwi took up the challenge of insults. "Senior? You are no more important than I am, Caledon. Just because you are from the high hills that makes you no loftier than I am, coming from the Taexali plains!"

"I have no need to be more important than you two are because my rumbling insides are always noisier than yours," Beathan grinned. "When I am fully grown my Brigante challenge will be unbeatable."

The banter continued, bragging improving as the time went on, their boasts sounding angrier as they railed at their fettering wrists and what they could do to each other if free. Hefty shoulder nudges were aided by rippling chains as the threats increased.

"Enough, sneaky Caledon! I will pay you back for that," he shouted, when his leg got in the way of a restrained kick that Derwi had aimed at Gillean. "And you, Derwi of the Taexali plains, will feel my wrath as well."

Within the bounds of their chained hands, even the exhausted Gillean managed a creditable squirm of legs, launching ineffective kicks at each other with more sound than real rage.

"What is happening here?"

Beathan rolled off Gillean's shin and attempted, unsuccessfully, to untwist his manacle. He knew that voice and it was not any of their usual guards.

General Agricola looked down at his still sprawled position and gave his other foot a nudge to separate him from Derwi on the other side. It was not the first time that Agricola had stopped by when he was being unchained, though most times, so far, it had only been a momentary silent scrutiny before the general moved away. He liked to imagine that Agricola's stare was of concern, but realistically it was only to see if he still thrived. This time, though, Agricola gaped at all of them before his gravelly voice drawled.

"I can see that you three have far too much vigour. Come dawn we will take steps to rectify that."

Having made his pronouncement, Agricola turned on his heel and walked on, away from the mansio and around the nearest corner to where Beathan assumed the bathhouse was, since the location of that facility tended to be a separate building in behind the lodging area.

Though called on by Agricola to serve his food later that evening, no educational conversation occurred. The general was joined by a military officer who was also spending the night at the mansio, the person travelling north. He listened well, but their talk was mainly of military men that he had no knowledge of, and the forts mentioned also meant nothing to him.

Boredom was difficult to keep at bay as he stood alongside waiting to serve drinks when required. He hated how tedious it was being a wine-serving slave. And he berated himself for selfishly wanting the general's exclusive time to learn about the reasons why people like him became captives, slaves and hostages.

He was not too surprised when the following day it was his neck ring that was chained to the wagon, and he was forced to plod alongside it. He loathed that fettering most of all, tied like a draft animal, but Agricola had said he would take some sort of action, and the general was a man of his word.

That thought actually made him smile.

How could he know anything about the man who was Governor of Britannia and Commander of its mighty legions?

"What has got you looking so smug, young Beathan? Have you seen something you want to hide from us? Perhaps to do with Agricola's men being in a better temper today?" Derwi's assumptions were rarely off the mark.

He had thought his chuckle was a quiet one, but agreed that the mood of the quarter-century of special guard was much less tense than at any other time during their long trek from Trimontium. He understood that Agricola was closer to home, but that did not explain why the men guarding him should feel the same relaxation. He needed to think more about why that should be so. He turned back to Derwi who plodded along behind him.

"We are close to where Agricola was reared."

"How can you know that?" Gillean's question was whispered, not due to fear of reprisal from the guards but more because his breathing was more awkward by the day.

He darted his glances back and forward, so that he could see the expressions of the other two. "The optio, from Agricola's personal guard, was grumbling yesterday about leaving the road that leads to Massalia, which it seems is the soldier's birth-place. He moaned about having to walk another three days to reach Agricola's family estates and then three back again."

"Do you suppose the optio is looking forward to some time at home?" Gillean's words were laced with his usual pondering.

"Are you thinking we can use that to our advantage?" Derwi chuckled, yet when he looked back Beathan could see that his Taexali friend was thinking about possibilities.

"And are you guessing that Agricola's personal guard will be drastically reduced, after we arrive at Agricola's home?" he asked. It was the first time he had thought of the possibility that some of those men were from the area and might be granted leave.

"Who can tell?" Gillean sounded almost cheered.

"I have no desire to rain doubts on that thought, Gillean, but I am sure that Agricola will have something organised at his estate." Derwi's face mirrored his reservations.

Gillean grasped the edge of the wagon to aid his flagging footsteps, his voice husky. "Just remember that we must take advantage of every opportunity that comes our way."

Lugh's warmth was low in the sky by the time the road Beathan trekked along began a gradual descent, sloping down to a flat plain that stretched towards the sea. Near the distant twinkling waters, countless buildings curved around a harbour.

"Look beyond the houses!" Derwi pointed out the direction his peering was focused on. "There are even more ships than we saw at Gesoriacum."

"By *Taranis* thunder!" Gillean groaned, barked up some thick spittle and spat it out. "I want to free myself from these chains, but escaping by sea was not exactly what I was hoping for."

The amount of buildings near the ships indicated it must be a large port. Partially screening his eyes, Beathan could see there were boats still sailing in from the open water, probably the last of the day's seafarers. The daylight blue was sliding through a pale, shimmering orange into a ribbon of dark burnt-orange and on to deepest blue-black.

Ahead of him, the vanguard of Agricola's column was already veering off the cobbled road onto a narrower one which was gravelled and led down to a sprawling, low-level house. Further buildings in small clusters were set at short distances away. To one side of the house, large field areas glowed with a white-gold crop, though other long strips had darker-hued plantings closer to the ground overshadowing the soil that people worked around. And on the other side, even more people ferreted around between rows and rows of palest-green bushes, though he could not work out why.

Their column had been spotted. He watched one of the field-workers closer to them turn-tail, after which the man ran towards the house, at speed.

Behind him Derwi whistled. "If that is General Agricola's home, then I am thinking that he must be a man of consequence in this territory – for reasons that are nothing to do with him wielding a sword like he does in Britannia!"

Chapter Eighteen

Gallia Narbonensis AD 85

The scurrying of figures, in and out of the curved arch which led into the building, increased. Up ahead of Beathan, the vanguard slowed down the line, and the standard bearing Agricola's insignia was raised aloft when they came to a halt in front of a much more genuine welcoming party than he had seen at any of the mansii they had stopped at.

He decided that the woman who stood central in the group of people at the doorway was important. Elegant, though simply dressed, her manner was calm as she awaited Agricola's approach.

The general's welcome back to his Narbonensis estate was then highly formal, an exchange of pecks to the cheek and verbal greetings that he was frustrated not to be able to hear properly, though he heard enough to be sure the woman was Agricola's wife. Agricola then hailed the others who stood alongside, though Beathan reckoned some of them might be servants who held the most senior positions, rather than family.

He saw none of the spontaneous physical gestures – hugs and kisses – between Agricola and his wife that his parents regularly showered on each other, yet the sparkle in the woman's eyes seemed to display a genuine, if reserved, affection.

He was taken aback when Agricola turned and marched towards him while he was being unshackled from the wagon, the woman following on behind. Along the way, the general dismissed his personal guard and pointed to the servant who would show all of the soldiers their quarters.

On reaching him, Beathan felt the force of one of Agricola's long assessing stares before orders were issued. "Your collars and armbands will remain but those chains will no longer tether you. The people who work on this estate drag no physical chain, but their well-being is dependent on working loyally for their livelihood. You three will do likewise while you remain here." Agricola's terse demands rattled out in the same form of the language of the tribes that his Gallia Narbonensis unit used. "Understood?

He could not prevent a questioning twitch from creasing his eyebrows as he worked out the implications. Gillean's coughing prompt was accompanied by a nudge at his shoulder, which was followed by one from Derwi on his other side.

"Aye, we understand," he mumbled. Agricola's stare intensified. Though unenthusiastic, he added what his friends had failed to mouth, "General Agricola."

Agricola beckoned over a burly man whose generously-folded, long tunic was more like the togas worn in Londinium. Switching to Latin, the general's tone was slightly less peremptory. "These three are hostages, but while they remain on the estate you may use them in any capacity you choose. Just be sure to keep them alive and never let them out of your sight."

"As you wish, lord." The man's facial expression showed no emotion as, after a head-dip, he stepped back a pace.

Agricola was suddenly right upon Beathan again, almost chin to chin, the language back to that of the tribes. "Sextus is the head of my household. Along with my personal guard, he will monitor your every move. He will issue your orders. If you, or your fellow hostages, fail to adhere to them be warned that you will no longer be an encumbrance that I need to drag with me, when I leave for Rome."

Agricola then turned to the woman. "Should the Lady Domitia Decidiana ask you to do something, you will obey without question. Is that also understood?"

A nod from him seemed unnecessary since Agricola had already turned to lead his wife away, the two of them followed by Sextus. Beathan was annoyed that the orders given to the overseer were too quiet for him to eavesdrop. He really wanted to know if he was involved.

Later that night, he was escorted to a room in one of the small storehouse clusters that sat at a short distance from the villa, the other two hostages there before him and having claimed their choice of bed. The thin floor-mattresses did not differ, only their placement within the room.

It seemed his lot was unchanged, since he was still closest to the door, but that no longer bothered him. The floor was swept clean and the plastered walls were dry to the touch. He stretched out on the low straw-filled mattress and popped his arms behind his head, careful not to have his metal ornamentation links clank together, since he had no desire to strangle himself.

The dim torch-light from a wall sconce set outside the door, that streaked through an iron grill near the top, was just enough for him to make out the shadows of his friends, but not their features.

"Who are we now, Derwi? Has our status been raised?" he asked, a chortle preceding the questions as well as following them.

"Praise be, indeed, to their Roman goddess *Clementia*. Sextus seems overly fond of telling us about her." Derwi's laugh echoed around the room. "But I will save my own thoughts on what we now are, young Brigante. Agricola is a difficult man to assess, and I still cannot work out what he wants to do with us."

Gillean's rough bark broke into their conversation. It was a few moments before he cleared his throat sufficiently to speak. "The way I feel just now, he will get no coin for me at all! But I will handle what tasks I am given in the daytime, so long as I can praise that lenient goddess at night from this soft bed. For at least a few more nights."

Beathan added a silent plea to his own goddess *Rhianna* to give Gillean the strength to recover properly. They had been given fresh bread and some form of cheese earlier, but it had been the thin broth that was the best nourishment for his Caledon friend. He had no idea what had given it the smoky taste but he could still feel its warmth sliding down his throat and savoured the memory of his belly ceasing to rumble.

Soft snores around the room lulled him to add to them. There were two of Agricola's men posted outside the door, so chancing an escape that night was clearly not being contemplated by the other two.

Loud thumping on the outside of the door wakened him abruptly, followed by peremptory orders from Sextus. Struggling to free himself from the best sleep he had had for a long time, he was surprised that neither of the other two had roused either, since a pinkish pre-dawn hue flooded the room when the overseer thrust it open. He put his own drowsiness down to the soft bed beneath him. It had been a long time since any kind of bed had been available.

"Rise you lazy…Britons." Sextus' hesitation was clear as he struggled for a word to use for them all. The Gaulish form of the language of the tribes sounded different when used by the man, but the words spoken were simple enough to work out. "Follow me."

As he trooped out behind the overseer, Gillean's whisper tickled his neck. "Keep alert. Remember. Any opportunity."

Agricola's special guards were on sentry duty.

Sextus nodded from one to the next as he filed past them and led on towards the back of the main house.

Beathan tried to count Agricola's guards. Either a good half were still asleep, which he doubted very much, or they had been given leave. But that still meant at least ten soldiers. The last detail escorting them from the previous fort to Agricola's house had been auxiliaries wearing chainmail. He could see no sign of any of those.

By the time Sextus had dished out their tasks, Beathan had also worked out who else appeared to be keeping their eyes open for Agricola – and that looked to be almost every worker around the estate!

Days passed, at the beck and call of Sextus. In some respects, it was similar to his time at Trimontium Fort. The current tasks demanded of him were not physically onerous, except when he was sent out into the fields to work when the hot sun beat down on him. From the workers he toiled alongside, he learned a lot about Agricola's estate, handed down via his father and grandfather who had both held important official posts in Rome.

Sextus was particularly good at dropping that kind of information into any talk. Though, they could not be named conversations since Sextus clearly wanted no responses. He found it difficult to comprehend that the workers on the estate were all slaves, yet they harboured no grudges about being there.

"Do you not yearn to be a free man?" he asked one of them as they worked their way along the rows of vines. The searching out, squeezing, and removal of harmful beetles was the allotted task.

"Why would I leave here? I was born here and will die here, like my mother before me. I am well fed. I have a place to rest. And Sextus only beats me if I do not work hard enough."

The same question was put to different workers, but the reply never varied. Beathan was unsure what to think. The food was simple, yet sufficient. He had been told that the workers regularly enjoyed a ration of the wine produced on the estate, though what he was given had taken a bit of getting used to.

However, the place to rest was questionable. Sextus was lucky to have his own room near the kitchen, but for many of the other household slaves it was a very different matter. Some of them slept on the floor of the place they worked in, like the cook in the kitchen with the other menial kitchen slaves ranged around him. Other house slaves lay on thin rolled-out mattresses outside the doors of the main sleeping rooms occupied by Agricola, his wife, and the guests who flowed in and out of the house like a meandering burn. Those slaves were at their beck and call all night long…and then all of the day after.

He supposed, in a peculiar way, that the slaves bedded down outside the doors of those rooms for sleeping in was also a kind of security, though not like having an armed legionary on guard. Simply put, those slaves were expendable. In the event of any kind of turmoil, he had worked out that their lives were easily forfeit before entry could be gained to Agricola, or his guests – any resulting noise expected to warn the guards at the main doorways.

His own situation was puzzling. Having a tiny room to share with the other two hostages overnight was much better than those menial slaves. Why was Agricola permitting that? What drove the man's thinking?

Chapter Nineteen

Gallia Narbonensis AD 85

As the days moved on beyond a half-moon, Gillean's cough gradually disappeared, which benefitted all of them since the wracking irritation no longer disturbed their sleep. And a good rest meant more hope that the coming day might be the one they awaited.

"Yet another day and no sign of him leaving?" Derwi's grin was the usual wry one as they passed each other in the *posticum*. He was leaving via that servants' entrance and Derwi returning with an over-laden weighty basket of dark-green leaved plants at his shoulder.

Beathan felt his head-shake was becoming too familiar. He had been inside the house much more than Derwi and was in a position to hear more of the on-goings. "What is that?" He pointed to the contents of the shallow carrier.

Derwi's shoulder hitched up the tiniest bit, his expression whimsical. "The name sounded like caulis."

Beathan had seen the Taexali tribeswomen make a slushy soup from green leaves, but the fat hen plant leaves were nothing like those Derwi carried. He was interested in all food but, for sure, whatever the cook produced from those green plants was not likely to pass the lips of the likes of him.

"Where are you off to, then?" The guard snarled at him from the low wooden stool that he sat on while polishing his helmet earflaps, always attuned to what was going on around him. The heat from the god *Lugh* was at its strongest, so it was no wonder the man was always irritable at this time of day.

He thought that the large amphora cradled under his armpit was a good indication of where he was heading, but it seemed the guard needed to hear it.

"The cook wants more oil," he muttered as he made sure to be at more than an arm's length from the man on bypassing, the soldier's swipe not something he wanted repeated. The helmet polishing over, the man was lifting a whetstone to make a start on the gladius blade that was to hand.

The smallest of thumb gestures indicated the way to the cluster of outbuildings set at some distance, though it was totally unnecessary since he had been to the different storage rooms many times already, and the guard was well aware of it. The shrill whistle sent on as a warning to the next soldier, who was just visible beside the nearest outbuilding, also seemed to be unnecessary. Beathan had easily worked out the observation system that was used to guard Agricola's property.

Content to be outside for a while, he hummed a quiet tune as he ambled along the earthen pathway to the area where the wine making would take place after *Lughnasadh*, the celebration of the end of the summer. It was a song story that he had learned from his Uncle Brennus. He still struggled to overcome pangs of wistfulness, triggered by something as simple as one of Brennus' tunes, though had slowly come to terms with missing his family. He could do nothing immediate to be reunited with them, however his decision to cherish memories of happier times, he knew, was a positive one. And if he forgot that for a while, he was lucky to have Derwi remind him that being still alive meant that fortunes could change.

The short walk also gave him time to ponder on all that he had already learned of Agricola's estate. Sextus was a fount of information and was gradually more accommodating about answering questions. He could not pin-point why, but the overseer boasting of how he was soon to gain his freedom, and of how he would then own a small plot of land, was something to consider. It was, of course, conditional on Agricola keeping his word and granting Sextus his freedom – but Sextus was very confident about Agricola's intentions.

From his limited experience of Agricola, he was finding the man had many different facets to his character. He had witnessed the general being brutal and relentless, yet the man could also be…almost…kind.

"Hurry up with those baskets, or you will feel this whip!" Sextus' bawls came from behind him, back at the villa entrance. The overseer had learned how to make his voice heard from a great distance.

The man was vicious when riled, Beathan had already seen what that whip could do, yet the estate workers genuinely believed Sextus to be a just and impartial superior.

When he thought about it, he knew that he had seen much harsher punishments meted out in the Roman forts he had inhabited.

He squinted his eyes to shield the bright light of *Lugh*, to take note of everything around him. Field workers scurried around at the far end of the long wheat strips, overseen by Sextus' second-in-command, but the bulk of the outside workers were still on the lower slopes checking and replacing the willow canes that supported the rows of vines, the leaf growth much heavier than when he had first arrived on the estate.

Agricola's soldiers were dotted around, distinctive in their glinting chest armour, and mostly within hailing distance of each other.

His stroll almost over, he expected to be accosted by the guard on duty at the corner of the building which housed mainly wines and oils, but the soldier was no longer in his usual position. Any previous time that he had been fetching something, the guard had observed his every step along the pathway.

There was a wide roof hang all the way around the stone-built storehouse which provided shade for large earthenware *dolia*, the containers holding large amounts of olive oils and wines. The dolia on three sides of the building were of wine, but the oil he wanted was on the fourth side where he could hear voices. Could the guard, for some reason, have realised he needed to access the oil dolia? It was an impressive assumption that made Beathan smile. Stopping at the corner, he took a peek to see who the soldier was talking to.

Instinct made him pull back out of sight.

Agricola's guard was nowhere to be seen but the Lady Domitia was at the far end talking to someone. While he hesitated, he could not shake the feeling that something about the conversation looked wrong. He had seen Agricola's wife visiting all of the external buildings in the cluster, but he had never seen her outside the villa without at least one of her female attendants, when not accompanied by Agricola or Sextus. Walking around alone seemed to be something that the Roman matron just did not do.

He snatched another glimpse. They were speaking in the local Gaulish version of the common tribal language. Domitia's words rang around, tight and angry. She was attempting to remove her arm from the man's tight grip, but failing.

"I already told you, he is not to be disturbed. Not by anyone!"

"And you are not listening to me. You will take me to him, now!" The visitor was thick-set and brawny, his actions more of a demand than his words, when he used both hands to imprison her.

Beathan ducked back, hopeful the person had not seen him spying since Domitia's body partially obscured his view. Unlike the slaves of the estate, he owed Agricola's wife no allegiance, but the man pinning her arms posed a threat to a defenceless woman.

Realising that making his presence known from his present position would do no good at all, he sped all the way around the storehouse. He stopped short of the far corner, forced himself to take stock, and adjusted the burden of the amphora he was still clutching.

"By *Jupiter's* Balls!" The oath came through gritted teeth. "You bit me!"

When he peered around this time, Domitia had staggered back a couple of paces, her alarm fixed on the man's fist reaching up to his belt. Before the thin blade could be slicked free from its sheath, Beathan launched himself around the corner. His two hands firmly on the handles of the clay amphora, he swung it aloft and brought it crashing down on the man's head.

Jumping on top of the prostrate, but still wriggling, figure he had no thought to whom he was issuing orders. "Sound the alarm down at the villa! There is no guard nearby."

The Lady Domitia needed no urging. She ran for the end of the building screeching and bawling much better than he ever could have. Her higher tones disturbed the birds in the nearby olive trees and set them up in a panicked flight, easily seen from a distance.

The attacker bucked and writhed beneath him, attempting to free himself from the tight neck grip that he had on the man's tunic, some of the backwards punches and lunges powerful enough to give him sound bruising. Beathan could not match the man's brawny stature, but he had the advantage of length and all but covered the assailant.

Grabbing fistfuls of hair, he banged the man's forehead on the ground, enough times to ensure no further resistance – an exhausting business that drained his strength, till one last muffled squelch emitted from below him. Unable to move, he hoped the totally slack body beneath him was not dead. He preferred to meet an enemy in face-to-face combat, but decided he was not really too concerned, even when a trickle of blood began to seep out.

He heard a swarm of people converging around the corners, the many feet of special guards and field workers. Raising his head slightly, he groaned and flopped back down.

The soldier who had recently been polishing his gladius near the villa was skidding to a halt, the point of his shiny, sharpened blade thrusting menacingly towards him.

"No! Not the Brigante!" the lady Domitia cried from a few paces behind. "The man beneath him is the one who threatened me."

Beathan had barely rolled off up onto his feet when the full force of Agricola's wrath descended. The general grabbed up his wife in a cossetting hug while orders fired out. "Where is Optio Narbona? I want a full investigation. How could this happen?"

Lady Domitia, emerged from the tight clutch and looked around at what seemed to Beathan to be everyone on the estate. "Husband." Her tones placated as she laid her palms squarely across her husband's chest. "I am not harmed." She looked around for Sextus, who had just arrived. "Get everyone back to work, now, please."

It only took one glare from the overseer for the crowd to disperse, their tones low, horrified that their mistress had been threatened.

"Sir." One of Agricola's guards dared to approach the general. "Optio Narbona is on leave."

Agricola nodded his acceptance of the information, just the once, then pointed to the assailant. "Turn him over!

Beathan stepped aside when two of the soldiers rolled the man over, but was unable to prevent his gasp. The thin weapon that had not been properly out of its sheath earlier was now embedded in the man's chest, right to the hilt, the eyes above lifeless

Agricola looked down dispassionately at the figure. "Have you ever seen this man before today, Domitia?"

The Lady Domitia looked horrified by his tone but her answer was steady. "Never."

Agricola whipped around to Sextus. "What about you?"

"No, Lord. I have never laid eyes on this man." The overseer's head shakes threatened to remove it from his neck.

Beathan felt the full force of Agricola's glare turn to him. "And before you killed this man, what did you witness?"

"He was threatening your wife. But I did not use the knife on him, he must have done that himself when I pinned him down."

Domitia interrupted the inquiry, her cry much more alarmed than before when she looked around at those still in attendance. "Where is Agatha? She was with me in the storeroom. When I heard someone outside, I told her to continue to check the damaged amphora – that was why we came over here. That man was outside."

A loud noise at the doorway of the building answered her question, the limp body of Domitia's slave was draped over the arm of one of the guard. Beathan knew he could not be the only person to have worked out that there had to be at least two assailants.

Amid Domitia's distressed cries and wails the soldier's words were solemn. "Strangled, sir."

The approach of another soldier had all of them turning around. "Lollius is in one of the other buildings. Whoever it was, must have really caught him by surprise. His throat was cut from behind."

That explained why the guard was not at his post.

Agricola once again took his wife into his arms and indicated her servant's body be removed.

"Follow me, Brigante."

On the way back to the house, walking a few steps behind them, Beathan took stock of what had just occurred. From the grim set of Agricola's jaw, he worked out that the assailants' main target was not Agricola's wife. But who could possibly want to threaten the man who had been in charge – was probably still in charge – of the whole of Britannia?

It did not make any sense.

Chapter Twenty

Gallia Narbonensis AD 85

Agricola paced around the courtyard garden, more than ample for a provincial villa, though not nearly spacious enough for his present mood. He had known this moment would come but had hoped to have a bit more time to spend in the tranquil presence of Domitia.

The last weeks had dissolved the strained atmosphere that had persisted between them, after the death of their baby son, not yet two years ago. The last thing that she needed was to be involved in the political mire that he had found himself in. His esteemed Emperor Domitian's tentacles were too close, but why had the emperor sent inept assassins? Domitian's brother Titus had employed much more successful Praetorian spies and assassins.

It was unfortunate that the one caught fleeing the estate had not survived long enough to reveal either the full purpose, or to confirm his suspicions over who had sent them.

He knew that the Emperor Domitian was not the only one in Rome who had not appreciated his success in Britannia.

"There you are." His wife's arrival calmed his patrolling.

"Domitia." He reached for her hand, led her to the nearest bench and sat alongside her. "I thought you were still asleep?"

"Me? Asleep at this time of day?" Her jest was accompanied by a watery smile. The loss of her maidservant had hit her hard, her weeping weakening her into a forgetting slumber.

Gently placing his palms at her ears, he kissed her forehead and then made sure she absorbed his concentrated stare. "I have already vowed to our household *lares*, and to *Invidia*, to ask her to wreak vengeance over Agatha's needless murder."

Domitia's profound grief flayed him, her response predictable. When Domitia gave allegiance to something, or someone, she was true to the very end.

"She was my friend as well as my servant. I intended to grant her freedom at her next birth day celebration, but that cannot happen now."

Taking her into his arms they talked of Agatha, the companion who had journeyed far and wide across the Empire with them, to Aquitania, and to Britannia. Servants came and went across the peristyle, the gardener trimming the hedging and another quietly sweeping the paths of dried leaves. It was important that she see that the business of the estate continued to run as normal, even if their servant count was one less in number.

"I know how fervently she hated the cold of northern Britannia, but she never complained. Not once. She feared for my life, was ever watchful of any barbarians coming near to me, yet she never feared for her own life in that hostile place."

A momentary silence descended, each thoughtful till his wife continued, her tones stronger and more animated. "Why did her life become forfeit on this estate that she felt so secure on? What did she do to deserve such a poor deal from the *Parcae*? Why did *Morta* deem it her time?"

He surprised himself by his answer. "Only the supreme deities know that answer, Domitia. But be heartened, Agatha was a wise woman."

Domitia's interruption was vehement, distress returning. "When we rose at dawn, Agatha looked out at the cloudless sky, which was not different from most of our daybreaks. She heaved a sigh, turned to me with my stola in her arms and said that she was getting too old. She held out one hand towards me and joked that she feared being wrinkled like a dried fig. For that, she said she was ready to die young."

The expression on his wife's face was a mixture of bewilderment and anger, her words trailing to silence. "I laughed it off, told her that nearing forty was not young but no great age either. Could she have known?"

He shook his head, though he was always inherently reverent of those who could make predictions.

"She was a wise woman, but I doubt she had become a seer. Though she did look after all of your needs so well, including your safety, for many years."

Domitia's watery smile broke through. "She defended me from predators many a time, animal and man. How do I find that security again, my husband? Tell me how? Is there another slave in your employ who will fill her shoes and slay my unknown enemies?"

After a silent pause, where he felt the full gaze of her scrutiny, she continued, "Or your enemies? For you must acknowledge now that you do have many of those."

He could not deny her. It was so true. "In Caledonia I, at least, knew who my enemies were." When her silent enquiry continued, he nodded. "You know I cannot delay my return to Rome any longer?"

"Do you now have a date from the senate, for your celebratory return?"

"You jest, my love." He laughed, but it was a hollow one he felt curdle his stomach. "You know that I will not return at the head of an army. There will be no major events marking my many triumphs in Britannia. Domitian cannot risk having my re-entry overshadow any of his own recent exploits, you know that too well."

He was surprised at Domitia's vehemence. "The favours of Rome are never fair, or just, when the emperor is himself the recipient. No expense is spared when an emperor adds Germanicus, or Britannia, to his titles but the same can never be allowed when it is a mere general who has achieved the subjection of the barbarians!"

Agricola pulled her close, unwilling to have her earlier distress return over something they were unable to change.

"Hush, Domitia. I will set forth come the dawn. A reduced guard is sufficient for my ride to Massalia, and for the two voyages. Those on home leave will be recalled, to help those left here to guard the estate."

His wife's tears dripped silently. "But is less than a quarter-century sufficient to keep you safe from Ostia to Rome? Will you let me come with you? I must know that you will be safe."

After kissing the drips free of her chin, he pulled back to see her properly. "I vow that I will send for you. When I know your safety can be secured. This day has proved to both of us that Domitian can diminish me by attacking you. And if that was not the work of Domitian, the same applies to any other man who seeks to destroy me."

"For the first time ever in all of our years together, my husband, I beg you to think carefully about what you do next. Domitian does not deal well with those he does not favour – and the same can be said of his cronies."

Well aware of her deep concern, he relented and told her he would stay one further day and leave on the following daybreak

"Then, I shall make sure we enjoy tomorrow."

He continued their hushed conversation but made sure to talk of brighter things.

Chapter Twenty-One

Ostia, Port of Rome AD 85

Beathan trudged along completely awed by everything around him. The port at Ostia was like bees buzzing at a hive. People came and went seemingly from nowhere. They swerved in and out to avoid each other in the throngs of bodies, animals and carts that forced their way in two different directions along the cobbled street.

He felt as though he was being forced through the neck of an amphora lying on its side. The street he was on could not be called narrow. Yet, it was not built for the bustle that hemmed him in, even more than the reduced personal guard had done when he had been lined up and fettered, thankfully only at the wrists, after disembarking the ship. The soldiers were struggling to flank Agricola who walked directly ahead of him, leaving just two of the guards behind Derwi at the end of their hostage chain. The crowds around Agricola were kept at bay by the every-ready pila carried by his armed men, but after bypassing the general, the oncoming traffic almost overwhelmed him.

He was not surprised that the ostler kept the horses somewhere beyond the quayside, the stables being their destination, according to what he had heard.

From behind him, Gillean's growl was just discernible as he fought to keep pace. "Have you ever seen the likes? What will Rome be like if the port is this crowded?"

Beathan turned back to grin. "One thing is certain. It will not be quiet like your Caledon mountains."

"I swear by *Taranis*! His thunder is noisy but this is…"

Gillean had no chance to finish. Beathan saw the blade even before he saw the man who darted around an oncoming body and surged towards Agricola

"Look out!" he cried.

Propelling himself forward, he crashed into Agricola's shoulder, toppling the general to one side. Yanking up the chain that bound him to Gillean, it prevented the blade from stabbing beneath Agricola's chest armour though was not forceful enough to prevent it from slicing into his own forearm before he landed on his knees.

When Gillean fell on top of him he had no love for his friend's droll humour. "You should have asked the goddess *Andraste* to help you know who your friends are, young Beathan!"

Gripping his ripped skin to prevent more blood loss, his retaliatory remarks were drowned out by the clamour that ensued around him. Optio Narbona, who had been recalled to duty, and two of the other guards, dealt swiftly with the attacker, the crowds rippling back from danger as though the tide was ebbing past a shipwreck.

Back on to his feet Agricola towered over him, his instructions furious. "Find something to bind that wound."

A small blade flashed in front of Beathan, making him flinch, though the cut was not to his person but at the bottom of his filthy tunic, after he obeyed the command to stand up

Following a quick inspection of the dead assailant, Optio Narbona declared, "Nothing of note to give us any idea of who he might be, sir."

It took only a few blinks before their small group were on their way again, the attacker abandoned where he lay on the cobbles.

Gillean's voice behind him sounded impressed. "Did you see any of the crowd looking in the least disturbed by that little happening, Derwi?

His Taexali friend's low whistle was familiar. "Not a one. It looks like an everyday occurrence to me. Are you faring well, up there young Beathan? Having saved the life of the man who is holding us hostage?"

Was he? He had fared a lot worse after the battlegrounds of Beinn na Ciche. Beathan had no idea of how he felt about having saved his hated enemy. Pure instinct had driven his call.

"I am alive and intend to be so for a bit longer, *mo charaid*!" he grumbled.

It was good that at the next corner he could see they had reached their destination. It was even better when Agricola ensured his guard encircled them while horses were brought forward. And even better still when he and the other two were shunted onto a small cart along with some of Agricola's belongings.

"How long will it take to reach Rome, Beathan?" Derwi asked.

He got as comfortable as he could while still chained together, cradling his arm against his stomach to prevent jarring from the cart side. The ride was a bumpy one on the cobbled street, since this time there was no leisurely pace set.

"One of them said a whole day's ride, but since *Lugh's* light has shown itself for good while already, Agricola might find a suitable mansio to stay in."

At that point he really did not care. All he wanted was to take a nap, since he felt as weak as a new born chick.

A jostling at his elbow woke him up.

"Are you still with us, young Beathan?" Derwi's face loomed over him. "I think the mule is slowing down."

Beathan could not tell from the expression if his Taexali friend was concerned. Derwi's face was in shadows, full-dusk almost fallen.

"Have we been riding all this time? No stops?" he asked.

Gillean wriggled up into a sitting position against the cart side.

"We have had the finest feast you have ever seen, but you slept soundly through it."

Derwi peered at him and chortled. "Agricola made the guard shake you to prove that you still lived, but then let you sleep on. His concern is so admirable."

The Caledon's sarcasm surfaced. "Ha! If he was so concerned for our young Brigante's welfare, the general would have freed him before now."

He struggled up to a sitting position alongside Derwi who put a piece of dry bread into his hand. "Not as fresh as it was when we stopped earlier. You'll have to make your spit slip it over since they took away that horse-piss they call vinegar wine."

Tearing off a piece with his teeth, he slowly savoured it.

"Gillean and I have had plenty of time to talk, but we cannot work out who would want Agricola dead," Derwi said.

Wiping his teeth with his tongue before speaking, Beathan answered. "It has to be someone in Rome. Someone of high authority."

Derwi lowered his voice to a whisper. "You mean the Emperor?"

"His attacker, the one who sliced you, was not exactly the best man for the job. If he was from Domitian's superior troops, surely he would not have failed." Gillean gave him a gentle nudge. "Just as well, though, or you might also be dead."

"Give the lad his due, Caledon. If Beathan had not been so alert, Agricola's assailant might have been successful."

Beathan grumped. "And if I had not been so vigilant maybe, just maybe, Agricola would be dead and we might be free."

Gillean nudged him playfully.

"Nay. We discussed that while you slept. Derwi was chained to one of Agricola's rear guards."

Derwi exhaled loudly. "Pity. The crowds would have masked our flight."

This time he was aware enough to avoid Gillean's hefty shoulder. "The next time Agricola is attacked, you need not be so honourable, Beathan the Brigante!"

"And next time we run whether, or not, we have to drag a Roman soldier in the mud, having already strangled him with that chain of *Succellus*."

He had thought hard about both of those things, too.

"Out!"

Beathan felt the guard could have been more civil when the whole party settled to rest the horses.

Forced to sit down at the roadside, he accepted a wineskin when it was brandished at his face. He thanked *Rhianna*, since it was better than nothing. Some of Agricola's small guard milled around them while torches were being lit, the scrape of the iron firestarters against flint intrusive. He knew it might be his overwrought feelings, but everyone and everything seemed so tense. He could taste the strain.

The sounds of a hard-ridden horse slowing down towards them was not unusual, since the road they travelled had been busy during the day, though it was not that way now. The guard immediately surrounded Agricola, except Optio Narbona who took hold of one of the lit torches and risked a central position on the road.

"I seek General Agricola with communication to be handed to him personally," the dispatch rider declared, after he yanked his horse to a standstill.

"Then give it to me!" Agricola sounded frustrated from his perch upon a stone that was flattened from many rumps.

The dispatcher dismounted and looked around cautiously, his gaze counting the small escort who encircled the general.

Beathan watched Agricola lift his glittering helmet from where he had dumped it on the ground before the general got to his feet. Donning it with precision, Agricola stepped forward, right up close to the dispatcher. He pulled himself up to his full height, though that was on par with the *eques*.

"I am General Gnaeus Iulius Agricola, Governor of Britannia…"

He had no need to finish declaring his full credentials. The dispatcher saluted, swivelled around and fumbled in the leather satchel attached to his horse to withdraw a scroll.

After receiving it, Beathan watched Agricola's polite dismissal of the deliverer. The general indicated that Optio Narbona should hold the flare ready, before he stepped a few paces away to read the missive. The rest of the guard hovered near the dispatcher who was remounting his horse. All of Agricola's men were suspicious of anyone who went near the general.

"We will eat at the next mansio." Agricola rolled up the scroll and headed towards the pouch that was attached to the back pommel of his horse.

"As you say, sir! Do we leave now?" As ever, Narbona was expressionless.

Agricola's only response was to remount his horse.

Chapter Twenty-Two

Rome AD 85

Beathan gleaned a few more snippets as they continued the journey, slower now because they only had a few lit torches to guide them along the darkened road. The guards were tucked tightly alongside the wagon he was glad to still be riding in.

"They are not happy about how Agricola will be entering Rome." He made sure his whispers could be heard by his companions but drowned out by the rolling of the wagon on the stones of the road.

"What do you mean?" Derwi asked.

"Optio Narbona thinks Agricola should be having a great welcome with people lining the streets. He says they should be applauding him for being a great general. They should be declaring him a wonderful Commander of the Legions of Britannia."

Gillean grunted. "Does that mean we will have the fine opportunity of being humiliated while he struts in front, and we are dragged along behind by our chains?"

Beathan had not even considered that horror, though now that Gillean had uttered it, he found it impossible to erase the very thought of it.

"The dark of the night will shield us from the worst of that dishonour but by *Taranis*, defending Agricola will be even more difficult than earlier today." Derwi swore by every other god of retribution that he could think of.

Gillean sat up and peered over the side of the cart, the weak moonlight poor for long sight. "Better ready yourselves because the dark shadows I can see up ahead are moving. They are not a mansio, nor are they the first buildings of Rome."

He struggled up onto his knees and looked out over his side of the wagon. A good-sized band of horsemen approached them. He could only hope they were not going to be bringing bad news.

The following morning, he and his companions had an unexpected visitor in the tiny storeroom that they had been dumped in at some point before dawn. He thought they had entered someone's villa, but it had been so dark it had been difficult to tell.

Agricola loomed large over him as he sat on the dusty floor, his back propped against the wall.

"Take off their collars!"

If Optio Narbona was surprised at the order, he never showed it when he produced a set of iron keys. Clank followed clank as the iron collars were dumped on the floor.

Agricola yanked at the chain that bound Beathan's wrist manacle to the iron ring on the wall.

He failed to prevent the gasp of pain that flashed up his arm.

"Attach the chain to his other wrist."

There was no concern in Agricola's voice, only practicality, as the optio bustled about doing the general's bidding.

"The bleeding has stopped?"

Beathan nodded. He had not even looked at the cut, still covered by the grubby piece ripped from his tunic.

Agricola stayed exactly where he was, still staring down at him. "Remove the binding."

The order was so dispassionate that at first he thought it had been issued to Narbona. The intent question in Agricola's eyes eventually made him realise otherwise. He peeled free the blood-stained cloth that stuck to the hair on his arms, determined not to show even the tiniest wince.

The cut was long, though not ragged. The blade used had been sharp. Only the top layers of his forearm had been laid open, and thanks be to *Andraste*, it was not nearly deep enough to bare the bone.

Agricola looked down, and then indicated he should re-wrap it. "I have seen worse."

Turning away from him the general addressed Optio Narbona, pointing to the bundle of neck rings. "Take those away."

Beathan then felt the full force of the man's gaze return to him.

"But the hostages will all remain inside, till I give further orders."

He expected Agricola to leave with Narbona. However, the general lingered at the door.

"Stand up, Brigante!"

Weary already of what might now be coming, he finished tucking in the end of the cloth wrap and slowly got to his feet.

"Did you ever think that one day, Brigante, you would be in Rome, right at the heart of my Roman Empire?" Though an odd question, the expression on Agricola's face indicated a genuine response was wanted.

He shook his head. "Nay! I never did." He then felt the urge to add, "But when I went to battle at Beinn na Ciche, I never expected to be captured by you, either."

Agricola strode forward to peer up at him because regardless of his limited food intake, Beathan had still managed to grow taller.

The general almost looked amused. There was just hint of something playful lurking in the depths of his deep-brown eyes. "And I expected that you would be a useful hostage."

He then watched Agricola stare at his companions alongside the wall before the general shook his head. "I had fewer hopes of making great bargains with you two, but nothing can be predicted just now."

In response, Gillean cleared his throat and then howked out a stream of spittle. Not near enough to hit Agricola's boots, but close enough to make his point. The Caledon's expression showed no fear.

After a last intense stare, Agricola swivelled towards the doorway, and halted there for a moment. Half-turning, his parting words lacked any emotion. "You have no audience with Emperor Domitian this morning, but I do."

The door banging shut was salutary. Beathan realised he had been holding his breath too long during that last exchange. Though Agricola had faced Gillean, he knew that the general's threat was shared by them all.

Food and watered wine arrived later that day. As ordered, he was not allowed outside and neither was he expected to do any menial slave work. The long, hot day passed slowly, the stench of the small room increasing – sweat vying with the contents of the buckets in the corner. Solid and liquid.

"They expect us to use them?" Derwi had laughed and laughed, pointing to the buckets.

The boy who had delivered the buckets had explained their use very slowly. By the time the lad was finished, Beathan decided he had learned a lot more Latin than the young servant had. Wherever the slave had come from, the boy had not grown up speaking Latin.

He knew from his time at the fuller's tent in Eboracum what the urine was used for.

"Rome pays coin for full buckets of piss. They use it to bleach cloth."

Gillean had snorted as well. "So, Agricola expects to make money from us?"

His answer was quiet. "I think the slave was telling us that any money earned from the sale of that piss will get the servants of the house more food. The coin does not go to the owner of the villa."

Given that information, there had been a grudging acceptance of the buckets.

The second day moved on and a third came and went. It became almost impossible to keep any kind of conversation going. Tempers were on a knife edge; except they had no knife between them to sever the strain. For such a long time they had been on the way to Rome, but now they were actually in Rome, the reality bit deeper than ever.

Four walls of the room that encased them.

Beathan faced the fact that at any time now he could die on the end of a Roman gladius. He even came to the conclusion that was preferable to being sold in the slave markets. Whatever situation, what bothered him most of all was the prospect of being split from his companions, the two men who were now as close as his kin had been.

The soft snores of Gillean to one side of him almost made him smile. He could not sleep but was amazed that the others were able to forget for long enough to drift off.

"Are you still awake, Derwi?"

No response from that side gave him an answer, of sorts. He lay on his back and tried to exhale deeply through his nose. He closed his eyes then opened them again. He was about to puff out through his mouth when different sounds came to him. Footsteps headed away from the door. The guard had gone?

Holding his breath, he waited. And waited for a bit longer before he heard a scrape. Not footfall, but iron touching iron.

Someone was definitely outside the door. The tiniest of creaks as it opened had him tense all over. To sit up abruptly would be too noisy, but he was too far from the door to do anything useful.

"Stay silent."

The low tones of Agricola were a complete surprise, after the door closed again. Thin streaks of moonlight filtering through the iron grille near the top of the wooden panel shed enough illumination for him to see Agricola step towards them.

He wriggled himself up onto his knees.

"What is happen…" Derwi's sleepy voice was cut short by Agricola reaching forward to gag him with his open palm.

"Be silent. The guards must not hear you."

Beathan detected a repressed fury behind Agricola's words.

Reaching over to Gillean, Beathan whispered a warning into his friend's ear as he shook him awake.

The light clink of the chain link being removed from the wall hook by Agricola made him even more uneasy as he got to his feet, the other two doing the same.

"Come closer, Brigante." Agricola brandished something held in his hand. "This is a key, not a weapon. Hold up your wrist."

Beathan stepped closer and held out his manacle. He was mystified by the general's actions but felt there was no threat coming his way.

When he was free of the iron bracelet, Agricola pushed him towards the door and then turned back, his words directed at Derwi at Gillean. "Beathan of Garrigill is free to go. I will not stop him, and neither will my guards, though…only if they do not see him. I have not changed their orders, and they do not know what I am doing right now."

Beathan hesitated. Freedom for him but not for his friends? And why had Agricola used his name for the first time? Agricola's next urging gave him no time to answer his last question

"Go! There are no guards posted outside this door just now, but other guards are watching all of the entrances and exits. Once you are out of this villa, I cannot help you. It is entirely up to you if you live or die, but you will no longer be on my conscience."

Derwi's urging was even more forceful than Agricola's. "Go home, Beathan. Tell our story when you get back to Caledonia."

"You have been good at making up new endings to those song-stories told to you by your uncle when you forgot the climaxes. Make up a good one for us, young Beathan. But for now, I vow to *Taranis* that you shall take flight like a bird and fly home."

The droll addition from Gillean, to avoid a sailing, made up Beathan's mind as nothing else could.

He held out his wrists to the general. "Put the manacle back on. Where they go, I go."

"Ha!" Agricola actually sounded pleased. "The only weapon I carry is this key. There are three of you and one of me. Though, if you attack me now, the guards will be alerted."

Derwi held out his arm. "Free us, and we will look after him. We will make sure he does get back to his family."

That seemed to be assurance enough for the general.

Once they were all free of fetters, Beathan opened the door a crack and popped his head outside. The courtyard was empty, though the light of the moon illuminated it quite well.

"Wait!" Agricola whispered.

Beathan froze. Was Agricola playing a tasteless joke?

Agricola held out a soft purse of leather. "Coins. They will help pay for some food and passage on a ship. When they are used up, you will have to make do with your own ingenuity." Handing the purse to Derwi, the general continued. "The kitchen exit door is down that way. I will distract the guards from over on the other side, if you give me time to encircle the courtyard."

Before Agricola slipped past his shoulder, the man's last words stunned him. "A long time ago, I was in the same room as your father and mother. By *Jupiter*, and by your supreme god *Taranis*, may they still be alive. So that you can send them my greetings. Tell them they should be proud of their noble son."

Beathan watched while Agricola disappeared into the shadows, as silent as a cat. He had barely controlled his erratic life-blood when a clamour from the next part of the house shattered the quiet of the night.

Agricola's distraction had begun.

"Get moving!" Gillean whispered, leading the way along the pillared walkway.

Chapter Twenty-Three

Ceann Druimin Caledon Territory AD 85

"Torquil! *Fàilte! Ciamar a tha sibh?* Come away in and join us."

Enya of Garrigill indicated a space right next to her in the large roundhouse she and Nith shared with her Garrigill clan at Ceann Druimin, most of whom were ranged around her at the fireside.

"We did not expect you to come back with Ruoridh. It has been long moons since we talked."

Torquil, chief of Dunrelugas, chortled as he looked down at her hands splayed over her rounded stomach. "The time has passed well for you, I see. Will there be a bairn by the feast of *Imbolc*?"

She patted the bump that stretched her dress. "Aye, if the goddess wills it."

Torquil reached behind her to give a friendly slap to Nith of Tarras' shoulder. "I imagine you had a hand in the making of this bairn? Is this the reason why it was young Ruoridh who has been doing the travelling of late?"

Nith laughed, and then covered her hand with his own, tenderly caressing both her fingers and their unborn child. "Aye and nay. Enya and I have been searching, but to the south. Ruoridh opted to check the northern territories since it was a while past that we had any word from you."

She leant into Nith when he turned his attention to her brother Ruoridh.

"You have not found any traces of Beathan at all?" Nith asked.

Ruoridh slumped to the floor and rubbed his hands towards the heat of the dwindling fire, his expression a dejected one she knew only too well. "Nothing, but I will let Torquil tell you what he has heard."

Enya's mother, Fionnah, bustled around with food and drink, handing it out to everyone. And once everyone was served, Torquil began.

"I have no proof of Beathan's whereabouts, but there may be a possible sighting."

Enya's insides flared, though she knew her raised hopes could be nothing compared to Nara and Lorcan's for their missing son.

Torquil continued, "My source for the following story is reliable. After the Battle at Beinn na Ciche, one of the Taexali chiefs – who lived not far from my hillfort – was taken captive, along with some warriors of his clan. Chief Derwi has never returned, though his warrior, Farrahll, managed to escape."

"An enterprising man," Lorcan of Garrigill commented. "Getting away from Roman clutches takes a special kind of warrior, or one in the favour of the gods."

Torquil smirked. "Farrahll would say he was neither, but that he was in the right place at the right time. His slave line – sent south from that 'many-fisted' Roman Camp at Moran Dhuirn – was being marched to a fort in southern Votadini territory when disaster struck. The slaves had been halted at the road's edge, to allow a Roman convoy of wagons to pass by, when a wheel sheared off from one of the heavily-loaded carts. The contents spilled forth, crushing the kneeling captives. Two of them were killed."

"*Ceigean Ròmanach!*" Enya spat at the fire. "The Roman scum would not be pleased at that. Fewer slaves would mean less coin for the Roman Empire coffers."

She felt Nith's affectionate patting of her leg. She imagined it was to keep her calm, but really it was just because he liked the loving contact. He leaned closer to her ear to whisper. "More likely it was less profit for the rapacious slave traders."

Concentrating on the conversation, she pulled her attention back to Torquil. "How did Farrahll escape?"

"While the Romans were sorting out the mess, the slaves were uncoupled and herded into a huddle, so that they could remove the dead and assess the injured. Farrahll scurried away during the confusion. He saw Derwi being loaded up onto one of the carts, but he reckons that his chief must just have been stunned. The Roman patrol tossed the bodies of the dead behind roadside bushes, before they moved the line on."

She sent a quick prayer to her goddess. "May their lives not have been in vain, *Rhianna*."

"What happened to the rest of the slaves?" Nith prompted Torquil to finish his story.

"Farrahll followed the patrol in the growing dusk. Some of the carts, including the one that Derwi and the other injured slaves were on, turned off the road to a small fortlet the locals name as the place of many oxen."

"So, the other captives went somewhere different?" she asked.

Torquil nodded. "Aye, the main slave file was harried further down their southern road in the darkness to an auxiliary fort named for the three distinctive hills nearby."

A gasp from Nara halted the talk.

"What is it?" Enya asked her aunt, realising that Nith and Nara were exchanging some very strange looks.

Nara's eyes were raised to the roofbeams, her murmurs a plea to *Rhianna*, before she turned to Torquil. "I am Selgovae born. The hills you speak of are where you will find the hillfort of the Selgovae High Chief."

Enya felt Nith's arm tighten across her shoulders though his words were for Torquil. "I went one time in Callan of Tarras' warrior guard, when he visited our Selgovae High Chief. Don Eil's hillfort was on one of those three peaks that you speak of. It had an impressive command over the land, but his clan numbers were very few compared to what the site had harboured in ancient times."

She watched Lorcan of Garrigill soothing the restlessness of Nara's hands on the pile of nuts that she was shelling into a small wooden bowl.

"Keep the memories of your blood kin treasured ones, Nara. There can be no happiness in comparing what was in your youth with what now occurs in that area." Lorcan turned to speak to Torquil. "The news we had of Don Eil seasons ago was not good. That was when we heard about the Romans invading his hillfort."

Enya watched the small twitches to Nara's lips but knew her aunt was strong in spirit. The older woman had survived much hardship already and would survive more, if necessary.

Though she also knew that talking through troubles would help Nara to get through the continued absence of her son, Beathan.

"Can you tell us what you know of this fort that the slaves were taken to?" Enya asked Torquil, keeping her tone calm.

"Nay, I know very little."

Brennus of Garrigill spoke from the opposite side of the flickering fire, the newly added wood smoky and spiralling in front of him. "The Romans name that fort Trimontium. Many seasons ago it was impossible to get close to. It was garrisoned by Roman cavalry who patrolled a very large area around it every single day. Though, I have no recent knowledge of it."

Torquil accepted the new information with a nod. "I believe the Roman presence to be unchanged. Farrahll remained in the area only long enough to be sure that the local tribesmen would be no help at all in rescuing his chief."

The murmurs of disgust came from most around the hearth.

Uncle Lorcan's nostrils flared before he spoke. "The last thing we heard was that Votadini were living in Don Eil's hillfort, the remnants of the Selgovae all gone."

"If the locals that Farrahll encountered were Votadini, they would have betrayed him, rather than helped him. He was doubly favoured by his god, if he managed to get home safely." Enya was vehement. Her tossing of a log onto the fire caused a flurry of orange-red sparks to fly up towards the central roof timbers. "The Votadini were never to be trusted!"

"When did this incident happen?" Nith asked.

Torquil could not be sure. "Some days before the festival of Imbolc, but it took many moons for Farrahll to make his way back home, hence the delay in the news coming to us."

Uncle Lorcan interrupted. "It makes my heart glad to hear that Farrahll escaped, but what has this to do with my son Beathan?"

Enya felt a shiver run through her. Her child was not yet born, but she feared for the pain a lost child would leave, whether new born or older.

Torquil's words were earnest when she saw his attention focus on her Uncle Lorcan and Aunt Nara. "I do not want to give you false hope, because I cannot be sure. What Farrahll can confirm is that Derwi made friends with a stripling named Beathan, even before they were set on the march from the Moran Dhuirn encampment. The lad Farrahll speaks of claimed that he was a Brigante, and not from a Taexali tribe, when questioned by Agricola's men. He is sure the boy was not injured and was leading the line that marched south to the fort of the three hills."

Enya watched her Aunt Nara's flare of hope because Torquil's words were the best they had heard for a very long time. To have had no sight, or word, of Beathan for so long had been dispiriting.

"My thanks to you, Torquil. Your words now fill me with hope that he will return to us." Nara's lip quivered.

Enya watched Lorcan's gentle grasp of Nara's hand. "If the young warrior you speak of is our son Beathan, then we will find him. Even if it means we are endangered by the traitorous Votadini, as well as the Roman scum."

Enya's chest felt tight just thinking of Tarras, the Selgovae hillfort where she had first met Nith. She remembered Callan of Tarras quite well. Most people had found Callan a nasty old man but, for some strange reason, her missing cousin Beathan was unusual in that he had formed a strong bond with his maternal grandfather. Though, nice or nasty, it had made no difference to the Roman invaders when they descended on Tarras. Death and destruction followed their arrival when it was clear that the Tarras Selgovae were resisting with their every breath.

Enya felt Nith's hand reach out to engulf her smaller one, the squeeze a gentle reassurance.

"I mourn my lost kin," he said, addressing those in the roundhouse, "but I am heartily glad we all left Tarras when we did. It is one thing to know that your place of birth has been destroyed, but to watch it happen would have been to die along with them." The pat to her rounded bump was a proclamation. "I look forward to providing a secure future for this little one, though how to do that is in the hands of *Taranis*."

Nara's low invocation to her goddess *Rhianna* rippled around the fireside as the others repeated the plea to keep Beathan safe, long enough for them to rescue him.

After a short pause Enya shunted aside to allow her Uncle Lorcan more space to get to his feet, since he was less agile than he used to be.

Following refilling their cups with Nara's recently-ready barley beer, Lorcan stopped at Torquil and gently laid a hand to the man's shoulder, his vow clear. "This is the first real possibility of us finding my son. Come the dawn, I will set off for Trimontium Fort. I do not yet know how, but if Beathan is held captive there, I will free him!

At Enya's side Nith jumped up to stand alongside Lorcan. "Some of us will definitely go to Trimontium but it should not be you, Lorcan. Your negotiations with our Caledon allies are too important to be halted just now. Should those Romans who are still stationed near our Ceann Druimin territory decide to venture into our mountains, then you will be needed here much more than I am."

Enya rose up to raise her wooden goblet. "I did not find my cousin during my last foray, but this time I will. And no matter what you may say *màthair*, I am not so far gone with child that I cannot travel. And I will do this knowing that Nith is all the protection I will ever need."

Enya's mother, Fionnah, made no sound at all. She merely nodded her approval since she knew it was an unfinished task.

Nith took her into his arms. "I will always be there for you, Enya, but I am also practical. Perhaps Ruoridh and Feargus of Monymusk will join us?"

Ruoridh raised his beaker. "You can definitely rely on me. But where is Feargus, so that I can ask him?"

Enya grinned. "Maybe leave it till later? He is visiting Màiread just now. She lives two roundhouses down from here."

Her brother's eyes gleamed, his tiredness suddenly banished and his crossed-teeth grin wide. "Does Màiread have any sisters?"

Chapter Twenty-Four

Eboracum Roman Fortress AD 86

"Whatever made me think that Eboracum was a large settlement?" Derwi's question was reflective, his head cocked to one side.

Beathan bent over the horse's head and peered into the distance. Having experienced so much of the Roman Empire, on a journey that had lasted more than four full seasons, Derwi spoke the truth. Everywhere was so much smaller than Rome.

"I look forward to welcoming countryside that has no towns at all." The further north they got, the more Gillean became increasingly desperate to see his Caledon hills.

They had talked, at great length, about whether to avoid entering the township of Eboracum. But he was keen to make contact again with his aunt Mearna, on a visit that would be just long enough to carry news of her to his family in Taexali territory, when he found them. He had convinced himself that at least some of his kin would have remained close to the battlegrounds of Beinn na Ciche.

"What will you do when you reach your beloved mountains, Gillean?"

He had asked the same question many times as they trudged northwards along the Roman road from Gallia Narbonensis to Gesoriacum. The journey had been almost the reverse of what they had covered as Agricola's hostages. However, it had taken the three of them almost four times as long, because the weather had deteriorated when the winter season had arrived. They walked every step and had had to steer clear of Roman convoys on the roads. Thieves, and some desperate men they had to assume were deserters from the legions, had also been avoided.

Gillean's answers to the question had varied, but the constant thread was that once he arrived back to his hill country, he never intended to leave it again. "Ask me that when we are close to Obar Dheathain and I will give you my answer!"

"Ha!" Derwi chided. "Are you now doubting that we will eventually get there, my Caledon friend?"

Had they not been on horses now, Beathan knew that there would be a bit of their friendly shoulder nudging and banter going on.

"Nay. Never that, Derwi," Gillean said. "Our progress has been slow to approach Eboracum, but I see no reason why we cannot pick up the pace now that we have these horses." Gillean's jaw was set, not always a good sign.

"You call this beast a horse?" Derwi's chuckling disturbed his mount, a fidgety one at best.

Acquiring the rides had involved an exchange of their physical toil for more than half a moon, at the stone quarries near the previous Roman fort on the Roman road that led them north from Lindum. The overseers of the quarry got the stone they wanted hewed for them, but Beathan felt the barter they ended up with was a lot less favourable than they had anticipated. Worn horses, too old to carry the Roman soldiers from quarry to fort, were not what he had expected.

"Are you now an experienced judge of horseflesh?" Gillean frantically clicked his tongue to urge his ponderous beast forward.

Unbidden, some memories came to Beathan that made him grin. "My Uncle Gabrond was in charge of the horse herds at our Garrigill Hillfort. I can vaguely remember him putting me on a horse for the first time. I was probably unable to even run, but the remembrance of surging off, with his hands holding me secure in front of him, still lives with me."

"Not your father? Nor your mother?" Derwi was always interested in his tales of Garrigill.

"Nay. Perhaps they were away from the hillfort. They were Brigante negotiators."

"Would that have been when Agricola said he had met them?" The question came from Gillean, always intrigued about the conversations he had had with the general. They had discussed the man and his actions towards them many times, yet had never managed to come to a satisfying conclusion

Why Agricola had freed them still remained a mystery.

"My father and mother went a few times to meet with General Cerialis, but I never heard them say that they had spoken to Agricola."

"Would Agricola have been at the treaty signings because he was Legate of the *Legio XX*?" Gillean prompted.

Beathan shrugged. "He was definitely the commander of *Legio XX* during the time that Cerialis was Governor. Agricola may have been at Eboracum, as a senior soldier, but he was not the one conducting the talks."

Derwi whistled. "No matter! What we can do is thank the Roman goddess *Fortuna* for Agricola giving us our freedom,"

Predictably, Gillean was thinking differently, his laugh even more droll. "I would much rather thank *Fortuna* for him giving us that very generous pouch of coins. We would not be here now without them."

After their escape from the villa in Rome, they had stumbled around trying to find a way out of the huge city without making themselves seem obvious runaways. The streets were so confusing, thronged with multitudes of people speaking many different tongues. Just remaining close together had been exhausting. Beathan had learned how to truly grow up.

Few people had given him good directions. At first he had thought them uncooperative, but he then realised that the bulk of the inhabitants of the city of Rome only knew the parts close to where they worked, and lived. Ostia was heard of, but they had no idea how to get there.

Though he would not want to experience again the feelings of insecurity – and at times terror – that he had felt in the seedier districts, a part of him was glad that he had seen some of the magnificence of the place the Romans called the heart of the empire.

Derwi grew serious. "How can we ever forget those buildings in Rome! So startlingly white but also luridly coloured. There can be no other place like Vespasian's amphitheatre, though I am glad we did not linger there."

They had only seen the striking new building from a distance. As they approached it, Beathan had asked people nearby what the huge amphitheatre was used for. Everyone asked had gushed about being desperate for the next public event to take place, with a fervour that was strange. He had understood enough to work out that gladiators fought against fellow combatants and against outlandish wild animals. When he heard about the gladiators fighting against captives snatched from across the Roman Empire, he had nudged Gillean and Derwi in a different direction, and well away from the sheer bloody horror of it.

Gillean's chuckles grew more unrestrained. "Why would I want to remember that building? I would much rather remember the women we had after running away from that Flavian wonder. Do you think Agricola knows what we used some of his coins for?"

Women, especially young ones, had become a distraction in Rome.

"Probably." Derwi was even more amused by the memories. "But I wonder if he would have appreciated just how picky you were about our entertainments, my Caledon friend!"

The first coins used had paid for food and drink. It had taken them hardly any time at all to work out which coins to use for a flagon of wine, and which for a round of bread. Beathan recalled Gillean's eruption when the Caledon realised that the coin used for one jug of wine was also enough to pay for the three women who were dragged out by the roadside *tabernae* owner, for them to have sex with.

At first he had though his friend angry that he needed to part with so much. But then it dawned that his Caledon friend was appalled at how little value was put on the women, and that the slave women had little choice. Unlike the women back in Caledonia who usually did most of the choosing.

"You probably paid too much, *mo charaid*, but I thank you for your selection." He grinned at Gillean.

In some ways, he cringed at the recall. Using him as an interpreter, Gillean had grabbed the coin pouch from Derwi and slapped two of the coins on the table. With the promise of a third held tight in his fist, Gillean had made the owner bring out all of the women who were available, until the Caledon was satisfied that the ones chosen by him were suitable. Gillean wanted to be sure the women would not kill them and pocket their precious purse. The man of the mountains also wanted to be certain, as sure as he could be in the circumstances, that the women were in agreement to sharing their bodies with them. Using some fairly crude gestures, Gillean had also made it clear that Beathan should have a good introduction to sex.

When the negotiations were concluded, Beathan found himself the popular one. He had learned a thing or two that night about what he and a young woman could find pleasure in.

Their evening with the slave whores in Rome had been a risk, but it had been a confirmation that they were still alive and not dead on the floor of the massive Flavian amphitheatre. After they had strolled away from the tiny partitions in the back of that tabernae, caution had sat on their shoulders.

Derwi grinned. "No one I know will believe my stories of Rome." More memories made him chuckle harder. "How do I explain those marks on the walls?"

Beathan was not so sure that he would be believed, either. Rome's incredible buildings, and streets, and forums had been full of visual reminders of mating. There were colourful drawings on the brightly plastered walls, and above doors and windows. The writing was a mystery but the simple images were not.

His own people worshipped many gods and goddesses, but the marks the people of Rome created for their gods, especially for the god they named *Fascinus* were memorable. How the people made their vows and intents, at street corner shrines, was very different to how his Garrigill clan worshipped.

"If I get the opportunity young Brigante, I will tell your people of how many times I had to drag you past some of those statues in Rome." Gillean's chortles were rich. "Though perhaps not. You were an immature lad back then."

That was true.

Thankfully, he was well-past the time of wondering if his body had matured properly. He could now laugh about how exaggerated some of the statues and wall scribbles were.

They had spent more than half a moon going in wrong directions in the swarming city of Rome. They avoided the soldiers of the *cohortes urbanae* by day, the legionary city guard who seemed to appear on every corner. At night, they prowled around till they found places to curl up and sleep, avoiding the *vigiles* who patrolled the streets at night and put out the numerous small fires that sprang up regularly.

Eventually, they had made their way to the port of Ostia, terror that they would be discovered still stalking their every step. However, it did not take long to realise that many of Rome's inhabitants, and the travellers on that road from Rome to Ostia, had their own furtive reasons for choosing dawn, dusk and the dark of night to make most progress, and especially when the light of the moon was bright enough.

The experience with the whores in Rome had not often been repeated during the long trek homewards, survival having taken precedence, though when it had no coin had been exchanged. Those women had not been slaves.

And it had been during the days at Ostia, when they had to linger around waiting to take passage on a ship to Massalia, that he had eventually told them of Agricola's strange parting words.

Chapter Twenty-Five

Eboracum Roman Fortress AD 86

Beathan slowed down his horse as they approached the first raggedy streets of Eboracum. "Do you really think General Agricola gave us our freedom because he had met my kin here?"

Gillean's bellow startled Derwi's horse, anew. "Nay, lad. You saved Agricola's skin when that assailant attacked him, but I favour his clemency was more because you saved his wife, Domitia Decidiana, from a knife at her throat. He owed you!"

"Aye, indeed." Derwi clearly agreed. "That General Agricola is rightly a strange one. If he had not been such a Roman turd in Britannia, I would almost say that – for a Roman – he is an honourable man."

"Hold the gossip! That ostler over there will do just fine for us." Gillean pointed to one of the wooden huts nearby before dismounting. "I am not for leaving these beasts unattended for a single blink. Pathetic as they are, they are valuable to us. I will just stay right here with them, and you two can go and find Mearna."

Beathan led his horse over to the large wooden building behind Gillean who wasted no time in gaining the attention of the horse-handler.

"We need fodder for our beasts." His Caledon friend's tone conveyed an urgency, yet was civil enough.

The ostler looked at their huddle of horseflesh and smothered a smirk. "Aye, they need a bit of feeding right enough. But what coin have you?"

Gillean pulled forth a brace of hares. "Will these do, instead?"

Beathan was sure that the barter was more generous than it needed to be. Though, since they had no intention of staying overnight at the mansio, they had to make it worth the man's while."

The ostler grabbed hold of the reins and headed towards the open door of the building. "Hay now, and some for later?"

Gillean stepped in front of the horse handler. "That sounds good, but tether the beasts on these hooks outside."

A glower was followed by a shrug as the ostler accepted the conditions. After securing the horses, the man shuffled into the building.

"And I'll be waiting right here for you two," Gillean shouted, a grin bracketing his face when he slumped down against the wall.

Derwi fiddled in the pouch at his waist. "I have coins in here somewhere that will buy us food." He glared at Gillean. "Since we now have nothing left to eat."

Gillean was in a playful mood. "I am feeling generous. The day is fair, and the goddess *Brigantia* is good to us."

Beathan snorted. "In what way?"

"She got us here safely, did she not?"

Derwi tucked his pouch out of sight. They had all learned a thing or two about snatch thieves during their journey. Even though they were as ragged as the poorest they could see around the streets, they were not locals. That meant they were a prime target.

Beathan looked around him. "I recognise none of this street, Derwi." He had to be honest. When they had left as hostages of Agricola there had been no need to note the streets while they were leaving.

"If we find the forum, will that jog your memory enough to work out how to get to the riverside and to the fuller?"

"Which way to the forum?"

Gillean's bellow startled more than him. A young lad came scurrying out of the stable.

"You want the forum?" the boy asked.

"Nay, lad."

Beathan smiled as Gillean pointed to him and Derwi.

"Those two really want the riverside markets, but the forum will do."

Two different directions seemed too confusing for the boy. "The forum is up ahead, around that corner up there."

When he and Derwi remained where they were, the boy turned tail and pointed down the street, in the opposite direction to the forum. "But you can see the river from those warehouses."

When no coin was offered to him, the boy shrugged and returned to the stabling.

"I am sure," Beathan repeated, after they had rounded the tall warehouses and were close to the riverside. "This is the place."

"Well, the fuller's tent is certainly not here now." Derwi gestured to the huge empty space between the ramshackle buildings.

Beathan went to the person who tended a small leatherware table nearby. "There was a huge fuller's business over there, not so many seasons ago. What happened?"

The man looked up at him, nodded just the once, and put down the awl that he was using to pierce holes in a leather belt. "Fire. All of his empty barrels were aflame in moments. The whole place was gone as quick as I could grab what work I could cradle and flee."

It was beyond belief. "But there was so much water around here. How could it happen?"

The cobbler shrugged his shoulders. "That stuff they used to add to the water fired the flames. And with all of those drying clothes hanging everywhere they had no chance of getting out quickly."

"What happened to the slaves who worked there?"

"Some died. The fuller got trapped in the back with his favourite slave." Beathan found the man's leery grin repulsive. "Picked a bad moment to get his cock out."

Beathan felt the heat of his anger rising as though he were experiencing the flames himself. "What about the older slave-woman?"

"Mearna? She died the day after. Nobody could have survived those burns."

Beathan had the presence of mind to ask, "What about the young lads who trod the clothes?"

"Sold. The fuller's wife got rid of them all, some of whom would have been better dead, like Mearna."

Derwi nudged his elbow. "Time to leave."

Beathan could not have said which upset him most while Derwi bought some bread that was almost fresh, and a cloth wrap of ground oats. Was it because he had only met his aunt that one time? Or that he was unable to free her, and take her home to his Garrigill kin?

He realised that had been in his mind for a very long time.

Chapter Twenty-Six

Vinovia Roman Fort AD 86

Beathan's horse plodded northwards along the road to Vinovia Fort. He remembered little of it from his previous visit, though Agricola had stopped at each and every fort when he had marched south from Trimontium to Eboracum. So much had happened since then, and so many new places mingled in his head.

"Hold still." Derwi was riding in front, the best place for his nervous filly. He brought the horse to an abrupt halt. "Listen!"

They were about to crest a long incline, the countryside beyond sheltered from view by thick stands of trees to each side. The growth closest to the stone roadway was of spindly saplings, now above man-height, and low bushes which had colonised the area after the levelling of the land when the Romans had constructed the road.

"I hear it."

And what he heard, he did not like the sound of. On the Roman road, the clatters of small patrols, or the dispatch riders who often rode at full pelt, were a frequent noise.

This was different.

Gillean urged his horse forward to come abreast of Beathan's.

"That is more than a small patrol that approaches. Maybe we should head off the road and into the forest. Till we see what is coming?" Gillean sounded sure.

Beathan needed no more urging. He followed Derwi as he forged a way into deeper tree cover. They had often been on the Roman roads when a small patrol passed by, or a mounted turma of some thirty horsemen, but what he had just heard was more than a few feet. The raucous call of a centurion, or his optio, was urging the men to double-pace as they climbed the hill.

Hidden from view, Beathan watched as line after line of legionary soldiers passed by, four-abreast. After the first wave had passed by there was a lull, till the beasts pulling the baggage wagons hauled their burdens to the summit. Then came more and more infantry.

"They are from the *Legio II Adiutrix*."

His friends agreed with him. An image of a horse with wings on the banner that was held aloft at the front of the column declared their identity.

"That must have been a whole cohort of them."

Gillean's whistle was soft and speculative. "Now why would so many of those soldiers be heading south towards Eboracum?"

It was a good question. They had seen no signs of native unrest while they had journeyed north from Londinium. Everywhere they had passed through had seemed well-resigned to adopting everything Roman. And it had not only been Londinium that had had a Roman forum built, with daily activity centred around it.

Derwi's chuckle was loud. He seemed unconcerned after the whole column had passed by. "Perhaps my Taexali kin, and yours too, have done something drastic enough to send them scurrying away?"

To Beathan, that did not seem like the reason. He had learned long ago that whole centuries were deployed from one area to another – to assist with new fort building, or some other particular work detail. Moving units around was fairly normal procedure. Though a whole cohort, a troop of five hundred, being moved south might be more significant.

The light of *Lugh* was low down when Derwi encouraged his mount to move faster along the dirt track they had been following. "There are people up ahead near those bushes. Can you see them?"

Heathlands surrounded Beathan, dotted with small stands of bushes and trees. "Perhaps they are making for that hamlet you heard about earlier?"

They had no intention of spending the night anywhere near the fort at Vinovia. They used the Roman road by day, since it was the easiest way to go north, but they avoided arousing suspicion by staying near the forts that were regularly placed along it. Their usual shelter for the night was a well-chosen spot where they could light a fire and bed down around it.

Beathan moved out in front, the track well-enough trodden to catch up to the figures who halted when they heard the clops of his horse.

"*Feasgar math!*" The woman said, though the smile that bracketed her face was a wary one. Her main movement was to tuck the baby at her front closer in to her body, and to tighten her grip on the young boy at her side who stood watch over the laden basket of blaeberries that she had put down at her feet.

"Good afternoon to you, too." Beathan returned the greeting, sliding off his horse to stand alongside her. "Are we close to the hamlet of Giuthas? We have no wish risk our horses going lame in the dark."

He was aware of the woman looking them over before she answered. "Nay, you will not reach the place of the fir trees before dark." After a moment, she seemed to make a decision. "Though, if you are not expected there this night, my hearth lies beyond that next copse of birches, in one of the small cluster of roundhouses. You will be welcome to share it. My nose tells me that the coming night will be a very cold one."

"We have no need to trouble you, we just need to know if we are on the right path."

Before the woman could answer Gillean coughed, one of his rusty throaty ones, though he no longer had a problem with his throat or chest.

It was a signal that they should investigate, find out what was happening in the area. Sharing the hearth overnight of strangers was not usual, in fact it was the opposite from their normal caution.

"You may wish to carry on, young Beathan, but I would be very pleased to share this woman's fireside to get out of this bitter blow."

"Leave the basket to me and run now to your father, Aodh. Tell him to expect three visitors."

Beathan's sling had been used well earlier that day and their barter of some plump birds was more than acceptable to her hearth-husband when they reached the small roundhouse.

"Where are you heading?" their host asked, urging them to sit with him around the hearth which emitted a welcome heat. Finding a space was less easy though, since it was crowded with a number of children of differing ages, and a dog that was so long in the tooth it made barely a whimper when they entered.

Beathan and the other two had already discussed the best reason for them journeying in this part of Britannia. He let Derwi answer, his Taexali friend always good at being genial.

"Our friend Beathan here was born in northern Brigantia. We are accompanying him to the hillfort of his upbringing."

"Move along, Maeldun!" the man chided. "Let our guests sit close by me."

Beathan was not so certain his son was happy about being moved from prime position next to his father. Of a similar age to his own, the young warrior looked to be the oldest of the brood. When Maeldun moved along a bit, the dog also shuffled aside coming to rest between the son's crossed legs after he had settled down.

When organised next to his host, Beathan offered his hand for the dog to get used to him. Her rheumy eyes were trusting, the time long gone for the bitch to guard anything. That the animal was around the hearthside, and not tethered outside, indicated the bond must be deep between son and dog.

The woman handed out bowls of broth and some bread that was past its best.

"Aye, that is the way of it," Beathan said. "I was raised for a time at the Hillfort of Garrigill, till around seven summers old when we had to leave."

It was too far distant for the warrior to know of it himself, but the tale of Beathan's family fleeing north when the Romans invaded was one their host had clearly heard many a time.

He reached forward to take the bowl the woman indicated was for him, the sleeve of his tunic baring the dark marks around his wrist that no amount of washing seemed to erase.

"I have salve that can tend to that bruising."

Before the woman could say more her hearth-husband brushed her offer aside. "The young man is fine. His healing will be done at the whim of the goddess *Brighid*."

Beathan thanked the woman for the broth and ignored talk of his wrist. He had no intention of mentioning anything about the lasting reminder of his slavery, and set to supping the thin soup.

While Derwi led the conversation, he looked around the roundhouse, one of four in the cluster. There was nothing in the room to make it different from any other tribal home that he had been in. He could see no Roman influences, though the small hamlet being situated so close to a Roman fort meant he needed to be cautious with any details that he shared.

Gillean wiped drops of well-made small-bere from his moustache, prior to speaking. "Before we headed west along the track towards here, we saw hundreds of Roman legionaries marching south. Does that happen often from the nearest fort?"

Their host grunted. "They come, and they go, but not often in such large numbers. My neighbour told me of some who recently left Vinovia Fort. What you just saw has to be the second cohort that has gone south to Eboracum these past days. There cannot be any more of the *Legio II Adiutrix* left still further north of here. My neighbour says the Roman emperor has recalled them all."

The woman settled down at the fireside having made sure her hospitality was not lacking. Beathan knew well-enough to pass his beaker back to her as quickly as he had finished it, since it needed to be refilled and shared around her children.

She joined their conversation. "There must be some reason for them not remaining in the north, but we have no-one to tell us why."

He tried not to draw attention to the smirk and twinkle in Gillean eyes. The Caledon was clearly delighted with the notion that his lands could be free of the Roman scum. But he would not believe it, till he could prove it.

He risked a tentative question. "Do you stay well clear of the Roman fort?"

The man spat at the low-burning fire; his disgust evident. "Aye. Till they claim our grain for their taxes. You have already crossed our moorland. Where they expect me to grow the amount of oats they demand from me is something only the goddess *Aine* knows, and the deity has not enlightened me."

The conversation continued, friendly enough, but Beathan had learned well that he and his companions could trust nobody till they were certain of where loyalties lay. Gradually, the children disappeared from the fireside to lie down in little sleepy huddles around the edges of the room.

Gillean eventually rose to his feet.

"I must check our horses. They are old, but we do not want them to go a-wandering in the night."

Beathan rose and followed him outside, an excuse to have a few words together.

"Do you think them to be resistant to Roman rule, Gillean?"

Gillean retied the tether of Derwi's horse and tested that the wicker divider of the animal pen was secure. "It is not easy to tell. These people have little to feed themselves on. I would heartily resent giving up any of my heard-earned food to the usurpers, but the Romans have been in that nearby fort for a long time now, and the locals are well-used to Roman ways. Your age is testimony to how long it is since the Romans have settled here."

"Aye. My whole life has been spent being affected in some way by the Roman scum."

Beathan woke to a silent urging, Derwi's palm at his shoulder giving him a slight shake. He was on second watch, a habit they had got into during their long journey, Gillean always preferring to take the third till dawn. Their caution was normally to ensure no animal predator harmed them, or that no Roman patrol would come upon them unawares. It was an unusual situation for them to be wary of a fellow Celt.

After a while of thinking about recent happenings, and things from long before that, he found it a harder task to keep awake while still lying down. Huddled next to his two friends, close to the low-burning fire was comfortable enough, but he could not forget he was the stranger in his host's roundhouse. It was not his place to sit up and tend to the embers, as he would be doing if it was their own campfire.

A rustling near the doorway had him hold his breath, the smallest swish of the dog's tail and the tiniest snuffle alerting him. Leaning up on his elbows, it was too dark to see more than a vague shadow. From the height of the person following the dog out of the entrance tunnel, it was unlikely to be the father of the family. The person leaving was tall and the father was not.

There were few reasons why Maeldun would go outside in the dark of a near-winter night. The dog might be the reason, yet instinct told him otherwise.

What was Maeldun's purpose?

Practised at moving without noise, Beathan sneaked out of the roundhouse and dipped under the overhang of the roof. Thick cover obscured the light of the moon goddess, *Cereduin*. Maeldun would know his way around the cluster of roundhouses, but he did not, and dared not risk tripping up. Cocking an ear, he heard only the noises made by small creatures who thrived in the darkness.

Wait outside? Or inside?

He crept back into the space next to his friends, deciding not to risk the dog alerting the boy to his presence outside. It was a good choice because Maeldun returned almost immediately.

For the rest of his watch, he heard only the soft snores of people and the old dog. It gave him time to think about his own situation. He desperately wanted to get back to Caledon and Taexali territory to seek out his kin. Though, like trying to make contact with Mearna at Eboracum, there was also a hankering to see Garrigill Hillfort one more time – even though to reach it would take them away from the main Roman road that lead northwards. His memories of Garrigill were happy ones, till they had had to abandon it, but after so long away he wondered if he would even recognise anything about it?

The other consideration was that his friends were also desperate to get back home. Especially now, if there were fewer Roman troops marauding around northern Caledonia – perhaps even none at all?

Was it fair to make them take another detour?

Chapter Twenty-Seven

Near Vinovia Roman Fort AD 86

"It is quieter today." Gillean's comment broke the silence as they clopped their way along the paved road towards Vinovia Fort.

The orb of *Lugh* was already overhead, but Beathan had not seen anything like the troop movements of the previous day. Some vehicles carrying hopeful merchants headed north, and others with empty carts headed south. Their greetings on passing by were courteous enough, though he felt a tension he could not quite identify.

"Have you two felt that the traders on this stretch of road have been over-wary of us?"

Derwi nodded. "Aye, young Beathan, they have been exactly that."

"What draws their attention?" he asked. "We had no such suspicion coming north from Londinium. It is only since we left Eboracum, that I have been aware of it."

Gillean clicked his horse to move faster. "Three men of native origins riding north seems to be less than usual. They are curious to know why we travel together, and what our purpose might be, since we are clearly not traders."

"We carry no obvious weapons, so surely they cannot regard us as rebels." As he said it, he found the notion inherently appealing.

Derwi worked harder with his heels, urging his filly to keep pace when they climbed a low rise. "Our last host mentioned there have been some stirrings in northernmost

Brigantia. None have yet taken up arms against the Romans in their small forts but, according to him, the resentment that has remained under the surface for a very long time is bubbling again, like an oatmeal brose that is ready to eat."

Beathan looked to the east. It was brighter there, the land slipping down from the road. Beyond a belt of spindly saplings and low bushes, there was a vast expanse of tussocky moorland. The only signs of habitation in the distance were tiny smoke trails from a cluster of roundhouses spiralling upwards in the calm day. If there were risings of rebel forces, he thought they were unlikely to come from the territory close to this important roadway.

To the west, the forest cover was dense. It encroached the road edge and dimmed that side. The land cleared by the Roman road builders was just enough to leave a short strip alongside the sloping camber.

"What is wrong with this beast?" Derwi moaned, trying in vain to settle his animal that shied away from the road's edge and nudged into the space used by Gillean's mount. "It is the most nervous animal I have ever come across."

Beathan laughed at Derwi's antics to control it. "You need instructions from my Uncle Gabrond. He was the best horseman in the whole of Brigantia."

"Quiet, you two!" Gillean pulled his horse to an abrupt halt. "There is something…"

A surge of Roman legionaries erupted from the trees; the clanking of their armour now noisy enough to set all three horses prancing. It was far too late to acknowledge that Derwi's horse had better hearing than he had.

"Get down!"

The Roman optio's order was unnecessary since Beathan was hauled down anyway and made to stand alongside Derwi and Gillean, a wall of soldiers now to all sides, and of at least a quarter century of men.

On the flick of the optio's pilum, a hand reached forward and pulled forth Beathan's small eating knife, the only blade he carried. The legionary continued to inspect the other pouches around his waist belt, giving his optio a brief list of the contents. "Blade. Sling stones. Grains."

The legionary cut free the pouch containing his slingstones and tossed it to the optio, but added the knife to his own pugio scabbard. The optio tipped Beathan's stones onto a palm before discarding them into the nearby trees. His horse was checked, his friends and their horses also having similar treatment.

"You carry neither swords, nor long knives?" The optio sounded incredulous, yet also amused. "How do you defend yourselves?"

On the point of retaliating, a flicker of Gillean's eyes warned Beathan not to rise to the bait.

Derwi kept his tone even. "Do we need to defend ourselves on your Roman road? We thought this the safest way to travel to the north."

The optio chose not to answer, his earlier humour replaced by a sneer. Questions were thrown their way, the man striding back and forth in front of them, Derwi answering most of them.

"Taexali territory?" The optio nosed up to Derwi, his suspicion a menacing growl. "That is a long march from here."

Beathan refused to flinch when he became the soldier's focus. The man was taller than most Roman soldiers that he had encountered. He tried to mask his surprise when his wrist was grasped and held up and away from his body, the man peering at the underside of his forearm. His other arm got the same treatment.

"Those marks tell a tale much better than any excuses you might mouth at me." The optio's lips slipped up into a parody of a smile before he issued orders to his men to create a tight formation around him and his friends, one they could not easily escape from.

After a long oppressive trudge, entering the gates of Vinovia fort was not part of his earlier plan. He and the other two had meant to skirt clear around it, and find some night shelter somewhere to the north of it.

When the detail marched the three of them into the centre of the fort, there was a familiarity to the via principalis that he wished he had no knowledge of. The freedom that they had experienced since leaving Rome was over, for the moment, but he refused to allow despair to creep in. He had broken no Roman rule that he knew of by using the Roman road to go north…but his free-man status was another thing entirely.

The optio halted the procession and presented himself at the doorway of a room which lay on one side of the principia courtyard.

Beathan did not want to look at the centurion who soon appeared in front of him, but the memory of the damage a vine rod could inflict was too strong.

"All three have slave marks but no branding, you say?" The centurion did not sound convinced.

The order to have him stripped made Beathan stifle a groan. Expecting to be beaten he forced himself to pretend indifference, like the other two seemed to be managing.

Both centurion and optio walked around him, forcing his arms away from his body. Seemingly satisfied, at least temporarily, the centurion pointed the vine rod to his pile of clothes.

"Get dressed!"

After Derwi and Gillean suffered similar treatment, he was pushed into leading their line to the far end of the pillared walkway of the principia, a smaller guard than before walking alongside to ensure he complied. Rapping the vine rod at one of the closed doors, the centurion waited till entry was authorised.

Shoved forward towards a table loaded with scrolls was too much of a repetition for Beathan. When barked at by the figure seated behind the table, he gulped, his eyes stretching wide.

"You!" The officer laughed outright, a rumbling hearty chortle. "And the other two, I also recognise. Well, well."

Alongside him Beathan felt the optio bristling. The soldier had no idea of what Legate Liberalis was referring to.

"Leave us, Optio Ovidus. Though, station enough of your men outside the door to kill them all immediately, should they try anything stupid."

The centurion took up a position near the table that would allow him to defend his superior officer. Brawny arms folded around his vine rod, his glare daring Beathan to move from his position.

Legate Liberalis stared at him.

Beathan had thought he would never see the man again, but it was clear that the goddess of war – *Andarta* – was not playing fair.

"Why has it taken you so long to reach here?" Liberalis was no longer amused, though his expression dripped curiosity.

Beathan held his tongue. So did his friends, except that did not last long. The centurion's staff twitched at the edge of the desk, mimicking the blows the man would soon inflict.

"You could surely have walked faster than you have done, so what – I repeat – have you all been doing since the last time I saw you?" When no reply came from him Liberalis nodded to the centurion.

Beathan knew the goddess had completely failed to listen when he was the first to receive a whack from the vine rod. His shoulder stung, but it was surprisingly not the force it might have been. Or, maybe he had grown stronger, or more inured to pain.

The legate's exhaled breath sounded frustrated; his expression resigned. His next words were also unexpected. "Leave this Brigante with me, but take the others and lock them up. I'll deal with them one by one."

If the centurion was surprised by the order, he showed none of it.

Liberalis waited till Derwi and Gillean were bundled out before he spoke again, his tone now quite flat. "I have no time to waste, Beathan of Garrigill. I know exactly when you escaped from the villa in Rome."

He could not hide the flicker of alarm but could only stare at the man whose head nodded a few times.

Liberalis continued, his expression questioning, though no longer threatening. "I also know the circumstances of that escape, but I would like to hear your version of it."

A cold trickle of sweat slid its way down Beathan's back. There was only one version that was true, so what could the legate mean?

"You will not be punished for telling me what happened in Rome. You have my word on it."

Liberalis was serious. In his heart Beathan knew he was, but how could he tell this man that the general had let him escape, had probably committed some form of treason against the Roman Empire in doing so.

The legate got up, paced around the table and sat on the edge of it, right in front of him.

Beathan swallowed down the noxious stuff that wanted to erupt from his mouth. With some difficulty, he managed to maintain a stare.

Liberalis' voice softened to a whisper. "General Agricola was my superior officer, but he was also a friend. What he did to free you three in Rome was insupportable, though I respect him for the choices he chose to make."

Beathan licked lips that were drying up, as was his mouth. Liberalis continued to confront him.

"Did you know that Agricola's plan was to use you as evidence of his conquests in Caledonia? To prove to

Emperor Domitian that he had succeeded in conquering not only the Caledonians, but that he also held the last remnants of the Brigante rebels?"

Beathan found himself answering. "All I know is that he must have decided I made a useless bargain."

Liberalis chortled, again. "You definitely were. After hauling you across half of the Roman Empire, my friend Agricola confirmed that the emperor was not interested in anything from Caledonia, nor from Brigantia."

The legate's conspiratorial tone returned. "Tell me about when you arrived in Rome."

Beathan was confused. He had still not answered the previous questions.

"There is only so much that is safe to write in a letter, Beathan. Agricola is still my friend, but I need to know why he chose his fate."

Beathan felt his brows cross. Was the general dead? Was that why Liberalis was asking such strange questions?

Liberalis' fingernails tapped against the undersides of the wooden table edge. "This is how I believe it to have been. Agricola intended to spend a night at a mansio between the port of Ostia and Rome. But he changed his mind, continued on and entered the city when it was dark. Inconspicuous, though much safer."

Beathan could not avoid the legate's upward stare, their faces being so near each other.

"Your nod will suffice, if I have it correct." Liberalis waited for a reaction.

He dipped his head the smallest bit.

"Agricola then made his way to the villa of Senator Marcus Cornelius Nigrinus where you and your friends were locked up."

A nod was not too difficult to manage since the statements did not seem incriminating.

Liberalis continued. "What you have no idea of is that on the third day after your arrival, Agricola had a very short audience with the emperor. Domitian had purposely made him wait for days, and then barely acknowledged the general's impressive achievements in Britannia. After that, the emperor made Agricola an offer of a new posting, which my friend refused. It is a very dangerous thing to get on the wrong side of a Roman emperor who wields incredible power. You do not need to know the details of the offer, but thank all of your gods and goddesses that it happened, because you would otherwise now be in your otherworld. Agricola's decision to decline the post gave you a chance to survive, something he could not even be sure of himself."

Beathan looked at the floor, the compulsion to be cautious was overridden by the need to find out more about the strange man who had been so powerful in Britannia, and then so contrary in Rome. He had wished the man ill so many times, but now that it might be so, he did not know what to feel. Liberalis waited, probably sensing his indecision.

When he lifted his head, he knew what needed to be said. "Is the general dead?"

Liberalis' head shook. "No, but he might now wish he was. The last I heard – written, naturally – was that he is alive and living quietly with the Lady Domitia at his estates in Gallia Narbonne."

Beathan felt a strange sense of relief before recalling its dangers. "It is not safe there, either. His wife, Domitia Decidiana, was attacked. Before we all went to Rome."

"I know of your part in that incident, and I also know that you saved Agricola's life in Ostia. Since then, there have been a number of other attempts to assassinate General Agricola but so far, they have been thwarted and long may that be the case. Though I doubt they will ever stop. He lives from day to day wondering if it will be his last."

Beathan could not help himself. "Is there anything you do not know?"

Liberalis smiled. "I do not know why it took you so long to get here." The man seemed to enjoy repeating his own question.

"Have you been tracking our progress all the way from Londinium?"

Liberalis' guffaw was genuine. "My spies work well for me, but they have enough to do to keep abreast of the intrigue within the Roman Empire." He sobered a little. "No, Beathan. This meeting is chance. Some might say that my goddess *Fortuna* has been playing tricks on both of us."

Later that night, Beathan wondered if he had made up the strange conversation. It was difficult to grasp that Agricola faced an even more uncertain future than he did – from being successful at what he did in Britannia, to the life of a rural farmer.

Apart, that is, from the lack of final victory in Caledonia. Agricola had not triumphed there. The Caledon Allies had held him to account in a way they could never have envisaged.

He wished he was with Derwi and Gillean to tell them his news. He had no idea where they were, or what had happened to them. He was not chained to the wall. However, the door of the tiny storeroom was definitely locked. He suspected a guard was outside the door, but there was no iron grill at the top for him to check. Since it was totally dark, he tried to sleep.

Days later, he was still there.

Chapter Twenty-Eight

Vinovia Roman Fort AD 86

"Out, now!" The guard bellowed before he even had the door properly open.

Beathan struggled to his feet. They were the most welcome words he had heard for days.

Prodded in front of the guard, he was hassled along the pillared walkway of the principia, the sounds of tramping feet reaching him well before he got near the wide exit doors. Once outside, and onto the street, his guard pushed him against the wooden wall, using the length of his pilum to block him in. The via principalis thronged with wave after wave of legionary soldiers walking four-abreast, all of whom headed out the far gate.

He had seen the legion's emblem recently: the winged horse that was the emblem of the *Legio II Adiutrix*. After a half-century had marched past, a series of baggage wagons followed, hauled along by raucous, braying mules.

He felt the tip of the pilum slicing his cheek when his guard yanked it away and upright. "Move now. Along to the praetorium."

"Where are the *Legio II Adiutrix* going?" His question seemed to startle the soldier. Not so much that he had dared to ask, but he felt more because he knew which legion was on the move.

"Eboracum." The guard was not exactly talkative while they awaited entry at one of the doors along the praetorium's walkway, but Beathan persisted.

"I have never seen a whole century, with baggage wagons march right through a fort like that, along its via principalis."

The guard stared. "How many forts have you been in to know anything?"

"Quite a few." He pretended indifference to what had been an insult. "I have been in forts all the way to Rome itself." That latter statement was not quite true, but the guard could not know that.

The legionary's guffaws were loud enough to draw the attention of the sentries back at the entrance.

"Rome? Are you telling me that a menial tribesman like you has visited it? And that you walked our Roman roads to get there?"

Beathan could not blame the man. It did sound like one of his Uncle Brennus' tales around the fireside. On that thought, he felt a smile appearing. When he got home, he would have no end of stories to tell, though they would all be true.

"If the *Legio II Adiutrix* are heading for Eboracum does that mean they have been replaced by another legion?"

"You know nothing!" The legionary was dismissive. "The whole legion has been recalled by Emperor Domitian. They are heading for some proper engagement in Dacia, not the furtive little forays of those cowardly Caledonians."

He gulped, but he made sure his thoughts were not revealed in his expression. He had no idea where Dacia was but the *Legio II Adiutrix* had been supporting the *Legio IX*, and *Legio XX,* in northern Caledonia. If his kin were still in Taexali, or Caledon territory, then there must be fewer Roman troops occupying the far north.

That would mean less of the enemy's oppressive presence.

Pure excitement gripped him. He needed to escape to find out.

"Have other troops been sent north to replace this legion in the forts across Caledonia?" he asked.

Once again the guard stared at him as though he was an imbecile. "Most of the northern forts have already been abandoned. Those are the last of the *Legio II Adiutrix* to go south."

Beathan's insides were erupting. He could barely contain the elation he felt, but he wanted more information. He made himself sound incredulous. "Has Trimontium been dismantled?"

The soldier chuckled again. "Ha! You might want that, but no. Trimontium has been re-garrisoned."

He chose not to respond to the mocking, but when he looked at the soldier the abrupt change to livid scorn on the man's face was startling.

"And everything that General Agricola annexed north of those three hills is now in the keeping of the cowardly Caledons!"

Beathan's head was in a whirl. The man's contempt was palpable, but it was hard to determine if the soldier was blaming Agricola for the loss of the territory.

He could still hear the tramping of feet and the loud trundling of the wagons which probably meant a whole cohort was on the move. Understanding dawned, his smile even wider than before.

"Vinovia is a good-sized fort, but it cannot house so many extra soldiers overnight. Were they camped on the north side of the fort? And they now travel southwards using the via principalis right inside the fort?"

The legionary's small nods and glowers made him continue.

"Did the site builders of Vinovia make a mistake over where they placed the main road? Or were they just very clever?" He could not keep amusement from his tones, though his guard did not appreciate his humour.

The man grumped. "I hate being on sentry duty at the main East and West gates. Every single person, animal or vehicle has to be double checked at both ends of our via principalis." The soldier lifted his chin and peered at him. "If you have been in so many of our forts you will know that almost nowhere else allows civilians to prance their way right through our defences."

Beathan agreed. He had never been on any Roman road, used by the public, that went right through a fort, but it was good knowledge to have.

"Bring him in!" The call came from a non-uniformed person. From the stylus still in the man's hand, Beathan guessed him to be a secretary.

In moments he was standing, once again, in front of Liberalis who was having one of the straps of his moulded breastplate adjusted by a young servant.

"Leave!" the legate ordered. When the secretary hesitated, Liberalis waved him out, too.

Beathan felt the power of the man when Liberalis stood before him fully armoured. The man's polished helmet poised on top of the uniform stand drew his gaze, and his awe. The metal ornamentation was even more impressive than Agricola's, and though more battered the general's helmet had been stunning.

"You have given me a problem I could well do without, Brigante Beathan."

He stared. It was not a question, so he gave no response. He had plenty of problems of his own.

"Rome gives men frequent marching orders."

Beathan absorbed the terse tones and tried to interpret the legate's words. Although the room was cleared of his staff, it was possibly still not a totally private conversation.

"You mean that the *Legio II Adiutrix* has been recalled to Rome to go to fight a…less cunning enemy?"

Liberalis almost smiled. "The emperor demands their presence."

He nodded since Liberalis' expression seemed to indicate it was necessary.

He dared to add a little more. "I have heard that the *Legio IX,* and the *Legio XX*, have also been withdrawn from Caledonia. From all of the northern forts."

The legate's expression was calculating. "You learn the most fascinating information, Beathan the Brigante. Perhaps General Agricola was correct and that you do need to be handled very carefully."

He chose not to reply. Handling was something he had plenty of experience of.

"You have seen many of our forts but not, I think, Pinnata Castra?"

He had heard about that one from Ineda of Marske, his Uncle Brennus' hearth-wife, but he chose to only nod.

"Agricola was very proud of that fortress." Liberalis sounded reflective. "I believe he would have liked to show you it."

He found he could not hold back. "It has also been abandoned?"

Liberalis' chuckles were bitter. "I am glad he was not there to see his beloved *Legio XX* leave." The Legate's smile became snide. "You, on the other hand, might have been impressed by the situation."

The glare that came his way made Beathan refrain from asking any more questions.

Liberalis' tone dipped again. "Like General Gnaeus Iulius Agricola, past Governor of Britannia, I am also recalled to Rome. Though unlike Agricola, I will be embarking a ship well before Londinium, to take me to the shores of Gaul." Liberalis' voice quietened to a rasping whisper, as intense as his stare. "Agricola and I share a friendship and probably the same fate. But presently, I have no desire to leave any unravelling threads which he saw fit to loosen."

Beathan felt his throat seize up. What was the man talking about?

Liberalis leaned forward, closing the gap between them, his words a murmur. "Rome seems to have had no place for you…and neither does this fort. Because of the acquaintance I share with Agricola, I will not kill you, but you will go where you are less likely to cause yourself an early death."

For a brief moment Liberalis looked away. Beathan waited. He could tell there was more to come since the man seemed to be fighting with something unseen. When Liberalis returned his focus on him, he could not avoid noticing that a deeper anger was now interlaced with the earlier threat.

"I have been unable to keep your arrival a secret, so news of you being here has already caused some tongues to wag. You are not as inconspicuous as you may think you are, Brigante. And I cannot afford to be tarnished with allowing a fugitive to escape, again."

Beathan swallowed. Was Liberalis saying that even he had foes around him?

"Yes. Brigante. I do have my own enemies. I may, or I may not, manage to arrive in Rome hale and hearty." Liberalis broke off to laugh quietly, but it was a snide, bitter one. "Unfortunately, I will not have a champion like you to defend me – instinctively, or otherwise."

Beathan could not help the disbelieving frown that furrowed his forehead. Liberalis would make sure to set a substantial personal guard around him. Did the man mean he was not even sure that he could trust them?

"For some reason *Fortuna* appears to favour you, Brigante. I should like to drag you back to Rome as my personal good luck charm. However, I cannot acquire any form of remission for you. Neither could General Agricola, though he did try, to his own detriment. You are still an official hostage of Rome."

Beathan bit down the flood of bitterness that those words brought forth, his jaw tensing.

The legate continued his threatening whisper. "Though you are a mature young man now, you have still not learned to school that defiant expression, Beathan of the Brigantes. I advise you to remember some caution. You know already that Rome's centurions are trained to be vicious towards those who are slow to learn discipline."

Beathan felt his cheeks tighten even more. A sudden hatred of the man would not be quelled. He inhaled through his nose and forced himself to not reach out and punch the face that was close enough.

After a few long stares, Liberalis called for the guard to enter.

"Fetch Centurion Spectatus."

Beathan reckoned the man must have been close by since he strutted in almost instantly.

"This captive will go to Vindolanda Fort with the next shipment of goods. Double the usual guard and make sure he gets there. He is a slippery one. He will remain there till…" Liberalis paused to pop on his helmet and fix the neck strap. "…further orders are received."

"What about my friends? Derwi and Gillean? Where are they?"

Liberalis slid a knife from a pouch at his waist with great deliberation.

Beathan had never seen anything like the carving on the hilt, was not even sure what the hilt was made of. It was shorter than the pugio that most soldiers wore at their waist, but longer than an eating knife. His panicked fascination with the quality dwindled when the extremely sharp tip was tucked under his chin.

"Let us just say that they will be imprisoned in a fort that is closer to their home territory than where you are going."

After one long stare, Liberalis removed the blade and slipped it back into its sheath.

Beathan's last sight of Legate Liberalis was one he would never forget. A small smirk quirked up the man's mouth and a twisted amusement flashed across his determined expression.

The word captive resonated.
Liberalis had demoted him from hostage… to captive.

Chapter Twenty-Nine

Vindolanda Roman Fort AD 87

The flick of his broom was methodical as Beathan swiped the last of the musty layers across the wooden floor, and out of the door of the small praetorium at Vindolanda Fort. Piles of perfectly-dried bracken were ready to be scattered, the floor-covering designed to keep draughts at bay.

Praefectus Verecundus, in command of the auxiliary fort, considered the room his entertaining space and was obsessive about the floor being fresh. The man ate there, relaxed there on his own, though it was also his place of conversation with visiting officers who moved from west to east, and east to west, along the Roman road which stretched across northern Brigantia.

"Hurry up, you lazy Brigante!"

Publius, the supervisor of the praetorium, was as nasty to him as he was to the rest of the generous personal staff allocated to the commander. Lazy Brigante still grated, though he had learned to tolerate the abuse much better than at Trimontium.

The Hillfort of Garrigill, where he had been born, was not too far away, though he had no real idea of its direction. Gaining his freedom – returning first to Garrigill, and then to Caledonia – was what kept him going every single day. He had tried to take advantage of any opportunity that came his way to escape, ever since his arrival more than two seasons ago, though none had transpired.

Presently, he wanted to find out why there was a restlessness around the fort, for reasons that he could not fathom. He cast around the last remnants of the floor material, Publius at his heels, ensuring a good job had been done.

"Go and see if the carcass is butchered and ready for me. I have been waiting all morning and it needs to go on the spit." There was an urgency to Publius' words that was beyond the man's usual impatience.

Being compliant after arriving at Vindolanda Fort had resulted once again in the fairly quick removal of Beathan's chains, first the ankle ones and then the wrist. However, he still bore the slave collar that Legate Liberalis had insisted on. The very feel of it at his collarbones was a daily reminder of how much he loathed that particular Roman.

Vindolanda Fort was manned by a Tungrian unit. He detested them almost as much as Liberalis because it was likely that the very same auxiliaries had been in Agricola's armies at Beinn na Ciche. It was even possible that some of them had fought directly against his own kin on the battlegrounds. He could never prove such a thing, though he did try.

Now, they were used to seeing him fetching and carrying, their inquiries limply routine as to his movements, and some could even be lulled into conversation.

So long as he trod lightly.

And complacence, regarding their more settled existence in northern Brigantia, might be to his advantage.

"Hurry along now." The guard up at the East Gate tower urged Beathan around the corner onto the intervallum area, his shouts echoing around. "And you remember to go back using the via praetoria with that cart. This gate is going to be busy soon, and for some time to come."

He gripped the poles firmly and picked up speed, the small handcart bouncing along behind him. The East Gate was already being opened, and he could see a first wave of cavalry entering.

He glanced at the vexillum, the square standard carried by the front rider. More of the First Cohort Tungrians! *Ceigan Ròmanach*! After such a long time in the fort, Beathan knew its layout extremely well. Some of the cavalry barracks had lain empty, though it looked as though that was about to end.

In double formation, the stream of horsemen entered the fort behind the vexillum bearer and headed along the via principalis, the road he had just exited. Why they had not dismounted at the gate needed some thought. He had never seen that happen before.

And why they had not entered using the north gate was even more puzzling, since the unused barracks for mounted forces were at the northern end of the fort.

Pleas to *Andarta*, to give him strength to wreak revenge on the Tungrian turds, came thick and fast while he scooted his way down to the south-east corner to where the animal pens were located. Butchering was done close to the main sewer which drained away under the fort at its south-eastern end, where the natural slope was used to advantage.

He avoided being drenched by the soldier doing the butchering, the man casting a bucket of water around at his feet, to disperse the blood.

"What took you so long?" The soldier gestured at the prepared carcasses that lay on his table, his mood clearly irritable and cranky. "Hurry now, I need that table free again. I have given him two hogs, but no doubt it will be up to me to provide even more meat for the celebrations, and here I am with no slave to help me do the gutting."

"There is to be another feast?"

Since he had arrived the Romans of the fort seemed to find plenty of reasons to celebrate.

"Of course!" The soldier tutted at him. "Do you know nothing?"

When he gave no response the man continued, his tone as though speaking to someone senseless. "Part of our First Cohort are re-joining us, today. Years have passed, but we have never had the opportunity, yet, for all of us to celebrate together. Our battle triumphs against those gutless, barbarian Caledonians are worthy of a great feast."

His mouth felt gritty. "Caledonians?"

The auxiliary waved him to the other end of the first carcass. Together, they hauled it off the table and onto his little hand cart.

The man bragged. "It was our Tungrian auxiliary units who were responsible for General Agricola's victory in that battle against that Caledon Calgacus' puny tribes. And now that more of our unit gather together, we will celebrate our prowess!"

Beathan held his tongue and helped wrestle the second carcass onto his cart. The burning sensation inside almost engulfed him. He was so close to the table on which lay a perfect gutting blade, but he needed to kill more than just one of these bastard Tungrians.

Deep in his own mire, he saw little of the intervallum when he returned the long way to the praetorium. At the junction of the via praetoria and via principalis, he stopped to watch the last of the newcomers turn and clop their way up towards the North Gate.

Along the road, he could see that Commander Verecundus and the senior centurions still stood outside the praetorium entrance in full body armour, though the official welcome was now over. Now he understood why the North Gate had not been used.

Heading for the praetorium kitchen, he mumbled more pleas to his goddess *Andarta*. Now there were twice as many men in the garrison to kill, or what was probably worse… to flee from.

The day eventually dwindled into dusk, but it was little different for Beathan. He was still fetching and carrying, clearing the bowls and serving dishes that had been used in the prefect's living area.

The feasting had gone well though, naturally, he had had no taste of any of the specially prepared food. Commander Verecundus was in fine fettle and was still entertaining the recently arrived seniors of the First Cohort, and a tribune from another legion who had also marched into the fort.

The sour taste had not left Beathan's mouth. They all had plenty to boast about.

Armed with an almost toppling pile of dirty plates, he hesitated as he edged away from one of the low tables, unwilling to miss anything useful.

"And what would you determine is the mood of those pathetic Caledonians now?" Verecundus asked the visiting tribune.

"Little different from when General Agricola was in the north."

Beathan's glance took in the soldier tipping the dregs past his lips. The tribune then waved the glass cup in the air for a refill without even looking around. The wine boy was meant to be there…but not there, and of no consequence. Apart from docile servitude.

"I have no doubt the northern Caledons still bide their time skulking around in their precious, remote mountains." The tribune's tone was dismissive. "It is the Damnonii, and the remnants of the Selgovae, who currently make ineffective raids. I am talking about on the last of our fortlets in Selgovae and Novante territory, those which have not yet been given leave to dismantle and vacate."

Beathan set his pile near the wall and hastened back with the full jug of wine that lay waiting there. Publius had anticipated a long night of eating and drinking, and had prepared well.

Verecundus waved his own goblet for more wine, his tongue less guarded now. "What happened at Pinnata Castra?"

"The Caledonians had been rumbling in the nearby glens. Not in the huge numbers of before…" The tribune broke off to sip some wine from the refilled goblet, clearly appreciating what Verecundus had offered.

Beathan personally thought it to be rough. His head would have been off his shoulders if the commander knew he had tasted it, but the risk was worth it. Verecundus had snobbish social ambitions, always striving to give the impression of being highly cultured but, if by nothing else, Beathan thought his taste in wine gave away his equestrian status.

He had tasted good wine at Agricola's Narbonensis estate – not the early wine the slaves had been given every day, but some from Agricola's own cellars – and he knew what he was serving now was nothing like good wine. He felt a peculiar satisfaction in the knowledge.

The tribune continued. "Those northern Caledonians would not dare to gather in huge numbers again, but their sneaky attacks continued to be regular before the *Legio XX* dismantled Pinnata Castra."

Beathan took his time to take a step back, the wine jug in his hands an excuse to linger.

The tribune laughed though it sounded hollow. "You know how the emperor systematically withdrew our *Legio II Adiutrix* troops after Agricola was summoned back to Rome?"

Verecundus nodded.

"Well, those poor *Legio XX* bastards at Pinnata Castra had less than a half-cohort to clear the whole supply fortress."

A centurion of the First Cohort joined in. "They were Rome's most northerly troops by then."

The tribune set his empty goblet down. "They were. The nearest cohort was more than a day away to the south.

And at that time, all of the forts in central Caledonia were scantly garrisoned as well. And, of course, now they have all been dismantled, too."

Beathan brought forward the jug when prompted, though it would barely fill two cups and not the commander's third goblet. His thinking was not on the amount of wine, but on the fact that almost the whole of Caledonia had been freed of Roman presence.

His family would be overjoyed!

But would they have wanted to stay in the far north? Or, had they journeyed back down to the Selgovae territory of his mother's birth? Questions came think and fast to him, but he had no answers. How would he ever find them?

And gaining complete revenge for his captivity and current enslavement was another ambition entirely.

"Get moving, Brigante! Clear those dishes and fetch another jug!" Verecundus waved him towards the door, again without looking in his direction, and continued his conversation with his guests. "Are any of the southern forts in Caledonian still being maintained?"

Beathan took his time, his hands trembling on the empty jug, sheer rage taking over. The news was too much to miss.

The tribune nodded. "A few just over the hills from here, and Trimontium Fort. That will earn its keep for a while yet."

Praefectus Verecundus snorted, but Beathan thought it sounded insincere. "Just as well that General Agricola is far removed from here. Our withdrawal from Caledonia, and especially from Pinnata Castra, would never have sat well with him at all."

The tribune twiddled the stem of his goblet, swishing what was left of the wine. "I heard recently that Agricola is still in so much disfavour with Emperor Domitian. His retiral to his Gallia Narbonensis estates has been…problematic. Is that true?"

Verecundus thumped his fist against the couch cushion. "I heard the same. There is no safe place for him in the whole empire."

"Indeed!" The tribune's smile was taut. "Only Agricola would dare refuse an offer from Domitian and expect to come out unscathed."

Verecundus' response was another hollow laugh. "It takes a strong man to oppose the might of the Senate and our Emperor Domitian. The last I heard Agricola is still alive, but the same cannot be said for the ex-legate Liberalis. He was expected in Rome months ago but did not arrive."

Beathan found that news was welcome. If the legate was dead by someone's else's hand, he would not have to think about routing out the *Cèigan Ròmanach* and doing it himself.

He watched Verecundus wipe wine drops from his lips with the back of his hand when he stooped to collect the pile of dirty plates while keeping a grip of the pottery jug. Nudging the door open with his elbow, the last words he heard from the commander made him feel even more trapped.

"No. The Votadini will be no threat. That whole tribe acquiesced to Rome a long time ago. Trimontium will need to be slightly expanded by the incoming garrison, but they will keep our entryway to the north open. In case Domitian changes his mind about another Caledonian expansion."

The tribune's reply was almost a growl. "Or a different emperor?"

Beathan had only taken a few awkward steps out onto the pillared corridor when an acrid smell stunned his senses. Men erupted from doors all around the praetorium and rushed through the entrance, though he could see no sign of fire in the immediate vicinity. Hesitation lasted for only the tiniest moment before he dumped his burdens at his feet and rushed after the others who ran along the via principalis, turned the corner, and disappeared up towards the northern gate.

Flames sparked high from the roof of the barracks up at the far end of the street. In the distance, a chain of men already passed along full buckets of water, filling them up from the small cistern that lay on the edge of the intervallum.

He stopped stock still, buffeted by the men who surged from behind him. The fire was spreading across to the northern granary on the opposite side of the street, the evening wind strong enough for errant sparks to float across to it.

"That cistern is not nearly big enough!" he called out to no-one in particular. He knew just how much water it held because he was one of the slaves who regularly filled it up from the stream just outside the walls.

"Get up there and help!" An optio manhandled his arm but he resisted, repeating his words.

"That cistern will be empty by the time we even get there. You need to use the larger one at the East Gate, or fetch water from the burn."

The optio, a man he had often taken orders from, began to holler. "Form the chain to the East Gate!"

The man then turned to him. "Get back to the praetorium, Brigante, and get as many buckets as you can out to the eastern cistern."

He found he was not the only man changing direction. It was in everyone's interest to ensure that the grain supplies were not burned to a cinder, but the fire had taken too good a hold. It was not long before Verecundus was ordering the East Gate to be opened, though by then it already had been.

Beathan was only one of a number of men who slipped their way down the slope to the nearby stream. More curses were sent to the gods because being a fort slave, he was nominated to stand in the freezing cold water and fill up the buckets.

After too many bucket-refills to count, the night around him darkened once more to a point where he was sloshing a bucket down into the water and listening for it filling, rather than seeing it happen. Fumbling fingers had been passing the containers, one to the next, for what seemed like a long time.

A hollering came from the guard up at the gate, echoed by the nearest man on the banking. "Hold it! No more buckets till they check the fire's progress."

Silence reigned, the only sounds he could hear were those of the burbling stream and the heaving breaths of the soldier next to him.

"The fire is out!"

The men on the slope above him clinked empty buckets together, their congratulations a raucous affair.

Slumping down onto the grassy bank, Beathan swung his numbed feet out of the stream. The stabbing pains that had begun some time ago were a continuous ache as he rubbed and rubbed his toes to get some feeling back into them. Lying down he tried a different technique. Knees bent he drummed his feet flat against the ground till the stabbing pains came back again, his own noise supplanting the fading voices all around him.

Swinging around onto his knees, he realised that the rest of the men had already hared back up the slope and were entering the gates which were closing around them. The hollering inside the fort was still a tremendous din.

His life force thumped inside him, almost as much as that still happening at his feet.

He would never have a better chance!

Slinking along the stream bank he kept low on hands and knees, scurrying like a field mouse. The urge was strong to get up and run, but the east wall of the fort was the wrong side to escape from.

Garrigill, the only place he could think of heading towards, was probably somewhere to the south.

Chapter Thirty

Hamlet of Alaunas AD 87

"Is he alive?"

Beathan froze, and not just his feet. When feathery touches of fingertips felt the skin of the back of his left hand, not flinching was impossible. He opened his eyes to find a face close up to his own, the kneeling young woman almost as startled as he was.

"He is definitely alive."

The first voice spoke again, the tones of a concerned young boy. "Is he badly injured, Torrin?"

He stared at the woman while willing his frantic insides to calm down.

Her brown hair was braided in the fashion of a tribeswoman. He fervently hoped he was not wrong, but it had been so long since he had seen females of any kind: especially a young and comely one, who was probably about his own age. The next all-over flush that came to him was familiar and was nothing to do with any injury he might have, or his initial terror at being discovered.

There was a question in her eyes, though the rest of her expression remained serious. She twisted up some of his low-branched leaf-cover to reveal his whole body.

"Are you?"

A gripping pain washed over him like river water cascading over a crag and robbed him of his breath. It was an agony that a sleep of exhaustion had held at bay. Breathing in deeply through his nose, he forced an answer that came out as a croak. "If this is not the otherworld…then I cannot be so bad, after all." He immediately regretted his feeble attempt at humour when her eyes creased in concern, alarm spreading.

When she rocked back onto her heels and stood up in one movement, he tried to unfurl himself from his protective curl. Squirming himself free of the twiggy branches was agony, his wincing intended to be unseen.

Once again, she stooped down and pulled back more of the branches to help free him from the prickly thorns which snagged his clothes and ripped his exposed skin.

The woman did not seem to present any immediate danger to him, but he gave thanks to the goddess *Brigantia* anyway, that she was not a member of a Roman patrol. Though where her allegiance lay, regarding the Roman scum, could still be a huge problem.

The raw stabbing at his knee told him that the injury of the previous night had not had the favour of *Coventina's* healing. The goddess of the nearby burn must go by a different name in this area since she, too, had ignored his pleas.

Struggling into an awkward sitting position, he rested his back against the jagged bush and bent his right knee. His injured leg lay splayed out till he steadied the life force that was threatening to burst free from his chest.

The woman's expression was solemn, level-headed. "Where do you hurt the most?"

At that moment he could hardly tell her. His left knee throbbed. One cheek smarted almost as much as the backs of his lacerated hands, but those injuries were compounded by a different other pulsing which he had little control over.

The gods, and all of the goddesses, were definitely not favouring him. What had he done that had been so awful for him to deserve this present plight? Unable to face her any longer, he suppressed a self-berating smirk and swung his gaze to the other person, till he regained some control.

The boy, he guessed, was no more than five or six summers. The young lad's eyes widened when they noted his slave collar, a swift step taking the boy so close to the woman that not even a feather could separate them.

The lad flinched even more when he raised one of his palms and placed it flat across his iron collar. Tapping it gently, so as not to scare the boy further, he said, "My knee may be broken, but this is what causes me the greater hurt."

"*Cò sibhse?*" asked the boy.

"My name is Beathan. And your name?"

"I am Cailean." The boy's head bobbed furiously before he pointed to the woman. "Torrin is my sister. She can make you better. She is good at fixing me when I fall."

"Aye. And that happens all the time." Torrin ruffled her brother's hair. "Though your tumbles have not been so serious as I think this man's might be."

Beathan was a bit wary when Cailean bent down and poked a grubby nail at his braccae.

"Your *Màthair* will shout at you for all of those tears in your clothes."

That made Beathan almost forget his aches and pains. His mother shouting at him for anything would be a very fine thing. Pangs of a different kind of longing banished the sudden desire that had flooded him. He looked at his loose woollen trousers. They had been in a very poor state before his tumble of the previous night, and now only thin threads and matted-blood held some parts together.

"I need to see what you have done to yourself." Torrin pointed to his leg.

He was sufficiently recovered now for an investigation of his own. He had a feeling that walking would be difficult, and foraging for himself would be even harder.

The glint of a small knife, when she pulled it free of the sheath hanging from her belt, slightly alarmed him, though he had no option but to trust her. He was taller and stronger than she was, and could most likely overpower her even in his poor state, but she wielded a sharp-looking little weapon which he had no desire to have a taste of.

He braced himself for whatever might come next. He had survived so many different physical attacks and could survive another.

Small flicks opened up the torn leg of his braccae even further. He sensed rather than saw her re-pouch her blade before her fingers began a delicate exploration around his throbbing knee. The rest of his torn and bloodied leg got the same search, her fingers strangely warm against his skin which he already felt hot as a hearth-fire.

"Lay this one flat."

He was confused because she was now touching his uninjured leg, though he complied. She rolled up the leg of his braccae to bare his healthy knee and studied it very carefully.

"Now bend it again and try to do the same with this injured one."

Sweat ran down into his ears, the pain almost unbearable. Bending even the tiniest bit was excruciating.

"Enough."

He felt her hands bracket his shoulders to prevent him from toppling over while he found his balance again.

"Cailean." After she got to her feet, he watched her point to a stand of thin birch trees not far off. "Fetch me a stout tree fall, a straight branch that comes up to here." She brought her hand to rest on her brother's shoulder. "Go quickly. We must get this warrior back to our roundhouse."

She turned back to him. "I do not believe the bone is broken, but something about your knee seems wrong, apart from the ripped skin and the swelling. How did this happen?"

He was in no fit state to run off. He would lose little in the telling and was more likely to gain more. He could not call her expression friendly, yet neither did she seem actively hostile.

"I have been completely lost and stumbling across bleak moorland for the last couple of days." He was deliberately evasive.

"You injured yourself days ago?" Torrin looked disturbed. "Did you find no-one to help you?"

"I have not come across anyone at all. It was last night, when travelling in the weak moonlight, that I tangled my foot in heather roots."

She pointed to his slave collar, a glimmer of derision changing her look. "I can see why that would have been the best time to be on the move, though you were clearly not too successful."

Unsure if she was poking fun at his expense, he bristled. "I was following an animal track. Though, as you can see, it led to me being at the bottom of the fell slope much faster than I intended."

She slid onto her knees, putting her face right up close again, her expression back to serious. "And you were already weak from lack of sustenance?"

He felt Torrin's light fingertips feel around his shoulders and upper arms, her focus intent on his body rather than his eyes.

"Sit forward."

Caution failing him, he did as she bid, at least as much as his injured leg would allow.

Her fingertips continued to feel down his backbone as far as she could reach. The few unsuppressed winces told her where his other bruising mostly lay.

His fingers curled into tight fists on the ground as he battled with all sorts of feelings.

Pulling a water skin from her belt, she offered it to him.

"*Tapad leat*, Torrin."

"There is not much left, I am afraid."

"No matter," he said. "After my fall, I managed to drag myself to the burbling of a nearby burn where I lapped in as much water as I could stomach."

"Aye." She nodded. "There is one near here. And I am guessing that you dragged yourself to these bushes as the first ones you came across?"

That hint of scorn was back.

"They were. But last night, in the shadows, I did not realise till too late that they were hawthorns."

A brief ripple of her laughter made him feel just a bit less hapless.

"Weight bearing on that knee will need to be avoided till my mother can look at it. My brother sings my praises, but *Màthair* has not yet taught me all she knows."

Squirming around onto his good knee, he grabbed a fistful of hawthorn bush and hauled himself upright.

A second snigger was even more unexpected. "You know, I could have avoided you getting more thorns on your hands. I think you should not be so proud." She pointed to his slave collar. "You need help."

"My mother was also a healer." The words spilled free, though he did not know why he divulged them.

Antagonism now oozed from her; her teeth clenched. "I have no wish to be a healer." Her voice grew low, more forceful. "I want to be an avenging warrior, like the goddess *Andarta*. I want to wipe the Roman scum from my father's land and regain the life my grandmother had, and her mother before her."

Surprised by her vehemence, there was no hesitation over his next words. "My mother is both of those things. She is a fierce female warrior…" He broke off and had to look away, emotion almost getting the better of him. "Perhaps was – I do not know presently – but she also possesses unsurpassed healing skills."

"Then I shall look forward to hearing more of her later."

Torrin whipped off her bratt, folded it into a long length and draped it around his neck, so close her breath gusted his cheeks.

He wished her look to be…inviting, but it was not.

"That will cover you for now."

"I am obliged to you." Letting the bush absorb his weight, he raised his hands to tuck the material tighter around the iron band, before he tossed the long ends down his back.

"No thanks needed. Your tale of how you got that adornment can wait till we are in safety."

"This is the straightest I can find, Torrin. Is it good?" Cailean approached them at an awkward trot, dragging a stout branch behind him.

"You have chosen well." She patted her brother's cheek softly before she removed it from his grasp and set it up on its end.

She whipped her knife back out and stripped off some of the twigs, leaving a straighter shaft.

Beathan was not so sure of how much of his weight would be borne by it, but he also praised Cailean before grasping it firmly in one fist.

Torrin bent down to her brother, taking both of his small hands into her own, her tone grave. "Cailean, we need to get this man back to our roundhouse as quickly as we can, before a marauding Roman patrol discovers him. Be a good lad and lead the way for us, but no talking."

Her voice dropped to a whisper as she draped a brace of birds across the little boy's shoulders. "Mind me, well. No gossip. Especially if you see anyone at all on the way. Beathan will only manage to move very slowly, so you have to be our scouting eyes and give us plenty of warning."

He watched the beam almost split Cailean's cheeks. It was clearly an honour to take the lead, the boy stepping purposefully ahead after checking all around.

The tap at his arm alerted him to Torrin's mouthing. "Do not fear. He knows how to go, and it is not so far."

She slid both arms around his waist and snuggled herself under the shoulder on his poor side, her body so tight in against him that each of her steps then became his steps. If he had not needed to pour all of all his strength into moving, he might have found it more arousing.

They got into a rhythmic slow hobble using the prop of wood. His injured leg hung just barely off the ground, and they only stopped for him to regroup his strength. Cailean ran back and forth, like a blackbird darting around waiting for a juicy worm to appear when farmers till the ground for seed sowing. The boy's constant grin indicated his enjoyment of his responsibility.

It was after they had eventually crested a second low hill that he noticed signs of a single roundhouse down in a hollow, below the summit heathlands. A tiny wisp of smoke rose up towards the sky god *Lugh*. A couple of figures were working in one of the three field areas that he could see, thankfully the only people they had encountered.

"Run ahead now, Cailean." They had moved so quietly on the track, reserving their strength, that Torrin's words startled him out of his near stupor. "Tell *Athair* that we will be looking after a guest for a while. Ask him to come and help me get Beathan down the hill so that I do not fall, as well."

Cailean set off at a run down the slope.

Beathan sent fervent prayers to the goddess *Brigantia* to keep him from the humiliation of collapsing before they reached the sanctuary of Torrin's home at the place she just named as Alaunas.

Chapter Thirty-One

Hamlet of Alanaus AD 87

"You escaped from Vindolanda Fort? How did that come about?" Aonghas, Torrin's father, asked the questions, though halted on seeing the look on his wife's face.

Beathan sat propped on a pile of furs. His injured leg was stretched out and his back was supported by an upturned wooden tub, padded with bracken, that had been pulled free from a cot that lay against the low interior wall of the roundhouse. The contents of the small beaker that Torrin had given him, and the warmth from the fire, were making him feel drowsy already.

Alongside, there was a bowl holding a mushy-paste redolent of the sweetness of honey, and some herb he was too exhausted to guess at. Two strips of willow wood also lay ready for use. Young Cailean had described the injury very well to his mother, Niamh, who knelt in front of him.

Niamh sliced away the tattered leg of his braccae, revealing the full mess of his injury. Using both hands, she felt the knee-swelling and probed and poked around the rest of his leg, a lot less gentle than her daughter had been.

"Can you feel this?" The pinching at his toes was almost as painful as his knee.

"Aye." His grunt was feeble, but he was almost beyond caring.

The woman chattered non-stop asking him this and that about how his injury had happened, and how it now felt. He watched her place one of her hands firmly at the side of his knee. But when she gripped his ankle with her other, and yanked hard, his yell proved he not been expecting the treatment she meted out. The noisy pop at his knee had caused a silent hush around the roundhouse. And then the whoop of amusement that came from Cailean made even Beathan smile. A tremulous one, but a smile of relief since the agony was instantly much reduced.

"I should perhaps have waited for the swelling to abate, young warrior, before doing that, but then you would perhaps have known me better and would have been more resistant to my attentions."

Niamh's brief smile was one of reassurance, rather than regret, when she set to removing grit and other bits of plant material that had lodged into his torn skin.

He hardly dared breathe while she wielded a small and sharp bone needle to pull bits of his torn skin together, before she slapped the herb mixture around his knee and secured it with a piece of cloth wrapped around a few times.

"The poultice will help repair the damaged skin and will reduce the swelling."

After that, she deftly placed the wooden strips to each side of the injury and secured them in place with strong lengths of leather. "The wood will keep your knee from bending too much just now, because it will take some days for that swelling to go down."

He had a feeling that might be so. And her next words were not so unexpected either. He had seen warriors with bad knee wrenches which never healed properly. He fervently hoped the goddess *Andarta* would not be so unkind to him.

Niamh continued. "If you are to regain normal walking, the strapping should be in place for a while after the swelling has gone."

Turning to Cailean, the woman issued more instructions. "Find more bracken that can be put under

Beathan's ankle. His leg needs to remain raised, for the feeling to become normal in his toes."

Niamh turned back to him. "For now, you must rest that leg."

"He has bruises all down his back." Torrin's words were unexpected since she had been silent.

"And how would you know that?" The twinkle at Niamh's eyes was teasing.

Torrin stiffened, her words defensive. "I felt his body, just like you have taught me to do."

Aonghas' deep rumble lightened the sudden tension at the fireside. "Well, that is a fine introduction to this stranger!"

"That is not what I meant and you know it, *Athair*!"

Beathan sipped more of the drink. He had no idea what it was, but its soothing was working, though not so much that he missed the antagonism that flushed Torrin's face.

Niamh gave a gentle pat to her daughter's cheek. "You must learn to take some teasing, if you wish to be more than a hearth-wife and a mother."

Getting awkwardly to her feet, Niamh lifted the emptied bowl of salve, and took it across to the entryway. She came back with a larger bowl of warm water drawn from the pot that sat on the hearthstones, and a cloth which she thrust at her daughter.

"Wipe those cuts on his face and hands while I get some food for him."

He felt Niamh's attention turn to him again. The woman was civil, even hospitable, yet she was stern as well. "You have been in more than one battle, young warrior."

"I have never met anyone who has escaped from one of those Roman forts." Aonghas prompted, now that the healing had been seen to. "There are hundreds in that garrison."

There was an element of doubt in the man's tone that Beathan would have preferred not to hear, but he had already learned how being wary was worn like a second skin.

"Apart from this knee injury, *Andarta* eventually heard my pleas and favoured me." He had had plenty of time to think about that when hiding the last few days. "The misfortune at Vindolanda Fort was to my benefit."

In between dispassionate passes of the cloth dampened with clean water to his face, and then to his arms and hands, he described the fire and how he had managed to free himself. Torrin obeyed her mother, but he could tell that there was no enthusiasm in the task.

"Three nights have passed since then. The moorland between here and Vindolanda Fort has little cover, so I hid during the day and moved by night, with no knowledge of where I was going. Apart from hoping I was going south and glad to be away from the fort."

"The goddess *Brigantia* has favoured you." Aonghas' look complimented the local goddess. "We must give praise to her that Torrin found you. This whole territory is riddled with Roman forts and small watchtowers."

After Cailean had stuffed enough bracken under his ankle to raise it to the height that was deemed suitable, Niamh handed him a wooden bowl with a thin oat brose in it,

Beathan thanked her, and set to supping it, noting that Torrin shared her mother's doe-brown eyes, but little else was similar. Where Torrin was slim, in face and body, Niamh was comfortably rounded.

Niamh's expression was calculating, which did little to make him feel safer. He was possibly even more vulnerable now than when hiding under a bush. He had been betrayed before, by Brigantes.

Aonghas drummed his palm against his thigh. "Three nights, you say? Then they will have been out scouring the area, seeking your whereabouts. Finish that brose quickly. We must remove the collar, though those Roman metal workers do not make that an easy task."

No easy job indeed.

When General Agricola had ordered the removal of his first slave collar it had been a matter of a twist of a special tool to pop free the tightly-fitting rivet that sealed the ring. Torrin's father had no such instrument. And, to cofound it, his present collar had been wet often enough for rust to make the task even harder. He had tried many times to remove the pin but had failed.

He drained the bowl.

After taking it from him, Niamh headed for the doorway. "I will keep watch outside."

Aonghas selected a very thin blade from the pile of tools in a metal basket near the entrance. "We will have to pray that this will do."

Torrin slipped a bunched piece of material under the band, the cloth long enough to cover his head and ear, the rest she tucked in to protect his already chafed neck.

"This will, hopefully, prevent you from being strangled while *Athair* gets to work."

Aonghas indicated Torrin should kneel at one side and Cailean at the opposite. Each gripped the band to keep it as still as possible while Aonghas sawed through the metal at the back. That made the position awkward since Aonghas had to sit on the up-turned tub and find space for his bent legs.

The horrible sensation of feeling prone to being strangled, murdered or maimed was only slightly alleviated by Cailean telling him about their nearest neighbours, and the whereabouts of the closest Roman watchtower. The boy asked him questions, but it was difficult to answer while trying to keep still, and the rhythmic screech created by Aonghas as the blade bit in did not make it easy to hear. The conversation dwindled, but his awareness of Torrin being so close did not. Occasional speculative glances at his face gave him some encouragement that given time – perhaps quite a long time – she might change her attitude to him.

However, in contrast to any possible friendliness, he could not prevent a different disquiet from creeping in.

Was Niamh still outside?

Or had she gone elsewhere?

The repetitive screech dulled while he considered his current predicament. He had had plenty of injuries during his captive period, though none before this one would have prevented him from running off, if the opportunity had presented itself.

He was tired of being caged, tired of feeling threatened, in fact just tired.

If he could have hung his head down he would have, but even that was not possible.

"Are you not finished, yet, hearth-husband?" Niamh asked a short time later, having entered through the entryway with yet another small bowl in her hand. "I did not think you such a weakling to take so long to break such a thin band."

For the first time Beathan saw a genuine smile appear on Niamh's face before she thrust the vessel at Torrin. "I see no signs of any Roman patrols, but I have been thinking. We must make it believable that he is kin come to give us news. Use this salve, Torrin, when your father eventually finishes his labours."

Aonghas' grunts changed to a hefty sigh of relief when the metal band eventually separated. Gingerly, his host and children bent the opening wider and wider, till the ring could be pulled free of his neck. Beathan's own relief was marked by a smirk he could not quite prevent.

Aonghas studied the piece of metal, the newly opened edges sharp enough to skin a hare. "Do you want to keep this?"

While Torrin wiped his neck clean of tiny metal shards, relief filled his reply. "Nay, I am sure you will find a better use for the metal than me."

The salve smelled awful when Torrin applied large dollops of it and gently massaged it around his neck area with her fingertips, but what mattered was the instant coolness that bathed the outside of his skin. Inside was a different matter. She was so near he could feel her breath whiffing at his chin, though she avoided looking at his eyes.

Niamh gently pushed her daughter away to inspect the damage. "The abraded skin will heal well enough, Beathan, but you will carry a shadow there for a long while, at least until the light of *Lugh* darkens all of you to a similar hue. Have you any other places that need attention?"

"Nay. The broken skin was easily borne, but the mark of servitude, in here, was not." He pointed to his head.

Aonghas returned his blade, and the piece of iron, to the basket near the doorway and then put an arm around Niamh's shoulders, giving her cheek a swift kiss in a manner that reminded Beathan of the closeness that had existed between his own mother and father. Pangs of nostalgia had to be quashed when he looked at the encouraging expression that wreathed Aonghas' face. "Freedom deserves a celebration. What can you provide for us my resourceful, spirited, hearth-woman?"

Niamh's smile widened as she snuggled in. "Thanks to young Cailean's successful hunt this morning – before they came upon you, Beathan – we shall enjoy the heather-birds he bagged. Torrin teaches him well to use his sling."

Cailean stepped around him to link arms with his sister, smirking up at her. "Did I not tell you what needed to be done, Torrin?"

From the returned doting and patting of the back of the young lad's hand, Beathan could tell who was encouraging whom.

Before he succumbed and slid into a short nap, the fields and their animals were described by an enthusiastic Cailean while the other three went off to do chores before the early darkness fell. He learned that Torrin was not the eldest born of the family, her brother having been gone from home for a while. He had a suspicion that Cailean was not supposed to talk about Seumas being elsewhere, which made the inadvertent mention seem even more secretive.

Chapter Thirty-two

Hamlet of Alaunas AD 87

"This would be a very good time to tell us more of your tale."

Niamh passed him a roasted grouse leg, and a piece of roughly torn bread, when they were all back around the fireside in the evening.

"Where to start?" Such a lot had happened to him that would not normally seem credible.

Aonghas pointed to his neck. "How you got that collar would be good to know. We do not see many Roman slaves remaining around here, though we do sometimes see them being dragged southwards on the nearest Roman road." His tones grew vehement, soft and menacing. "You may not have heard of northern Brigantes rising up against our Roman usurpers, but that does not mean that we have all grown to like them. Mark my words, our time for vengeance against their tyranny will come. We may not liberate all of our snatched tribesmen as easily as I removed your collar, but we will wreak vengeance on Rome sometime soon."

"And I will be there, *Athair*! Even if all I can muster is this small blade to rip open everything reachable below their protective chainmail." Torrin sounded so ferocious when she pulled forth her sharp little knife and mimicked the movements, her eyes glittering with determination.

"I was born at the Hillfort of Garrigill."

He felt Niamh's stare. "Garrigill?"

"Do you know of it?"

"My sister was hearth-wife to a warrior who lived there. Garrigill was not so far from here." Niamh's eyes glistened.

He felt his throat fill and had to swallow hard. "Then you will know that the members of the clan at Garrigill fled northwards when General Agricola's forces swarmed the area?"

Niamh nodded. "Aye, but my sister and her man were killed in battle long before that."

He found it hard to speak louder than a whisper. "Was that at Whorl?"

Niamh's eyes filled with tears. "Aye, it was. And her unborn child was still inside her."

Beathan watched Aonghas reach for her hands to gently squeeze them, before the man spoke.

"I was favoured by the goddess *Andarta* at that battle, my injuries insignificant, but many of my kin were slain. That encounter signalled the end of resistance for those who remained in this area."

"Why do you think that was?"

Beathan knew his question might seem insensitive, but there were sure to be things he had not learned from his father, nor his mother. He only knew what had happened at Garrigill, till his clan had fled north to his Selgovae grandfather, when he was seven summers.

"Smaller forts – like Vindolanda – were built across our territory by General Cerialis."

Beathan nodded his understanding of that Roman governor's importance when Aonghas paused.

"Aye, well, Cerialis was cunning. The *Legio XX* began to spread eastwards from their fort at Luguvallium, building towers and fortlets."

"Agricola was their commander by then?" he asked, though he knew the answer.

"Again, aye! And Cerialis, who commanded the *Legio IX*, began building signal stations and forts westwards from Coria. By then, we had few warriors left who were not sorely battle-bruised. We had little vigour remaining to make any objections. We could not move beyond our own farm areas without feeling the stab of a Roman pilum."

"I spent a short while at Coria, the one the Romans name Corstopitum." He halted on hearing the gasp from Niamh. "General Agricola held me hostage there."

"What does that mean, *Athair*?" Cailean blurted out, clearly troubled. He tugged hard at his father's tunic. "Will they come again and search our roundhouse?"

He wondered what the boy's outburst could mean.

Niamh put down the spurtle she had been using to stir a thick broth made from the grouse carcases and barley, intended as a meal for the following day. She sat down next to her son and removed the boy's tense fingers from Aonghas' clothes. "I am thinking your tale is a lot longer than we could possibly imagine, Beathan."

Torrin, who had been listening silently, chose to intervene, her tone hard to determine.

"Did they put that collar on you because they regard you to be a high-ranking hostage? Or, an escapee?"

It took a while for him to explain what had happened to him after the battle at *Beinn na Ciche*. Some details came in order, though many did not since Cailean, enthralled by his story, made many interruptions.

"I never met your father, Lorcan of Garrigill, but I remember hearing the name. His negotiations kept his Garrigill area mostly free of Roman presence, but that was not the same for us," Aonghas said.

Beathan could not understand how the situation had been so different for other Brigantes. "We had visits from Roman patrols during my early years. I remember them well, and was terrified at that time, but they did not pressure us to become Romanised. Was that not the same for you here, at Alaunas?"

Torrin's response was scathing. "This roundhouse seems isolated, but that was not always so. When I brought you here, do you remember seeing signs of habitation in the valley before this one?"

He thought about it for a moment, guiltily realising he had been so intent on getting to the roundhouse that he had noticed very little.

"There used to be three roundhouses there, but they were torched by Roman hands when I was little older than Cailean is just now." The rage in Torrin's stare was powerful. "Poor plotting of an attack on a nearby Roman watchtower was disastrous, and those neighbours all paid the price."

Aonghas spat at the fire. "Every last man, woman and child was cut down."

"Now we do not give our trust unwisely." Niamh's stare was penetrating when he turned his gaze in her direction. "We must all play our part in resisting hidden enemies, as well as rise up against those who wear the Roman armour!"

Beathan found Niamh difficult to determine. She had been generous in tending to his injuries, yet her words indicated she would not lend her trust so readily. The only interpretation he could make was that she suspected any stranger could be a Roman spy, until proved otherwise.

How he could do that seemed impossible. He could barely move, let alone find someone to verify his story.

Alongside him, Cailean began an addictive yawning. He was glad when the boy was told to go outside to urinate before bedding down for the night.

"You should also get some sleep. Aonghas will help get you outside before you settle."

Niamh's command was a welcome one.

Strain from the last days, and the fatigue of his injury, made him sleep late the next morning. A thumping in his head meant he was reluctant to open his eyes, but the sounds around him told him that the day was well advanced.

"*Madainn mhath.* The wind has turned much colder and the deep frost will probably not lift till later in the day." Niamh's greeting was matter-of-fact.

She was on her knees near her small loom, Cailean looking bored at feeding his mother the wool fibres while she used the drop spindle at speed to create the yarn.

Setting aside the work, she got to her feet using her son's shoulder to help her rise. Rubbing her back while she crossed to him, she pointed to his knee.

"We need to check it."

To his surprise, her fingers were gentle. Unlike her expression which seemed strained when she regarded him.

"The swelling is worse, Beathan, and you feel hot to the touch. You should sleep as much as you can today. Sleep heals almost as well as any salve."

He needed no urging to close his eyes again. Cailean was speaking to his mother, but the words were fading.

"Is he very ill, *Màthair*?"

"Just tired. I am sure he will be fine after more sleep. Torrin will be back from visiting our neighbour's son, before he is properly awake."

"She likes visiting him. She always has a smile on her face when she returns."

Cailean's words were sliding away. They had a soft, wistful sound to them that Beathan found somehow soothing.

"But it never lasts."

Niamh's soft chuckle followed. "Aye. Your sister's current pleasures with Cian are not of the lasting kind either."

He passed through a very sleepy phase that day, and his slight fever abated. He had not been awake for long in the early evening when he realised there was something different about Torrin.

Niamh had declared her daughter had learned all she needed to know about the type of injury, what needed to be done to aid recovery, and had passed the task of monitoring it on to her daughter. Torrin's many questions went from the general to the more personal. But since her antipathy of the previous day was gradually receding, he was happy with the development.

It was on the fourth day after his arrival that the calm of the roundhouse was shattered.

Cailean burst into the room, his little chest heaving. "They are coming, *Athair*!"

Niamh thrust aside the bowl she was cracking hazelnuts into and pulled her young son down onto her knee, rubbing his back to reassure him. Beathan thought her voice sounded remarkably calm.

"Who is coming?"

"A Roman patrol is marching down the hill."

An instinctive panic flooded him. His stare at the door was intercepted by Aonghas' raised palm. "Stay where you are, Beathan."

There was just enough reassurance in the man's tone to stop him from doing anything rash. Hobbling away from the roundhouse would be difficult, though perhaps not impossible. However, if he did that and was caught, then the danger was not only to him alone. Torrin's whole family would pay the price of harbouring him. And that could mean the death of all of them.

An even more immediate horror slammed into his head, so much his gripping hands sloshed water over the bucket rim. "Torrin is outside, alone."

Aonghas again made a calming gesture with his raised palm before he sneaked a look outside. "She is busy. She knows what to do."

"Did they see you running back here?" Aonghas picked up some rough stones and thrust them into his son's hands.

From the scared look on Cailean's face the answer was easy to decide on.

"Show no fear." Aonghas was firm as he passed over a small whetstone. "Now sit here at your mother's feet. Smooth these down like you have been shown, Cailean, to make them into sling stones. Bend your head, be very hard at work, and say nothing at all."

Beathan looked around at the chores they had all been tending to. He lifted his hands out of the wooden bucket of water that sat between his splayed legs where he had been bending thin willow branches, for mending a broken basket. After shaking off the water from his fingers, he yanked the tie from his long waving hair and pulled the tresses forward to cascade over his shoulders. The ploy would not shield the front of his neck, but if he kept his head down…

"Keep busy." Niamh's voice was low.

Torrin was speaking to someone. She was just outside the entrance, soothing the bitch that was whelping. It was presently their only dog and the reason that Cailean had needed to play at some distance from the house to give them some warning.

But was Torrin now declaring his presence? Betraying him?

The enormity of it almost destroyed him. Though only a few days had passed since he had come to the roundhouse, he had become accustomed to the family. And they to him – even Torrin.

Two Roman auxiliaries followed her inside, after which they stood one on each side of the entryway. One kept a hand at-the-ready on his pugio, the smaller blade that hung from his waist belt, while the second drew forth a small wax tablet and a sharpened stick from a soft leather pouch at his side.

The spokesman knew the language of the tribes well enough. He looked at Aonghas. "You are Aonghas and this place is named Alaunas?"

"Aye. I am, and it is." Aonghas spoke as few words as possible.

"We are taking a count of everyone who dwells in this territory."

Beathan kept his head down concentrating on his task of slowly bending the willow reeds. The Romans often made such lists on tribal lands occupied by them. Yet, perhaps this seemed too coincidental?

"How many of you dwell in this roundhouse?" The auxiliary prompted.

Without looking up, he sensed when one of the soldiers noticed his injured knee, easy to do since it was still uncovered. When no question came about how the injury happened, he drew in a short calming breath.

"We have no new additions since one of your soldiers last asked that very same question. It takes a while for my woman to grow a child, and she is not near the stage of birthing, yet. When you next ask, it may be that she will have swelled our numbers in this house, but that day is still a couple of moons away." Aonghas' tone was not surly, yet not so agreeable either.

Beathan wondered if Torrin's father enjoyed provoking the soldiers, though that did not seem like the best tactic if the man wanted to protect his wife and family. Aonghas' growing family. He had not realised that Niamh was with child, since her dress was worn loose at her waist. He had just thought her heavier with age, compared to Torrin's slender shape.

"How many?" The soldier with the stylus was clearly eager to add the details.

"Still five, like we were before. I have one daughter and two sons, as you see before you." Aonghas now sounded bored, but inwardly Beathan sighed with relief. The man had just risked his own life and limb.

The soldier with the tablet checked a different wooden slat from his pouch. Satisfied with the household number, he nodded to his companion.

"Should you see any strangers in the area, you will let us know." There was no mistaking that the command was for all of them, the soldier's gaze going from one to the next before the two of them left.

Beathan listened intently to the sounds of the auxiliaries checking everywhere outside.

After waiting for a short while, Torrin whispered. "I need to see if the pups have been born."

Her father nodded his agreement. "Aye, but I will come too."

Later that night, the tone of the conversation changed. Beathan could not say why but Niamh seemed less hostile to him than before.

"They will come back, Beathan, of that we can be certain, but by then their reasons will probably have changed."

He dared to ask what had been sitting at the tip of his tongue all afternoon. "Will they not find out that your son has been away from home and realise that you have lied to them?"

Aonghas broke the tension around the room with a hearty, gusty laugh. "It will not be my first time telling them untruths and hopefully, by the hearth goddess *Brigantia*, not the last. Our son – if all has gone well with his plans – will not be in a roundhouse whose count will be wrong."

It took him by surprise when Torrin squirmed right up close to him, took his hand into her own and gently squeezed. He felt her warm gaze linger on him, and liked it. Liked the promise he read in it very much.

Though, it was her father that she addressed. "*Athair*? Maybe now is a good time to tell Beathan where Seumas is? And where I want to be as soon as *Màthair* births my new brother, or sister."

"Aye. It probably is."

Beathan's heart gladdened with every word spoken by Aonghas. There were Brigantes resisting Roman repression, just like his own clan had done many, many seasons ago. He still desperately wanted to see his family again, but the far north would not be the place he would gain revenge for his injustices – if there were no Roman troops left up there. Brigantia was the place for revenge and retribution.

He had more than a hankering to join Seumas' band of warriors.

Chapter Thirty-Three

Hamlet of Alanaus AD 87

A handful of days passed by with no intrusions from Roman patrols. Beathan had to be content with mostly sitting around, keeping his knee at rest. Though even he was amazed at how many useful tasks he could still perform around the roundhouse, to share the burden of the daily chores. His preparation of birds for the cooking pot could not be called totally successful, since his movements were awkward, but he never ruined any food to the point of it being inedible. The resultant humour generated from his clumsiness brought him closer to his hosts.

And even closer to Torrin.

Her attitude had gone from being hostile on that first day, to treating him with less disdain. A period of open speculation had followed, her increasingly appraising gaze falling on him often. Then came the revelation about where Seumas was and what he was doing.

From that night onward, her sexual interest in him was blatant. She had begun to check his wounds with tender caresses, and not only to his knee. Those first swift kisses dropped to his forehead had progressed to lingering ones on his lips when he had shown no resistance, no resistance at all.

The first night when she had crept over to where he was sleeping had at first unnerved him, her intentions clear. Making love to her in the communal roundhouse was not the problem: keeping gasps of pain at bay when his leg got bumped were. Groans of satisfaction were muffled, but that was nothing out of the ordinary.

He spent many moments telling himself that his life had been starved of females, and that was the reason he found her so tempting.

Though, realistically, he would probably have had similar reactions whether she was attractive, or not.

"*Athair!*"

Cailean approached the roundhouse clearly agitated about something.

"Your father is in the copse gathering wood. What is so urgent?"

The lad must have run down the hill from the amount of gulping breaths that made his reply stilted. "Seumas…is coming."

The boy swivelled and headed for the stand of trees at the same speed as he had arrived, bawling at the top of his voice that his brother was coming for anyone and everyone around to hear.

Beathan continued to grind the oat grains on the quern stone wondering what Seumas was like. He now knew the young warrior was only four seasons older than he was. He would have preferred to meet Torrin's brother when properly on his feet. The swelling was gone, but Niamh's opinion was that too much knee bending, and accidental weight bearing, would undo the good that had been done during the last days. He had been hobbling around the dwelling, though only to gain access from one task to another.

Niamh approached from the direction of the nearby stream where she had been collecting water. "My thanks for that grinding, Beathan. That was my next task."

A smile came easily to him. "The partridges are prepared and ready for the pot now that you have that fresh water. And fetching water soon has to be my task." His grin grew wider. "You have not trusted me, yet, to fetch any in case I spill more than I bring back?"

Niamh turned to face the hillside, her own smile radiating relief, and happiness. "If my son, Seumas, was not about to scythe both of us down, I would send you right now. Cailean's hollers reach me even when down at the stream, but Seumas is fleet of foot, and bests anyone I know at coming down off the hill."

Her words were barely finished when Seumas skidded to a halt and crushed his mother to his chest. Almost as quickly, the young man made more distance between them, his palms still cradling her shoulders. "I am sorry, *Màthair*. Did I hurt you?"

Niamh's tinkle was reassuring, one hand patting her stomach. "Nay. We are both in fine fettle."

Beathan felt the force of Seumas' stare over the top of her head.

"And who is this?" Seumas asked.

The question was pointed, hostility barely at bay.

Seumas' question was probably for Niamh, but Beathan chose to reply. "Your family have given me shelter and sustenance, which I have sorely needed."

"Seumas!" Niamh disentangled herself, her tones only marginally chastising. "Stop staring, so. Beathan needed our help, and we have gladly given it."

The arrival of the rest of the family gave Beathan a moment to rethink his sudden surge of temper. Seumas' reaction was to be expected. Strangers, he knew to his cost, were not always a welcome addition in a Brigante roundhouse.

Beathan's tale was told again as they supped at thin brose dotted with dried berries, quickly produced from his oat grinding and the water Niamh had fetched from the stream. Though this time bits of his story were added by Cailean who remembered well.

The young boy jumped up and rummaged in the basket near the entryway. He thrust the metal band into Seumas' hands. "I had to keep this steady, along with Torrin, while father broke it open."

Beathan noted the tiniest uplift of Seumas' eyebrows on holding the band.

"I have seen slaves wearing these near Eboracum Fortress but have never felt the weight. It is not so heavy after all."

Beathan wondered how much Seumas believed of his story but was not prepared to have the importance of it shed so lightly. "The band could be any weight at all, thin or thick, but it is the enslavement that matters in here." He tapped his chest, unable to crush the animosity.

Aonghas retrieved the metal and tossed it back into the basket before confronting his elder son. His tones were solemn, an abiding anger burbling beneath. "It took me a lot of effort, but only a relatively short time to cut through that band. Beathan was the one who wore it round his neck for many moons. My fear is that most wearers will never have the chance to have their collar removed, Seumas. I will not liberate many of our enslaved tribesmen, but I am glad to have done this for Beathan. Now listen well, and hear the rest of his tale."

He thought Aonghas was finished, but there was more to come.

"If you do not share my opinion of Beathan's value then so be it, my son. But this Brigante warrior will shelter under my roof for as long as he needs."

It was not comfortable, at first, since Seumas' distrust took a while to dissipate. In contrast, he found that Torrin's defence of him grew, and that came not only through her words but also through her unhindered, visible gestures.

The atmosphere in the roundhouse gradually changed during the next few days.

Beathan shared parts of his story that he had not yet divulged, however, he could not quite bring himself to speak of the strange bond that had grown between him and General Agricola. He would have preferred to have the full confidence of Torrin's brother but could see that trust would have to be earned and that was, in itself, a good thing.

"What kind of attacks have been happening recently around these parts?" His question might not be answered, but he was curious.

Seumas groomed down his lengthening moustache, though he kept his chin free of hair. "The Roman supply chain is always a good target."

Beathan agreed and waited, absently thinking that his own dark beard was growing in nicely.

"Was your band not planning a more determined attack sometime soon?" Aonghas prompted.

Seumas' expression froze, a silence descending.

It was interesting to work out just how secretive Seumas could be. Alongside him, Beathan felt Torrin's palm squeezing his thigh. Her smallest grip had him almost lose concentration but her next words, made him understand her motives.

"Seumas, you told me I should master my spear throwing before you would consider me being one of your band. When Beathan is back to full fitness, we both want to join you when you attack those forts! By then *Màthair* should have birthed her child."

Seumas' expression was indulgent. "I am not the leader of the whole group, Torrin. I could recommend you, but it will take more than that to prove your loyalty and ability to join. And what gives you the right to speak for Beathan?"

Beathan was surprised at the flush that appeared to pinken Torrin's cheeks. And it was not caused by sudden anger.

"Beathan and I have talked about this plenty of times already."

He felt himself become Seumas' focus yet again, but that was good since Torrin needed time to gather her calm.

Seumas was direct. "What was it that you planned to do, after you escaped from Vindolanda Fort? I mean before your knee injury."

He chuckled, his expression self-mocking. "In all honesty, when I crawled away from the burn I had no plan in mind, apart from gaining my freedom and finding Garrigill Hillfort. The desperate urge to feel some connection to my Brigante kin was overpowering. My family are, hopefully, hale and hearty in Taexali territory, but that is far from here. Garrigill seemed more easily reachable."

Seumas had been whittling a piece of wood earlier and reached for it again. "And it would have been, had you not tumbled down the fell."

"Seumas! I will remind you of how many times I have tended to your injuries since you were a babe." Niamh's defence warmed Beathan in a way that was different from Torrin's.

"Aye, that you have." Seumas held up the carving and examined it before turning to his little brother. "Does this resemble your new pup, yet?"

Cailean's teeth topped his lower lip and his eyes widened. "Maybe if you work on it a bit more?"

"That was the answer I expected, my brother. And in the same way, I will work harder at getting to know this warrior who has taken the fancy of my sister!"

Aonghas guffawed. "If that is meant to be divulging a secret, then I would not trust you with anything, my son. Beathan and I have already had words about Torrin's resolve to make him mate with her with great regularity. Though I will be sorely displeased with both of them, if he wrecks the healing that Niamh has encouraged these past days."

The last part of Aonghas' speech gave Beathan some heartache. Torrin's insistence that there were many ways to pleasure each other easily proved she had plenty of experience in lying with a man. He had also learned that the neighbour named Cian had not been her only local lover.

He was not yet sure Torrin actually liked him, but her carnal urges were something different, and momentary. In truth, he could barely wait for his healing to be properly done, so that they could enjoy each other even more lustily.

Beathan knew that Seumas' nod meant a better understanding was growing between them.

"*Màthair*? How long will it be before he is ready for a journey?" Seumas asked.

He felt Niamh look towards him before answering, her expression calculating. "The skin has healed well, and the bending is gradually improving. His use of the crook gets him further afield with every new day that passes. I think that he should regain sufficient strength to be without it after the next full moon. Though our weather god, *Ambisagrus,* might have some different ideas about that.

"Then that is when I shall return to Alaunas, and we will both make the short journey to what remains of the Garrigill Hillfort. In between, I shall make enquires and they shall be discreet, *Athair*, have no fear. I value my own neck and do not wish it to be decorated by one of those bands."

Beathan watched Seumas point to the metal basket at the door.

Alongside him, Torrin's fingers crept around his own. Holding up both of their hands, her declaration was firm. "There will be three of us making that journey, my brother. Of that you can count on!"

Chuckles rent the room. "Not allowing him out of your sight, in case he runs off?"

Seumas neatly caught the firewood log that Torrin lobbed at him.

Chapter Thirty-Four

Garrigill Hillfort AD 88

"Garrigill is over this last rise."

Seumas stopped near the top of the hill, his expression bearing sympathy and concern. "Are you sure you want to see what has become of it?"

Beathan had no hesitation. "I have seen many changes in my life, and this is another that I know I must bear. Should I ever see my parents again, I want to be able to tell them the truth of it."

Torrin linked her arm through his and snuggled close. He needed no physical support to help him walk, his fitness having been restored in less time than Niamh had predicted, but Torrin's emotional sustenance was given freely.

Smiling up into his eyes, she radiated confidence. "We will get through this, together. And we will soon be side by side, when we slaughter some of the detested Romans in our territory."

He felt the laugh burble up from his toes. Torrin was the only person to ever manage to twine positive thoughts with deadly ones so seamlessly. His swift kiss was inevitable. She was too tempting.

"Are we going to Garrigill? Or shall I just tell you all about it?" Seumas' words teased.

It had taken a while for Seumas to mellow, but he was now as familiar to him as any of his Garrigill clan had been. Heartily glad of that, Beathan used his free hand to encourage Seumas into motion.

"Lead me there!" he ordered.

Beathan looked down over the wide valley where the hillfort of Garrigill was located, a settlement he had left when he was seven winters old. His memories were clear about some aspects, less so of others, and seeing Garrigill from the hilltops was not a thing he had done often. He had been too busy playing around the settlement and secretly learning, even at such a young age, to become a warrior.

A lack of smoke rising from the roundhouses, down on the plateau that lay just above the meandering river, hit him hard inside. That was not what he recalled.

He felt Torrin's grip tighten around his hand. "Is this not as you remember it?"

"Nay, it is not. In my grandfather's time this was a very busy hillfort and the whole valley would have shown smoke signs of habitation. By the time I was born, it had fewer people and livestock after the battles at Whorl, but it was still busy enough."

Seumas pointed out the dark shadows behind the charred remains of the palisade. "There were only a few families scratching a living down there the last time I passed through this valley. The Romans razed this hillfort years ago."

"My parents led those of Garrigill who wanted to accompany them on the long trek to Selgovae lands. As I recall it, most people left with us."

"To the birthplace of your mother?"

"Aye. To Tarras and to her father, Callan." He found himself chuckling even though it seemed such an inappropriate time. "I liked some things about the cunning old rogue, but he was hated by most."

"I see smoke down there." Seumas pointed to the thinnest wisp rising from an outlying roundhouse and they set off in its direction.

His glance took in the tree level and down to the valley floor, all sorts of memories flooding back.

"Do you see that flat space over there?" He pointed out the direction for Torrin. "That was the training ground. Uncle Gabrond had very few horses return from Whorl, so raising new stock was his priority. Opportunities to learn to ride were precious, but he made every occasion great fun."

Seumas snorted in disbelief. "Do you mean that the Roman scum allowed you train?"

"Not openly with weapons. We had to do that behind the palisade and in between the numerous roundhouses. We could ride the horses, but chariot racing was a thing of the past. That was too obvious a battle tactic for any monitoring patrols – though they mostly left Garrigill alone. At least, until General Agricola came back as Governor of Britannia."

Beathan breathed deeply when they approached the lone man who worked in one of the field areas, near the only roundhouse that had a thin trail of smoke rising from its roof.

Chapter Thirty-Five

Hamlet of Alanaus AD 88

Niamh handed him a steaming bowl of thin barley broth the following evening. "From the forlorn expression I see on your face, I am thinking that the visit to Garrigill was not to your liking."

He pushed aside his sorrow and thanked her. "I had to go."

Seumas snorted. "Garrigill is just one of the many tribal centres in the north that has been obliterated by the detestable Roman scum. We have so many grievances that the Romans are responsible for."

Beathan finished supping, set down his bowl and rubbed at his knee. He had thought himself back to full strength, but his knee had another opinion. A dull ache still nagged at him when he walked over too much uneven ground. "I want to be alongside you, Seumas, when your band next takes vengeance."

Seumas' point to his knee was deliberate. "And you probably shall, but not till that knee stops holding you back."

He was affronted. Looking at both Seumas and Torrin his splutters almost put out the fire. "How did I hold you back? Did I not keep pace with both of you?"

Torrin snuggled in close and gave his cheek a quick peck. "Be still. My brother is right, for once. You did not hold us back, Beathan, but our pace was no more than a steady one. There was no urgency to it, as there would be on a raid."

He shrugged away from her grasp. "I could have gone faster."

The tinkle of her laughter softened his strain. "Nay. If you cannot be honest, then we will be honest for you. We are not attacking your courage, Beathan."

Niamh seemed to feel it time to intervene. "Some injuries take longer to heal than a broken bone." Pacing towards him, she indicated he should hand up his empty bowl since bending was now a challenge for her. "The warmer weather should make the aches come less frequently. I know that from experience."

After dropping the pile of empty bowls into a wooden bucket near the door Niamh turned back, a gasp of pain escaping while she clutched her swollen belly. "My own aches should lessen very soon now."

Aonghas jumped to his feet, however, Torrin was at her mother's side first.

"The babe is coming now?" There was both anxiety and excitement in her question.

Niamh's laugh held both relief and a chiding. "Not quite yet, though probably before the night is over."

The plans around the fireside between Beathan, Torrin and Seumas continued, but the volume was much more subdued than before. As the time for sleep approached, Aonghas cradled Niamh, supporting her as she paced the roundhouse. Torrin busied herself doing tasks her mother might otherwise have done.

Beathan could see Torrin's concern, had heard of the two babies that had come between Torrin and Cailean, the little mites not surviving more than a few days after their birth. Many women grieved for babies lost. And many warriors lost a hearth-mate during the birth, but that was not something he would dwell on.

He suddenly realised he had no idea how he would feel if he were to become a father, his thoughts not having got any further than having sex with Torrin when she initiated it.

Beathan watched Seumas bending down to give his mother a hug the following day, close to when the orb of *Lugh* was high in the sky.

The protesting little creature in Niamh's arms had appeared with the dawn. As yet, the little girl had no name but Seumas kissed both child and mother, drawing his forefinger lightly over the baby's downy cheek in a loving gesture.

"You must hand over the reins of the roundhouse to Torrin for a while and take plenty of rest, *Màthair*. I think it was difficult for you to bring this little one into this world of ours."

A sceptical grunt of laughter came from a yawning Aonghas. "What would you know of how long a bairn takes to appear?"

Seumas was quick to answer, his smile appreciating the sarcasm. "I held her hand when this little lad here was born, did I not?"

Beathan smiled when Seumas gave Cailean a conspiratorial shoulder nudge that toppled his brother over.

Aonghas' bellow was full of delight. "Aye. True enough, but you have no idea of long it took for you to come into this world. Your mother was plain exhausted by your contortions."

Torrin stifled her yawning and joined in the fun, her addition making the joke clearer to understand. "My big brother came to the world the wrong way, I'm told, and almost pushed my mother out of it. And he has been thrawn and ill-tempered ever since."

Though weak, Niamh made her farewells to her eldest son.

"Sometimes pig-headed is what is needed to survive. And I mean that you must survive my son, if you are to conduct all these raids and revenges that you speak of on Roman facilities. Go with my blessing and those of our hearth-goddess, *Rhianna*. Stay safe."

Seumas' departure was a timely one because, two days later, the snow began to fall. Big fat flakes stuck fast to the tree trunks and clothed the nearby shrubs in twinkling white cover.

Silence descended across the landscape. Biting cold permeated everywhere and it seemed that *Cernunnos* of the woods had robbed the countryside of every breath of wind.

Journeys Beathan made outside the roundhouse were only for necessities, and hunkering down around the fireside was most welcome. Bringing in plentiful stocks of wood for the fire was swiftly done, as was fetching fresh water from the burn. It sometimes took many spear prods to break the running water free from the upper icy layer and freezing fingers were gained in the process.

It was on the third day of snow that Aonghas nipped back into the roundhouse almost as quickly as he had left it. Beathan watched the man whip free a thick bratt from a peg near the doorway, although he already wore one. The surprise became greater curiosity when Aonghas carefully wrapped it around his hearth-wife who was dozing at the fireside, the baby tucked into her chest.

"This you must witness, my love." Aonghas declared, picking Niamh up as though she weighed no more than a feathery leaf.

Beathan looked to Torrin, intrigued by what was happening. Her finger to her lips cautioned speech. But after her father had dipped his body to exit through the low entrance, she nipped up to her feet and beckoned him to follow. Her little brother, too, at her heels.

Not far from the roundhouse they watched Aonghas stop and indicate something, his words to Niamh too far away to hear properly.

Beathan whispered in Torrin's ear, unwilling to break the almost total silence outside. "What is he doing?"

Torrin snuggled her body around his, since neither wore a shawl. "Can you not see where he points?"

He followed the line of Torrin's finger, though it took him a short while to see what she indicated. At the bottom of the slope stood an impressive, resplendent animal, completely motionless and only discernible by its darker antlers. The coat, at first glance, seemed to be pure white but on further inspection he could just make out faint brown patches beneath. The thick coating of icy snow gave the impression of a rare white deer.

Torrin brought herself around to fully face him, her eyes dancing with mirth. "My father names my little sister."

He could not resist the long kiss that followed, the cold banished by the heat generated between them. Or the next one because she was addictive, which led to them only stopping when Aonghas asked them to move aside and let him take Niamh back inside.

By the time Beathan led Torrin back into the roundhouse, driven in only by their freezing feet, Niamh had the baby at her breast. Aonghas was bustling around the fireside, getting wooden beakers set out on the hearthstones to fill with the small bere that Torrin had made before the snow descended. Cailean was following instructions to stir the barley broth and not allow it to stick to the bottom of the iron pan.

As soon as the baby had taken her fill, Aonghas lifted her from her mother and held her high above him.

"By the bounty of *Brigantia*, our earth-mother, the child will be known as Fiadh."

Little Deer – Beathan thought – was a perfect name.

The harsh winter weather deepened further and forced them to spend many days in the warmth of the roundhouse. The baby slept well, mostly, but when she did cry in the dark of night on the far side of the roundhouse, Torrin took advantage of the noise to be more voluble, and more playful, in their love making.

He realised he had not been so happy, nor so content since he was a little boy.

And after the freeze, the deep and crisp, icy layers slowly gave way to a soaking snow-melt that made the burn overflow, and kept the ground a cold mushy-mire from one new moon to the next.

Eventually, one morning when the earth underfoot became easier for walking, Beathan was surprised when Aonghas stuffed his boots with fresh, dried-herb linings. The man donned his bratt and made a declaration.

"Today, I will take news of Fiadh to our neighbours over the hill."

Beathan had not heard of such a tradition before, though made no comments since neither Torrin, nor Niamh, seemed to think it unusual. That he was not invited to go did not bother him, since he had never met any of the neighbouring folk. And he had no inclination to meet Cian, Torrin's previous lover, who lived in one of the roundhouses.

She had been out of the roundhouse recently, doing chores, when the weather conditions had broken sufficiently, though she had returned fairly quickly. That had made him think that he was her only current lover, but he could not be sure. He made himself believe it did not bother him either way, but knew he was definitely not inclined to be sharing her.

After Aonghas left, he undertook the man's chores, the day giving way to night.

Niamh showed no sign of concern when Aonghas did not return. "Nay. Do not worry. Aonghas has not visited our neighbours for some seasons. He will return tomorrow and be bursting full of news of what the Roman patrols are doing now."

It was the early evening of the third day when Beathan heard Aonghas hollering.

"Where are you Cailean? Come and help me!"

Beathan was intrigued when Torrin grabbed his hand and dragged him outside, her smile fit to burst.

"Your father called for Cailean, not for me!"

His mild protest was ignored. Torrin pulled him into a trot towards her father, Cailean predictably much closer to Aonghas by then.

Without any warning Beathan glimpsed a spear hurtling through the air well to the side of where Cailean was running.

"That little one is your very own, my son. Be sure to fetch it!"

It was at that moment that Beathan realised that Aonghas carried a bulky pile under his arm.

"Do you recall you telling me that I could make better use of the Roman metal that enslaved you?" Aonghas asked when he got closer.

Beathan nodded, the reason dawning, and his own grin as wide as Torrin's. "And it seems you have utilised it well."

He reached out to receive the three spears that Aonghas separated from the pile.

"These tips are made entirely from that slave collar. I guessed at the shaft length for you, but if they need adjusting, it can be done."

Torrin accepted the two new spears her father handed to her.

"These are a blend of the remaining collar metal and what the smith needed to add to create them." Aonghas' mirth dipped to becoming solemn for a moment. "Every time you throw them, Torrin, you can tell yourself that you are avenging Beathan's injustices. Those spear tips are as much a part of him as are the other gestures you share. Look after them well. A spear tip can last a long time, though lasting love and respect for a mate has to be worked at, to make it become hard and fast."

Beathan watched Torrin carefully lay down the spears before she removed the rest of her father's burdens, after which she gave Aonghas a long and lingering hug.

"Thank you, *Athair*, for all of that."

After she detached herself, Beathan found he was the next recipient of her crushing embrace. The man had just given Torrin his consent to become the warrior she so desperately wanted to be, but it was an acknowledgement of the way his relationship with her might also develop, as well.

He was not entirely sure that he was ready to declare Torrin to be a lifetime mate…though presently he was unquestionably enjoying her attentions.

"Why not go now?"

Torrin was like a dog worrying at a well-gnawed bone, as she rooted around in the long field-grasses before locating her second spear.

He found his three more easily and stomped back towards their start point. "Your mother still needs your help while Fiadh is still so young."

Only part of that was true. The baby was thriving well enough and Niamh was regaining her strength. Help with daily chores was convenient, but Niamh would manage without.

Her angered tones reached him from her bent low position. "You know that now is the best time to go north."

It possibly was, but he was not going to admit it. They had had the same discussion a number of times, and the distasteful result was already souring their joy in each other. She had been reaching for him less often and shrugging off his advances had become more frequent. Her expression was as pinched as her wan pallor. She claimed she was not sick, but he feared that something was amiss.

She had been absent from the roundhouse for two days, though refused to say where she had been. It was only Niamh's intervention that had stopped him from assuming that Torrin had turned her attentions back to Cian.

However, Niamh's conversation had not been altogether reassuring. Her saying that all actions brought consequences, sometimes wanted and sometimes not, he could easily understand since everyday life brought forth examples. Niamh had gone on to mutter about how some decisions that a resolute woman must take often come with sorrow and heartbreak. He began to wonder who Niamh was really talking to when she declared that regret is never banished, even when the goddess has made sure that results are favourable. But when she turned and spoke directly to him, saying that though some words may never be spoken they still lie deep, he got really confused.

The only thing he felt able to agree with during that odd encounter with Niamh was that Torrin's determination to become a member of Seumas warrior-band took precedence over all other things, her health included.

Now Torrin feverishly trained every available moment of the day. He did not mind that at all because he also needed to hone his spear skills. Fighting close combat with her, using wooden blades, sometimes drew her out of her fierce concentration and brought a return of their earlier closeness, though not always. He had a great urge to see a grin rather than a grimace. When he provoked that – and it worked – everything was well. Otherwise, when he could not rouse her humour, the whole day and sometimes night was soured.

One thing he decided was that he did not understand enough about young females to really know what drove Torrin's moods. Seumas had sent word that Eòghan, the group leader, was not looking to extend the warrior band till after the Beltane Rites. The moon would rise and fall more than once before then, so he had decided to tolerate whatever came his way from Torrin.

She picked up her spears and strode towards him in preparation for yet another throw at the target tree where both were polishing their spear skills.

"You say you want to find your kin, but I think you do not."

After standing alongside him, she nodded her readiness for their next throws, her tone belligerent. "You are afraid that they will be too different. In the way that Garrigill no longer resembles what you remember."

He did want to find his kin. He really did, but he also wanted to appease his growing urge for revenge. He could not shift the notion that if he found his family and got comfortable there, as he had already done at Torrin's roundhouse, then he would not want to come back and attack the Romans in Brigantia.

He could not tell Torrin that it was himself he feared. He knew she now felt obliged to accompany him to find his family, since she had said she would and her word was important to her. But she was resolute on wreaking her own revenge for Roman injustices as soon as possible and a journey would most likely delay that.

What now seemed a lifetime ago, he had trekked over half of the Roman Empire. He was aware of how long it could take to walk from place to place, but Torrin had no idea of how far away the Taexali and Caledon territories were. She had only stalked around her own part of Brigantia.

They had no horses. They had nothing to use to buy, or barter with, for any mounts that might shorten a return journey. She also assumed that when they eventually reached the site of Beinn na Ciche that he would immediately find his kin. He could not convince himself it would be that easy.

It was better to put off a visit for as long as possible.

Chapter Thirty-Six

Northern Brigantia AD 89

A pink pre-dawn had just slipped away above the treetops, heralding the mid-blue of what promised to be a fine morning.

Beathan inhaled a deep breath through his nostrils to enjoy the fresh morning air. Some of the scents of woodland plants, and the mustiness of the brackens and ferns nearby, were almost overpowering, but they grounded him to the land under his feet. The land that he and his fellow Brigantes cherished.

He looked across to where Seumas was taking cover in the belt of trees near the foot of the hill. The rest of the band were similarly well-placed, it being crucial that none of them made any errors that could lead to discovery. The further along the track the arriving Roman patrol got, the less cover there was for Seumas' warriors. The rebels occupied the best spot to ambush the Roman contubernium that would soon appear to do their daytime duty at the wooden signal tower, on the top of the hill.

The faintest sound of distant, clinking metal reached him at exactly the same time as he heard Seumas' warning bird-call. The padding of tramping feet and low chatter got closer and closer, though he did nothing. It was not his task to give the orders.

"Now!" Seumas bellowed.

The Roman decanus calling his patrol to form a protective huddle around themselves was not quick enough. The eight men of the contubernium team had no chance to organise themselves against the ten Brigantes who erupted from the woods. The Brigante spears winged near the ground to pierce the lower legs of the Romans, making them unstable and causing their shields to tilt before they got into a defensive position.

Into the chaos that the first spears made, Seumas' warriors let fly a second volley of weapons that aimed for undefended areas. Some bounced off shields, but enough of them made body contact, widening the gaps even further.

Like the darting of swifts, Beathan and the other Brigantes were upon the auxiliaries, their long knives piercing any parts that were vulnerable. The ambushers worked together, some parried the thrusting gladii and the others loosened shields from the grips of the owners before aiming their long knives under the chainmail and at necks and arms.

Metal clanked on metal. Cries of frustration mingled with those of sheer effort, and of agony, while the Roman patrol fought on as they had been taught to do. Blood spurted forth from many wounds to spray the faces and clothes of both attackers and the attacked, the ground under them all becoming slick with a tide of gore.

It took a remarkably short time before Beathan's hollering drowned out the last death throes of the Roman auxiliaries. The enemy around him had fought valiantly but had lost.

"Praise be to *Andraste*, goddess of Victory!" he roared.

Brigante long knives rose high above the grinning, panting victors.

Beathan, like the others, knew the next task was to ensure the Romans were all dead, and then to strip them of weapons and useful metal.

"Search for a firestarter on that one," he shouted across to Seumas, pointing to the Roman auxiliary he guessed to be the decanus, leader of the contubernium.

There was now no need to be silent, though they needed to work quickly and get well away from the area.

Torrin handed him one of his spears that she had just pulled free from the lower leg of a dead Roman.

"Next time you see him, you can tell my young brother Cailean that your spear has felled a detested Roman soldier many times already. But for now, you can find your other weapon by yourself." Her brief jest warmed him when she glanced up from removing her own spears and winked at him.

Since he had joined Eòghan's warrior group, a half-moon after the previous Beltane Festival, he had seen more of Cailean than he had of Torrin.

They had not envisaged being split up during their time in training, but that was what had happened. Eòghan's strategy of regularly changing the rebels in the smaller bands was a good one. They all learned to defend each other, regardless of who was in the patrol.

After wiping her spears on the grass at the side of the track, she held them aloft and declared, "May the goddess of War – *Andarta* – grant me more opportunities to use mine on our unwanted invaders!"

He was not sure when he would become inured to the carnage of an attack, but he did know that after almost four seasons' worth of raids, his need for revenge was not yet satisfied.

With hindsight, he admitted that his own feelings had been similar to Torrin's after their first attack on a convoy, the only other time they had been on the same raid. Training, for some moons, with Eòghan's warriors had not fully prepared him for the actual event. Thinking back, he wished he had vomited immediately after his first kill, like Torrin had done, because she had not needed to suppress queasiness like he had to do, on and off, for the rest of that day.

That sick revulsion had not clouded her expression now.

He set to tossing the items removed from the dead Romans onto the pile that would be collected by the group before they headed back to their base.

"Found one." Torrin triumphantly held up a metal firestarter that she had removed from one of the Romans.

Seumas shouted his approval and pointed up the hill. "Since you have found that, my brave sister, you have the honour of checking up there with Beathan, and then use that useful tool to best effect."

The rest of the band went off to gather wood.

There was no time for idle talk when he and Torrin sprinted up the hill, their first task to check that there were no stray Romans lurking around. Members of the band had been carefully monitoring the area, noting that the tower was only manned from dawn to dusk. The Roman soldiers were routinely back in the nearby fort over the night time, but a thorough check still needed to be made.

He knew that Torrin had no intention of using the metal basket that sat up on the platform of the tower. The message she was about to send to the next station would not be a welcome one to the Romans.

The broken branches, gathered by Seumas' men on their way up the hill, were added to the stock the previous Roman patrol had left ready for their signalling. And even more wood was added till the piles scattered all around the bottom of the wooden tower were substantial enough.

Grinning over to where he stood, Torrin brandished the pilfered firestarter before she pulled out a piece of flint and a pile of dried puffball mushrooms from the pouch at her waist. "You have such useful knowledge, Beathan of Garrigill. These Roman firestarters make a fire rise so quickly."

He accepted the compliment with a smile of his own.

"*Belenos*. Help us to avenge our Brigante slain!" she bellowed.

He was surprised when she handed him the flint and the metal that was formed into the shape of a wolf.

"The owner of that had really fat fingers! I can hardly keep hold of it."

After sliding his fingers through the finger holes, it took only a few determined strikes before sparks ignited the dried mushrooms that Torrin had placed above the mosses, brackens and other tinder that had been hastily collected. The crackling and popping noises of wood splitting began, as did the smoke from the damper wood. When there was sufficient fire, they all took lit brands and set them under the piles around the tower supports. Soon the reassuring hum of a solid blaze became a resounding roar.

Standing well back, Beathan heaved a sigh of satisfaction. "*Brigantia*. May your territory soon be free of the Roman usurpers!"

Torrin's reply was to grab him for a jubilant kiss. He wanted it to last longer, since any contact with her at all was rare. But it could not last.

When he was sure the whole tower would continue to burn, they all took to their heels to join Seumas at the bottom of the hill. The elation of the run was soon tempered by the weight of the extra metal that had been removed from the Roman patrol.

"Do not ask me, Beathan. You know now that I can manage." There was no hint of any light-heartedness now.

Draped in chain mail that was far too long for her, and bedecked with a helmet and extra knives around her waist band, Torrin was always determined to show that she contributed just as much as any other member of the group.

He had learned some time ago that the woman, who now so seldom shared her body with him, was fiercely proud. She was strong-minded but also ruthless when she felt the situation justified it. She called her brother Seumas the thrawn, confrontational member of her family, but Beathan needed no convincing that it was a shared characteristic.

If anything, Torrin had become even more fervently anti-Roman than before. She had changed, and he was not sure he liked the alterations.

Chapter Thirty-Seven

Northern Brigantia AD 89

"Our last raids on those convoys near the Roman road were great achievements. Your suggestions for attack worked just as effectively as the times we attacked the tower patrols, Beathan."

The speaker was Eòghan, the leader of the whole rebel group. The man poked a long stick at the cold empty space where a hearty fire should have been.

"And now," Eòghan continued, "we need to finalise our last attacks before winter weather sets in."

A general consensus of agreement rang around the room, the last raids having caused many disruptions to the local Roman routines. The insurgents had been organised and well-practised before Beathan had joined them, but his knowledge of Roman defence tactics and Roman army behaviours, had been used to full effect. Though, some of the gathering were carping about the retribution that local Brigantes had paid afterwards, purely because the raids had been so successful.

"Should we attempt another signal station raid? Or attack one of the larger forts? What do you all think?" Eòghan asked the congregation of around fifty warriors. Some of the warriors looked keen, though the grumblers were less so.

Eòghan prompted. "Beathan?"

He thought carefully about what his answer should be.

The harvest had been collected across Brigantia. Autumn colours brightened the countryside, but it was presently teeming with rain outside. Beathan was seated in the second row of female and male warriors who were gathered in a ramshackle roundhouse. Some of the roof timbers were bereft of thatching, the incoming rain making noisy plops onto the beaten earth now bare of its bracken and herb floor covering, if it wasn't dripping down the necks of those seated in the most unfortunate places.

The entrance tunnel was non-existent, which had positive aspects in that should the gathering need to rush away, it could be done easily. The advantage to the roundhouse was that it lay in a place that had been cleared of Brigantes many, many seasons before and was deemed safe enough for the present meeting.

The damp surroundings added to the recent trend of forceful suppression by the avenging Roman presence. Those in charge had not taken well to having their defences attacked.

Beathan had only on rare occasions gathered with all of the group assembled together, since it was a highly risky undertaking. Their meetings were mainly in open woodland locations, but for days on end the god *Ambisagrus* had been particularly good at alternately almost drowning them, and sending impossible winds that robbed the speaker of their words before all could hear them.

Inside the dank dilapidated roundhouse, they could at least hear each other speak.

Beathan eventually answered into the silence that had developed. "Not watchtowers. Their daily patrol groups now have mounted escorts, and they are much more alert to potential ambushes."

His opinion on that was agreed by most, though even after so many seasons with the group, he was not yet liked – or trusted – by everyone congregated.

"Do you mean that someone is feeding them our plans?"

He was quick to clear any misunderstanding. "Not as far as I know, but Eòghan will give you information on that."

Eòghan was visibly fierce. "They would no longer breathe, if I received knowledge of any traitors." The threat was added to by the thump of Eòghan's fist against his thigh.

The tension in the room was a tangible thing. Beathan waited for a nod from Eòghan to continue.

"If you threaten one Roman, you threaten them all, and they rarely allow mistakes to be repeated. Depending on what is targeted next, I will continue to work on strategies that might outwit them."

He sought out Torrin's gaze over on the far side of the fireplace. She, at least, should understand his next words.

"Like the hawthorn bush snagging its prey, we need to niggle the Roman Legions with many small spikes. And gradually wear them down while we build up our own strength and expertise for something greater."

Her light chuckle reached over to him, as did her cheeky smile. The less he experienced it, the more he found he missed it as time went on. None of the other warrior women in the whole group meant anything to him, like Torrin had.

The other female warriors were just as fierce and competent, and some wanted sex with the same enthusiasm as Torrin did. He had not shied away when approached by any of them, and sometimes he had even initiated the couplings himself, but they were no more than a fleeting relief.

Eòghan spat at the empty fire space. "Would anyone like to put forward a suggestion of what should be attacked next, apart from any convoys we hear about?"

Though Eòghan was clearly the leader, it was the tribal way to discuss any plans. In this instance, silence reigned around the room to the point of the lack of ideas being almost an embarrassment.

One of the founder members of the group, who sat in the front row, scorned. "Would you have more suggestions for us, if you became one of our spies, Beathan of Garrigill?"

He chose not to rise to the distrust. He had already told the group that he was not familiar enough with the territory and needed time to learn about what had been happening around northern Brigantia. He did not tell them the antagonism inside him would only be appeased by him being an attacker, rather than a gatherer of information.

Being associated with Garrigill had, at first, pleased him very much. However, there were enough people left in the area who knew of someone who remembered hearing about his parents, or his Uncle Brennus formerly known as Bran of Witton who had set up a spy network. Brennus' successes only existed now in tales told around the firesides.

As far as he knew, the current spy ring set up by Eòghan worked effectively. He thought carefully of what to say.

"To attack any of the local forts without more warriors would be futile. And the timing of a raid would be crucial. It would have to be when the garrison is at its lowest strength."

"How can we find that out?" The warrior who spoke was doubtful.

Beathan was not afraid to tell the truth. "I am sure that Eòghan's spies and infiltrators can relay useful information. We need to maintain the observation of the forts around here all through the winter."

"Aye, we can. But what has that to do with attacking them?" The warrior who scorned earlier had still not been appeased.

He maintained a calm temper. "The last of the troops who were in the north might be redeployed around Brigantia, even for a short time."

"That would mean the nearby forts will have even greater numbers than before." Eòghan's gaze ranged the room.

"Not necessarily," he said. "When new units are expected to garrison an established fort, the departing cohorts sometimes dismantle their interior buildings. The incomers build new blocks to suit their own requirements."

Eòghan grunted. "I have heard something of this process. So, we must monitor which forts are sending men away prior to destroying what they have been using?"

Beathan nodded. "Exactly. If we notice that happening at any nearby fort, we can attack when troop numbers are at their lowest."

They set to work, with Eòghan deciding first on new group formations.

He had expected Torrin to at least say a quick farewell to him before she left the roundhouse, but when he finished speaking privately to Eòghan, she was nowhere to be seen.

Seumas finished talking to the warriors in his new band and waved him over. "My sister is still rejecting you?"

He shrugged. "Your sister makes the most of her situation. I have barely seen her."

Seumas clapped him on the shoulder. "There are other warrior women would bed you, if you were not so glum all the time."

"I am not!"

The teasing expression on Seumas' face made him react with a friendly punch to the shoulder, his own grin mischievous.

"I think if you ask around, you will find that my couplings happen far more frequently than yours."

While he wandered off to the hovel he currently called home, one that he shared with a few of Eòghan's group, he considered Seumas' words. He wanted to be with the group attacking anything that was Roman, but there was something missing in his life.

He just wished he knew what it was.

Eòghan had agreed that his best time to go and seek his kin would be soon, before the winter bit hard.

It did not seem so long ago that Torrin had been desperate to accompany him to Taexali and Caledon territory. Now, that was not on her plans, at all.

Chapter Thirty- Eight

Vindolanda Roman Fort AD 89

Beathan eyed the looming outline with dispassion. The day had, so far, been an unusually fair one considering that the festival of *Samhain* had been celebrated a whole moon ago and the whitening of winter was not far off. Presently, only the tiniest hint of the deep-pink-tinged orb of *Lugh* was visible, the rest had completely slipped down into the night's darkest blue cloak, casting the east wall of Vindolanda Fort into deep shadows. From where he stood, lit torches on the gate towers were its only visible illumination.

He shivered. Not because of any foreboding, since his determination to make this a successful raid overrode any other feelings. It was more that the waning daylight brought in the nipping chill of night and he wore only a sleeveless tunic and braccae. No cloak covered his arms, since the guards on the towers needed to see that his wrist shackles were attached to the saddle horn of Seumas' horse.

He had no desire to set foot inside again but had been unable to concoct any other plan that would successfully get Eòghan's warriors into the short-handed Vindolanda Fort. The group of riders around him – a half-turma worth, to make it seem realistic – made no attempt to curb the plodding clop and clink that they made as they approached on the unevenly paved road.

Seumas kept his conversation low so that the Roman auxiliaries up on the gate towers would not hear him.

"Your advice to Eòghan to keep some of this chainmail and weaponry from out summer raids is about to bear some tasty fruit, Beathan. We could not have managed this kind of deception with the results as melted metal bars."

His own ironware sounded a noisy tune when he was yanked along, to keep pace with the gentle trot. He looked up at Seumas' smirking. The man was enjoying the role he was playing in Roman cavalry armour, on a Roman mount larger than he might normally ride.

"Just see that you remember how to use it to full advantage. And not on me!"

Seumas' chuckle was low. "Why would I use it on you? I have no reason now. You pose no problem with my sister, since she has moved on to yet another new warrior for her pleasures."

"You think to just the one?" His pent-up sarcasm growled free.

He might have punched Seumas if he had been able to and not in front of the gates of an equally-hated situation. But now was not the time to think of Torrin and her fickle feelings, though he was not sure she actually had any. Torrin, who was somewhere close by, and ready to enter the fort with the rest of Eòghan's warriors.

In answer to a demand from one of the guards on the tower, Seumas's voice rang clear.

"Decurion Augrinus of the Ala Gallorum Petriana, Corstopitum. We are returning a Brigante named Beathan who escaped from here some time ago."

"You are a bit late in the day to expect admission."

The guards might be correct…but their timing was perfect.

Beathan was relieved. Seumas had learned well the Latin words he had been taught in anticipation of this kind of response. One useful thing he had learned was that most of the ordinary soldiers spoke poor Latin, and basic phrases were all that passed between them.

A hurried discussion took place between the two soldiers on the gate with one of them saying there definitely had been a Brigante escapee. Beathan was glad to hear they spoke Tungrian which was close enough to his own tongue. That also meant Seumas' band should understand most of it. The short exchange resulted in the first guard drumming his way down the ladder to alert the senior centurion.

The second guard peered down at him over the rampart posts.

"Did you know that you have brought back our most-hated hostage, Decurion Augrinus? One who will never be forgotten?"

The Tungrian continued to address the rider at the front, the one he thought to be a fellow soldier of Rome.

"The stupid Brigante must know by now that Rome always manages to collect its dues. We knew that the *Brittunculi* would be found, given time."

Beathan stifled the responses that he wanted to make at the insult. He recognised the soldier up above as one who always had a sour outlook on everything, especially that his request for a new posting was always denied him.

After some disgruntled curses, the soldier continued. "Your charge had better say his pleas to every god and goddess he can think of. Commander Verecundus was furious when he escaped, but we were the ones the rage descended on. The whole fort was put on half-rations."

Beathan laughed raucously. His intention was to taunt the soldier, enough to keep the almost one-sided conversation going. The rest of Eòghan's warriors needed time to get themselves into positions at the bottom of the fort walls.

He called up to the guard. "You cannot blame me for those destroyed granaries. I did not set them alight! I was not the newly arrived First Cohort Tungrian who got so drunk that his torch flame set alight to the fodder in the northern barrack area."

"Oh, that poor bastard paid the easy price. He did not have to starve for a whole month like the rest of us." The guard continued an aggressive tirade. Against Verecundus' judgement, and against him for escaping.

Seumas' band kept their horses calm, not a single word being exchanged between them till the anticipated wait ended.

Half-expecting an escort to be standing behind the gates – led by the senior centurion – Beathan was delighted to see only the tower guard and two *millites*, second-stage recruits, who were opening the gates. He stifled a huge grin. He was not so famous after all, yet much better was the thought that the under-garrisoning of the fort must be even worse than they had heard from their intelligence sources. More smiles of satisfaction had to be hidden, even though the flares at the bottom of the tower ladders barely illuminated the area.

Before starting to climb back up the ladder, the tower guard sneered at him, though the message was for the supposed Decurion Augrinus. "You are to take him to Commander Verecundus in the principia. Try the aedes at this time of the evening."

He made sure his nod to Seumas was not noticed. They were being treated similarly to every other troop arrival, expected to know their way around any fort layout. Seumas clicked his horse into motion and hauled at his chains, yanking him through the gate opening and along the well-beaten via principalis.

Behind him he listened for the last of the horses trotting through. The rush of Eòghan's dark-clothed warriors came in behind, soundlessly. When he looked back, they had easily overpowered the gate-openers according to plan, and two of Seumas' band were creeping up the tower ladders. Eòghan would have chosen men well-suited to their murderous task, since it was critical to maintain the appearance of the towers still being guarded, and crucial that the other Tungrian guards along the walkway had no idea of what was happening below in the interior of the fort.

Seumas slid down from his horse, his whispers reaching Beathan in the near dark. The open intervallum area in front of them was shadowy and deserted: the illumination nearby being the torches set just inside the gates, and those at the corners of via principalis up ahead. Beyond that, the flares at the entrances to the main buildings were weak flickers, indicating only a few soldiers moving around.

"Hold out your hands." Seumas declared.

"You have been enjoying this role too much, I think."

"Not nearly as much as I expect to enjoy the next part, *mo charaid*! Does this bit of the fort look as you remember?"

Seumas unlocked his shackles and tested them. They needed to look as though still restraining him.

"The cistern over on the left there is the same, but the area on the right, before the taller praetorium building, is different. I think they may be dismantling that bit already, but I cannot tell yet what else might be wrong information that I have given." His confidence took a very slight dip but whatever the differences, Eòghan's warriors had to be trusted.

Seumas nudged his arm. "Have no fear. You outlined the fort well enough to the warriors last night. You are born to lead men, Beathan. They had no problems listening to you and they will follow through with your plans. They should find those on guard easily enough, and the weakest spots."

He gave no outward signs of his fear of being incarcerated again. The raid could not be allowed to fail. He had no intentions of dying in the process but would never allow the Romans to take him captive again. He watched none of the warriors creep their way along the dark intervallum to disperse themselves around the fort. He trusted them.

Leading the supposed troop from Corstopitum, Seumas strode confidently along the via principalis with his horse reins in one hand and Beathan's ineffective chain in the other, though they still maintained the appearance that he was being dragged along.

As he passed the praetorium entrance, the single guard on duty there aimed a jab at him with his pilum. Ready for such an event he avoided its bite, but not the thick spittle that spattered his chest.

"This Brigantian scum will wish he had been gutted by a wild boar by the time we get our hands on him. Though there will be little left after Centurion Spectatus welcomes him back!" His blast of hilarity was a waste of breath.

The satisfaction was Beathan's.

"Wha…"

The startled mumble became a death groan. The guard had been too busy with his malice to notice one of Eòghan's warriors slipping free from behind the horses. And he certainly had not seen the gleam of the blade that flashed across the unprotected neck.

Another warrior appeared out of the shadows to help cart the body away into deeper shadows, just inside the praetorium entrance. Nothing must seem out of order to any of the sentries who were stationed further up the via principalis.

Seumas nominated one of his band who wore Roman chainmail and a helmet, his instructions in a soft undertone. "Stay here till we come back and deal with any Roman who comes anywhere near you."

The warrior's expression, as he picked up the pilum that had dropped on the ground, was merciless.

Beathan stopped at the junction between the praetorium and the principia. "The surplus cavalry barracks were up there."

Two of Seumas' band led the horses around the corner. The rest of the men followed in behind Seumas.

"Stand up straight," he ordered them. "You are escorting an important prisoner."

Seumas grinned. "We are indeed. Lead me along to this headquarters building. I am eager to see it."

The unspoken was not what was inside, but who was inside.

Chapter Thirty-Nine

Vindolanda Roman Fort AD 89

With every new step on what was a familiar road, his resolve strengthened. This time he would not leave the fort without wreaking justice for himself. He would not be able to take out his ire on the ex-legate Liberalis, but he had another in mind. He did not care who Seumas tackled, or any of the other warriors.

The sound of their treads across the open ground of the inner courtyard got the reaction he had been hoping for, as they approached the far end of the principia.

Commander Verecundus came to the front of the aedes. Drawing in his considerable paunch, he stood with legs apart, and tucked his thumbs into the belt at his waist. The attempt to display his importance was lost on Beathan, he had seen that particular arrogance too often. Anticipation flushed through him. No breastplate worn meant plenty of flesh was accessible under the cloth of the tunic.

Centurion Spectatus was a step behind. Unlike his fort commander, the senior centurion was, as always, fully kitted out with chainmail. Beathan had never ever seen the man without it, but Spectatus would be Seumas' target.

"Bring him forward." Verecundus ordered, and then roared at him directly. "Had you not learned that escape from a Roman fort is never a good idea?"

Centurion Spectatus whipped forward his vine rod, an instrument Beathan was desperate to use on its owner. His instinct was to glance around the area, but he suppressed the urge. His quarry was directly in front of him. The many torches dotted around the inner principia made the area too bright for any of Eòghan's warriors to be furtive. But the opposite meant that Seumas' band who arranged themselves behind him, in Roman guise, knew exactly how many enemies they had to attack.

Verecundus shifted his gaze to Seumas. "Send my thanks to Prefect Quirinus. You have done us a very good service. How was this Brigante recaptured?"

The arrival of someone from a side room of the aedes had Verecundus turn his head.

"Ah, Signum Flavinus. I can only imagine that this escapee was caught after you left Corstopitum to bring me the news of the temporary secondment?"

Beathan acted the moment he caught sight of the white-blond hair and the distinctive nose beneath. Forcing the shackles free from his wrists he snatched the pugio that was at Seumas' waist and fired it straight at the throat of the startled Flavinus, who staggered backwards. With no knife to attack Verecundus, he launched himself forwards and toppled the stuttering commander. Quickly back up onto his knees at each side of Verecundus, his fists grabbed the material at the man's neck and he began a systematic thumping of Verecundus' head on the ground.

He was unaware of what happened around him, his only focus bent on destroying the man who had used him as his menial slave too often. The commander was not a small man, but too much socialising had left him unfit.

A tapping at his back almost distracted him, Seumas' voice at his ear.

"Use this. It will do the job more effectively."

A long knife appearing in front of his face almost made him laugh. Seumas really was enjoying himself.

A quick grab and one slit at the already stunned commander's neck was sufficient. Springing back from the spurting blood, he stood up and looked around him at the same moment he heard sounds of alarm all around the fort. Among curses, squeals of agony and triumphant shouts another word stood out.

"Fire!"

An exultant smile wreathed his face.

"Time to leave, Seumas."

Seumas collected the weapons that were close enough to filch. "Who was he?" He pointed a pilum at Flavinus.

"That was an arrogant signifer of the Ala Gallorum Petriana from Corstopitum. He would have known you were an imposter."

Seumas clapped him on the back before they took to their heels.

At the opened East Gate, he looked back. Dead littered the via principalis, and other soldiers ran around in turmoil. A cacophony of noises rent the air. Human screeching was almost drowned out by animal terror, both of those superceded by the sounds of roaring flames, the fires having been intensified by the fats added by Eòghan's warriors, which also created the black acrid smoke they needed for cover to flee from the fort.

Attack simultaneously with fire was the worst situation a Roman fort could face. In the flickering lights, parts of the fort were well-ablaze, though he could not tell if the dead on the via principalis were all Roman. Yet, he truly hoped they were.

"Where was Torrin sent?" He shouted above the din, compelled to ask her brother though he was not sure she would be concerned about him.

"Her task was to free the animals from the pens near the *Porta Praetoria*, their southern gate, and deal with any soldiers encountered there. Do not worry, she will have succeeded."

Seumas sounded confident she would have triumphed. He was, too, but… he needed to be sure.

"I'll meet you at the mustering place."

Before Seumas could say anything to the contrary he ran off, following the fort walls down towards the corner that led around to the southern entrance. The fire damage was still in the interior, but he knew that if Eòghan's warriors had fulfilled their tasks, then parts of the walls would probably burn, too.

Once around the south-east corner he could see what made the horrendous noises. Outside the Porta Praetoria, a few of his fellow warriors still fought with individual Roman auxiliaries. Pigs and hens squealed and squawked as they barrelled their way out of the fort, tripping up and bumping into anything that got in their way. A rush of mules and horses were not far behind from the sounds of the gallops. There had been no plan for the garrison horses to be sent out of the southern gate since the main stabling was to the north.

Something had gone wrong.

Worse still! A skirmish was raging in front of him, and he didn't even have an eating knife.

Kicking a pathway through some terrified animals, he headed for the nearest fighting pair.

"By *Taranis*!" The warrior's shout was jubilant, his long knife having gutted the auxiliary's insides, the last of many wounds to what looked to have been a very young recruit.

Beathan felt no sympathy for the soldier who by Roman recruiting rules would have been seasons older than he was. At that precise moment, he felt the weight of his experiences, but it was no time to dwell on such matters.

"Perfect timing. I need his weapons." Beathan's grin gave praise to the warrior's combat.

Scooping up the gladius from the ground, he noted that it was old, heavily nicked, and bore no glint of sharpness. It was probably the best that the recruit could muster, but it should have been in better condition. His optio, or centurion, was lax. However, the smaller blade when he pulled it free of its sheath was in much better condition. "My thanks, Roman."

For good measure he gave the body a kick to roll it down the slight incline before he brandished the knife that was not a proper pugio. "This will have to do."

The horses and mules had long cleared the gate by the time he went through. Both of the southern granaries were alight, though the fire there was barely getting hold. Down the intervallum was a different situation. The area where the animal pens used to be was well alight, the fodder making it easier for errant sparks to fly high into the air. The fat-laden black smoke was dense enough to make it difficult to see, but single combat was still going on. He was confronted by no-one when he sped along the intervallum, intent only on one particular pair of opponents.

Torrin was flagging, her enemy a good deal heavier than she was. Beathan could see that both combatants had been struggling with the gagging smoke for some time, in addition to trying to sustain their own inner fire. She was quick on her feet, but the Roman soldier was fighting with a gladius and a shield. Torrin brandished her long knife, her only weapon. The soldier butted with his shield, creating the cover he needed to protect himself. She worked her way to his left: he followed. He was the one defending, but her long knife would not easily dislodge the shield.

While he worked out how best to give her help, the answer came from behind like a bolt of lightning from *Taranis*. A howling cry startled the soldier sufficient enough for him to make a quarter-turn.

Torrin's knife was in his throat before he even saw the danger coming at him from behind. The spear thundering into the soldier's chainmail-clad-back drove him forwards. The shield flew askance out of his grip and slammed into Torrin who fell awkwardly onto her side with an ominous crack.

Beathan pulled the shield free from on top of her, dropped to his knees and cradled her cheeks tenderly before her brother skidded to a halt.

"You came back to help me?" Her voice was weak croak. An instinctive smile flashed up to him before she realised where she was, and what she had said.

"I did, but you needed none of my aid."

Her whisper reached him. "I do. Need you."

He could see the very instant the pain kicked in. Her doe eyes clouded over, and she clenched her teeth. The heat of roaring fire was creeping closer and more of the stinking smoke billowed around them.

"Is he dead?" Her question was driven by both fury and sheer agony.

He kissed her lips. Just once, quickly and soft. "Aye. You killed him before your brother's spear almost killed you as well."

Seumas' splutters were the work of a moment before practical needs took priority. "Hurry. We need to get out of here."

Torrin's lips winced. One of her determined, aggressive, expressions warned him that she was not ready to greet the otherworld. "Help me up. My arm is going to be useless for a while."

It was his turn to bear her weight as he helped her run out of the fort, Seumas finishing off the lone auxiliary who appeared, foolish enough to believe Seumas' support would be given as a fellow Roman soldier.

It took till near dawn, but when they reached the pre-arranged mustering place, they learned that two of Eòghan's warrior group had been killed. Most had sustained some kind of injury: some were worse than Torrin's, though many were more minor.

Roman armour was removed and went to join the pilfered weapons that had been dumped in a collective heap near the tethered horses. They now had a lot more horse stock than they had at the start of the attack.

Eòghan declared the raid a success, shared out the spoils and sent them home, the best places for them to hide.

"I can ride by myself." Torrin's tone was brusque, though her volume was as weak as a bleating lamb.

Beathan pointed to her almost dangling arm.

"You had better not jostle me, then."

Still bossy and independent even in dire pain, but that was one of the traits he realised he had missed, and loved about her.

Seumas handed over the Roman neck wrap that he had been wearing. Beathan used it to bind Torrin's arm tight in to her chest before Seumas helped hand her up to him on the horse he had chosen to ride.

Chapter Forty

Hamlet of Alanaus AD 89

Niamh handed Beathan a bowl of thick broth.

"What will happen now?" she asked.

It was a good question that Beathan already had some answers to. "The Romans will re-build Vindolanda Fort. Though they may reduce its size, depending on the incoming garrison."

Aonghas slurped the residues, not one to waste time eating even when the food was burning hot. After setting down the bowl, he wiped his grizzled moustache. "Will they choose a new site?"

"Nay." He thought that very unlikely. "They will probably move it over to a flatter area of the plateau to avoid the extra steps that had to be installed in front of some of the rooms. Some of the buildings had been sinking."

Torrin supped slowly, her use of one hand still awkward, it being only a few days since the raid. Niamh had pulled the upper-arm bone back into place as best she could, given that it had taken them a while to get back to the roundhouse at Alaunas.

An excited Cailean burst through the roundhouse entryway. "Seumas is coming."

"Shhh!" Niamh cuffed the back of her son's neck. "Fiadh has only just got to sleep."

Cailean rubbed his supposed sore bits, though the slap had been playful. "I thought you would want to know that he is with people."

"Who would Seumas bring at such a dangerous time as this?" Aonghas' censure was visible as he got to his feet, before he lifted a fire iron from the end of the hot stones, and went outside.

The Romans had not paid the roundhouse a visit yet, but Beathan knew retribution would come. Eòghan's spies would no doubt have information by now on who the new commander was going to be at Vindolanda Fort. He had enough experience to know that there was always someone ready to take the place of a dead officer – whether of high senatorial, or of lower equestrian, rank. A new garrison might take longer to install, but he was sure that reinforcements would be brought to the area to give temporary help to identify, and bring to justice, the perpetrators of the attack. That would, no doubt, get as much of a priority as reconstruction of the site.

Torrin was now the one propped up against the upturned tub, in the invalid's place. "My brother is not as reckless as he used to be. He will not bring danger to the door."

Beathan laughed aloud at her statement, though her mother wore a disbelieving expression. He had not managed to persuade Torrin that her injury was a hazard of combat, and that she had not gained it through incompetence. But he knew well that anything that hampered her movements made her feel inadequate, and frustration supplied the rest.

He did not expect to hear Aonghas having a conversation outside with the newcomers, rather than the usual greetings being exchanged once inside. However, the sounds of the man's cheerful laughter indicated that whoever Seumas had brought with him posed no immediate danger.

Aonghas straightened up once he had re-entered via the low entryway. Beathan watched him toss the makeshift weapon into the basket at the door before standing aside to bid the visitors enter. Aonghas' expression was hard to gauge. If anything, he thought that the man hid a smirk.

The warriors were young, older than he was, but were not part of Eòghan's warrior group. He had never seen this pair before. And yet, when he looked more closely, something about the one with the wide brows and long nose resonated. That warrior's focus was intent, but he knew it was entirely on him because the others in the room were being rudely ignored. He watched a gradual smile appear on the warrior's face; the man's large overlapping front teeth drawing more of his attention.

Those teeth!

A cold shiver coursed down his back. He stared; his eyes almost grown too big for their sockets. Jumping to his feet he started forward and then immediately recoiled. It could not be!

The man at the doorway began to guffaw, a very distinctive laugh that he definitely recognised.

"*Taranis* be praised! I never thought that I would ever find you alive, Beathan!"

He felt the last years roll away leaving him with an impossible vision. "But they…you…"

"I am alive."

"*Fàilte!* Be seated." Aonghas' polite interruption to the other visitor gave him a chance to breathe again.

A few steps took him to Ruoridh, the cousin he had thought killed by a Roman auxiliary. A death he had always felt was his responsibility.

Back clapping and full hugs eventually made him believe that it really was flesh that he was clasping.

"Enough." Ruoridh laughed. "You are crushing my bones. You have grown much sturdier since we last met."

Ruoridh's mock groans made him reluctantly let go, though his cousin continued to dominate the conversation, the rest of the room eagerly listening in

"If we had known that you have been hiding here all along in Brigantia, we would have been here much sooner." Ruoridh's chide was softened by two-palmed shakes to his shoulders, as though his cousin was also reluctant to break physical contact.

He grinned, beginning to feel his insides settle down to something more like normal. "Depending on when you arrived, you might have missed me."

Another mock punch from Ruoridh contacted his upper arm. "When we heard about a raid on Vindolanda Fort, a few days ago, I knew that the famous Brigante named Beathan – who led the attack – had to be you."

"I am not famous." He stood back to look at Torrin who sat as though bemused by the whole exchange and very interested in the newcomers. "I was not the leader and not the only one attacking that fort."

Niamh handed out beakers of small-bere to Ruoridh and the other newcomer. The silent exchange was simple enough to make him remember some conventions. He sat down after Aonghas had indicated places at the fireside for his visitors.

Ruoridh held up his cup and gave praise to *Rhianna* after thanking his hosts. "The way Feargus and I heard it…" Ruoridh stopped to introduce his Taexali friend, Feargus of Monymusk. "We were told that you created the plan for the raid, and it was your instructions that the warriors followed. Seumas here seemed to agree."

Beathan watched Seumas raise his beaker in salutation and then turn his focus towards him.

"Eòghan is a great leader, but he does not have the experience of the inside of a Roman fort like you have, Beathan. He will still command our warrior group – unless you want to challenge his leadership?" Seumas asked.

Beathan almost spat out the small-bere he had just glugged. "Nay. In time, I may want to be a leader, but for now I think I must rethink plans I made some time ago, which I cowardly set aside."

His gaze drifted across the fire to Torrin.

Her grin was laced with sass, but that streak of determination was also evident. "We will be going north, now that you have satisfied some of your craving for revenge."

"We?" He wanted to be sure.

"Aye, I said we and I mean it." Her eyes twinkled across to him, the firelight making them seem even more mischievous. "You were not ready for me, nor I ready for you. Now, it is different. I have a hankering to take a break…" Her attempt to indicate her physical 'break' made her groans loud. She continued, "A break from attacking Roman forts, and to settle down at a hearthside with just the one man."

Since her expressive eyes indicated him, he felt his own smile spreading.

"I can travel north with you while this heals. You will defend me from any danger, I know this now."

He watched her deliberately tear her gaze away from him to land on the visitors.

"I also believe it will be a good idea for Beathan, my famous Brigante, to be far away from here for a while. You must give me directions, Ruoridh, of how I can help him find the rest of his family."

Rising from his place Beathan went to sit down beside her, not willing for any new fickle changes in her allegiance. He decided not to even notice when she nudged him with her good arm, her words loud enough for all to hear and her cheeky grin infectious.

"I know now which one is your cousin Ruoridh, but tell me about the other handsome warrior who has come with him."

He snagged her gaze and held it, desperate to kiss away her brazenness. "I have no idea who he is, but if we remember our conventions, we might find out."

He vaguely heard Seumas' chuckling reprimand. "The famous Brigante in our midst needs to realise there are more people in this room than just my sister."

Reluctantly, he eventually turned his attention back to the company.

Ruoridh's grin was wide, his expression indulgent. "When you have time, cousin, maybe you can tell Feargus and I where you have been?"

He shrugged his shoulders and looked at young Cailean who was engrossed in the proceedings. "Where do you think I should start? You know a lot of my long story…"

Cailean had been silent for too long. As though the light of *Lugh* had appeared through broken clouds his face beamed, his words directed to the visitors. "Beathan has been everywhere. He even went to Rome!"

"I did, Cailean, but I am sure you can understand that before I tell that very long story, I need to hear about my family." He thought that would have cooled the young lad's excitement, but he was wrong.

Cailean bounced onto his knees alongside him. "I want to know about Caledonia, as well. Will you take me there with you when you go?"

Aonghas reproached his son. "Time now for you to listen to Ruoridh and not ask impossible questions."

Ruoridh began. "Nara and Lorcan, and my own mother and father, are all grey wolves now, but they have carved out a place for themselves at a place named Ceann Druimin. They fled to the village after the battlegrounds of Beinn na Ciche and at the invitation of the chief, Lulach, they have stayed there ever since."

A huge sense of peace flooded him. His mother and father were alive. He felt Torrin's hand sneak into his, her squeeze supportive and loving.

As Ruoridh talked of the other Garrigill Brigantes, a blockage of emotion sat in the back of his throat that would not dislodge. Swallowing got harder and harder. The tears he would not allow to fall made his eyes sting till a nudge from Torrin distracted him. Her whisper up at his ear was for him alone.

"Let them fall. Even just once, or you will have lingering regrets. They are happy tears, Beathan. You have held in your pain for far too long."

Her reassurance and care were sufficient. He swallowed the lump, wiped away the moisture and began his own inquiry.

"How did you know to search for me in Brigantia?"

Once again Ruoridh beamed at him. "Do the names Derwi and Gillean mean anything to you?"

A deep excitement flooded him and he felt a huge beam spreading. "You know something of them?" He was almost as desperate to find out about them, as about his own family.

"They came to us at Ceann Druimin. After you were all captured near Vinovia Fort, Legate Liberalis sent them north to the fort at Trimontium."

"I never managed to find out where they were sent. Liberalis told me nothing. I hated him for that alone."

Ruoridh continued. "They had no idea that you had been kept in Brigantia, at Vindolanda Fort. When more and more Roman troops were withdrawn from Caledonia it seems that Trimontium got to be a very busy place. There were a lot of comings and goings with many different temporary camps built around it, till the troops were redeployed in the south or sent away from Britannia."

He just knew the next part of the story. "They escaped?"

"They did, and they headed back home since they could find no traces of where you had been sent to."

Torrin grew more animated. "Beathan's friends found your family at Ceann Druimin?"

The parts of the stories meshed together, their talk going on well into the night. Beathan cradled Torrin as close as he could, given she was the injured one, and found out that he was not the only Garrigill Brigante in the room who had a tale to tell about insurrection and attacks on Roman forts. He would have loved to have been there with Ruoridh and Feargus when the Romans abandoned the fortress in Caledonia that was named Pinnata Castra. The one that Legate Liberalis had named the pinnacle of General Agricola's achievements in Britannia.

Torrin looked up at him with weary eyes. "You want to leave this very moment. I can tell my enervated green-eyed warrior, but first we will sleep on it." A merry tinkle escaped from her, drawing everyone's' attention. "Though, a cuddle is all you will be having tonight."

Niamh's hands rose in supplication, her laughter gaining a bigger reaction. "Thanks be to *Brighid* for that. We will all get some sleep!"

Beathan resolved to wait till Torrin was able to make the journey. Wherever he went – he knew in his heart that she was now ready to go, too.

Eventually, before sleep claimed him, he heard Ruoridh saying, "My parents were about your age when they were hearth-linked, Beathan. They are still as close as they were back then. Maybe you and Torrin will laugh and nag each other just as much as my folks do, and have done all of my life."

Chapter Forty-One

Ceann Druimin, Caledon Territory AD 89

"The end of your journey, Beathan." Ruoridh sounded almost reverent when he pulled his horse to a stop after coming out of the fringes of the woods. The rest of the small group following suit.

Beathan looked at the smoke rising high above each of the roundhouses that were spread out in front of him. The village was not large, but it cosily nestled in a small dip in the landscape, productive fields sloping very slightly around it. The winter season was already upon the foliage, the day clear and crisp, yet even in its dormant state it looked welcoming.

Domestic fowl pecked and clucked their way in between the buildings. A couple of pigs and a small sheep snuffled in the nearby animal enclosure.

Breathing became difficult. For so long he had had yearnings. He found himself swallowing down emotions he had no words for.

Alongside him Torrin lightened the tension, her words typically droll. "Do those poor beasts know that today might be the very day that a big knife will be wielded their way?"

Ruoridh chuckled, enjoying her wit. "The sheep will know that her milk and her wool is too important, but the pigs are another matter."

A small toddler burst free from one roundhouse entryway, a young woman in swift pursuit. "Come here you little runaway! Just you wait till I catch you."

The little one giggled heartily when caught up by the woman who only noticed the arrivals when she swung the child high in the air.

"Ruoridh!" she cried, and then looked to who accompanied him. "Oh, by the bounty of *Rhianna*!" Her voice rose to an impossible level, her excitement palpable. "Beathan has returned!"

The young woman rushed towards him, her tears dripping onto the little boy in her arms.

"Enya?" Beathan croaked.

Before he could dismount, the whole village seemed to erupt from the dwellings. He looked at the surprise and general delight on the faces, but most of all he focused on two of the figures who stood immobile, just outside one particularly large roundhouse.

The man put his arm around the woman, drew her in tight to him and dropped a kiss to the top of her head: one iron-grey haired and the other with grey streaks amongst the faded auburn. He could see that both of them trembled… joyful smiles on their faces.

He glanced at Torrin who had been riding alongside him and whooped. "My parents!"

He vaulted off the horse and ran across the open space.

Nara slid from his father's grip and held out her hands to him. He clasped them and then drew her into a wild cuddle. Somehow, his father Lorcan, managed to encompass both of them in his wide embrace.

He felt his mother reach up to stroke his hair away from his face, like she had done when he was a little boy. Her gaze into his eyes was intense, and jubilant, when she tapped her chest.

"I knew, here in my heart, that you were still alive." Nara's lips trembled.

Ruoridh, grinning as usual, belatedly shouted to all attending. "I have brought back Beathan of Garrigill." There was a tiny pause to ensure everyone listened. "The famous Brigante!"

He felt his mother's clasp slowly loosen, though his father's grip tightened across his shoulder, as they opened up their clutch and faced the crowd.

"Did you hear that, Nara? Ruoridh says our son is a… famous…Brigante."

Beathan could not miss the mischievous twinkle in his father's deep-brown eyes. His mother changed places to squirm herself in between, linking arms with both him and his father.

Nara's expression boldly challenged, but the beam in her eyes told its own tale. "You say that with surprise, my love. The goddess told us it would be so, long before he was born. Did you doubt it?"

His father looked over the top of his mother's head at him, his joy and love unconcealed. "Never."

"Look at the size of you!"

The giant who stepped forward pulled him free for a back-slapping hug. Uncle Brennus, still blond-haired, with just a touch of grizzling near the tips of his moustache, chortled heartily only needing to bend a little to stand eye-to-eye with him.

"I need to learn everything that has happened to you. And I mean everything. It will revive my storytelling prowess at the firesides."

Brennus' lopsided expression had been so badly missed that Beathan could not prevent the tears from beginning. Indeed, everything around affected him. He had had no idea that it was possible to grin and to weep simultaneously, but that was what was happening. Stiffening up his shoulders, he heard Torrin's whispers at his ear, which were not actually all that quiet.

"Do not dare repress them, Beathan! Let those tears fall. You deserve that every single one of them be shed."

"Take charge of your son before he runs off again." Enya handed over the child to a face Beathan easily recognised before she almost squeezed the breath out of him.

A smirking Nith of Tarras managed to hold his child while giving him a friendly shoulder slap.

"You and Enya made this squirming bairn?" he grinned, before turning to the next relatives who came forward to greet him. Some of the younger ones were difficult to place since they had grown so much since he last saw them, and were shy about coming close.

But like a thunderbolt from *Taranis,* he realised he had not seen his uncle Gabrond. He reached for Torrin's good hand, and stared at her, needing her emotional support before he managed to croak, "My Uncle Gabrond is not…"

"I am over here," Gabrond called.

Beathan swivelled towards the voice, understanding dawning immediately. He squeezed Torrin's hand and beamed at her.

"Do you remember I told you about the uncle who taught me to ride?" he asked her, pointing to the man who was inspecting the teeth of the mounts they had acquired at Vindolanda Fort. "He obviously prefers those Roman horses to me!"

"Not at all!" Gabrond strode forward. "I was just biding my time. Welcome home, lad!"

An old man Beathan had never seen before, who stood to the side of the crowd, cleared his throat before speaking, his voice surprisingly authoritative. The general noise immediately faded to listen to him. "You are very welcome at Ceann Druimin. This whole village has waited many moons for your return."

He drew Torrin towards him. "You must be Chief Lulach?"

A benevolent nod came his way.

"I am honoured to be here, to be in a place that has harboured my family so well, for such a long time." He drew Torrin closer to his side and clasped her hand. "Torrin and I would be delighted to accept your hospitality."

Through happy, stinging eyes he saw the speculation appear on both of the faces of his mother and his father.

"Come away inside, everyone. We will squeeze in. Do not stand out in the cold." Nara fussed, reaching over to take Torrin from him by her good arm, while inspecting the wrap that held her broken upper-arm close in to her body to prevent jarring during the ride. "You, I can see, have a story to tell me about that injury."

As an afterthought for Beathan and his father, Nara declared, "Let us all feast! We have many moons of absence to share."

Before his mother bore Torrin away, he snatched a kiss. "I did tell you that I have a large, noisy and bossy family?"

He loved her mock-horrified grin.

"Mother?" he asked.

Before he could say any more, Nara's chortles were contagious. "Have no fear, my very grown-up son. I can see that Torrin is going to fit in here with no problems at all."

For a long time that evening, the Garrigill roundhouse rang with laughter, with gasps of horror and sighs of contentment. Food appeared as though from nowhere to be shared around and everyone had something to wet their lips. The basics of his story had been told, but the fine details would come later.

"General Agricola said he had been in the same room as myself and your mother? Now that is hard to remember." Lorcan smoothed down some wiry upper-lip hair.

Nara was shaking her head. "I have no memory of him. Though, reluctant to praise a Roman for anything, I must nevertheless raise my thanks to the man for freeing you and your friends."

Beathan dredged up Agricola's last words to him.

"He also said…" He stopped to point to his parents who sat next to each other, Lorcan's arm casually draped across Nara's shoulders. "He was speaking about the two of you. Agricola said: *'By Jupiter, and by your supreme god Taranis, may they still be alive. So that you can send them my greetings. Tell them they should be proud of their noble son.'* I am sure those were his very words."

Across the fireside, Gabrond snorted. "Did he mean proud of you for destroying Vindolanda Fort?"

He had not yet told them all of the unusual, educational evenings spent in Agricola's company, but when pushed to think about the words again, they now seemed to make more sense.

"The Romans have a different way of worshipping their gods. He was very observant, devout, and…almost resigned to the belief that *Fortuna* no longer favoured him. He had made many enemies in Rome, though that was hard for me to understand. I think, apart from not being successful with people like you – the 'barbarian' Caledonian allies of the north, who were completely unpredictable…" He broke off to allow the spontaneous burst of laughter to died down, laughter which he appreciated. "Those high-ranking people in Rome were jealous of Agricola's other successes in Britannia."

His mother's expression was cautious. "In some way, you gave him your loyalty?"

"Nay! He always knew I detested him." He was swift to deny such a connection. "My loyalty was always given to Gillean and Derwi. When I acted to save both his and the Lady Domitia Decidiana's lives, I acted instinctively. When I shouted the warning to him, he was in just as defenceless a situation as his wife had been, even though his personal guards surrounded us."

His father reached over to clap his knee. "He respected you, my son. Your honourable principles appealed to him, and that is good enough for me." Almost as an afterthought, his father added, "Did he have sons of his own?"

Beathan knew that answer might need some time.

Uncle Brennus finished picking a bit of errant food from his teeth. "I have sent messengers to Gillean and Derwi. They will be keen to come and see you."

"You have?" He was delighted with that news.

Torrin leaned in close to him. "I will look forward to meeting the men who shared a lot of your adventures."

He stared at her. "We had no adventures. We were too busy keeping ourselves alive for that."

She nudged him, her gaze up at him playful. "I am sure there are things you still have to share about that fascinating city named Rome."

He spluttered into his beaker, laughter gurgling free. It was not the time, nor the place to tell everything about Rome.

Nara changed the subject, her expression quizzical, perhaps even secretive. "So, my famous son. Is your hunger for vengeance against our Roman enemy sufficiently satisfied now? Or, do you intend to go back down to Brigantia and wreak more disaster?"

He looked down at Torrin who was exhausted and almost asleep. "We will not go anywhere away from here till Torrin is properly healed, and after that we will decide together. Won't we, my love?" He realised he was mimicking the phrase his parents used often, to express their long-lasting love for one another. It sat well on his tongue, and he knew he was going to use it many, many times.

Torrin's smile warmed him to the core. "Aye, we will, my love. My famous Brigante. We have many things to sort out together."

Nara chuckled, one of her knowing ones as she gazed at a very sleepy Torrin. "I believe the goddess Rhianna has already taken charge of your future. The cycle of life continues, and time will tell."

~~~

TRIBES IN BEATHAN THE BRIGANTE

VACOMAGI

TAEXALI

CALEDON

VENICONES

VOTADINI

SELGOVAE

BRIGANTES

DUROTRIGES

Glossary

Note: Throughout the novel, I have used *italics* for the first use only of a particular term that appears in Latin, Celtic or Gaelic, to indicate to the reader that they will find a meaning here in the glossary. In the case of gods and goddesses, and Gaelic phrases, I have used italics throughout the story.

<u>Celtic Seasons</u>
Samhain 1st Nov – New Year, the beginning of Winter
Imbolc 1st Feb – the beginning of Spring/ the beginning of the end of winter
Beltane 1st May – the beginning of Summer
Lughnasadh 1st Aug – the beginning of Autumn

<u>Celtic Gods</u>
Ambisagrus – weather
Araun – underworld
Belenos – fire; sun
Cernunnos – horned god; master of wild places and things
Lugh – fierce warrior; storms; sun; thunderstorms
Manaan – sea; tides
Succellus – agriculture; carried a hammer and horn of plenty; domesticity; prosperity; wine
Taranis – carried thunderbolt and the wheel of the year; thunder
<u>Celtic Goddesses</u>
Aine – sovereignty; summer; wealth
Andarta – war
Andraste – victory
Brigantia – the high goddess
Brighid – domesticity; hearth; similar to Brigantia, possibly a localised name
Cereduin – light; moon
Coventina – burns; springs; wells
Rhianna – power of a giantess; strength of a horse

Roman Gods
Bacchus – agriculture; fertility; wine
Fascinus – masculine regenerative power; phallus symbol; sexual energy
Jupiter – king of the gods; sky; thunder
Jupiter Optimus Maximus – best and greatest
Mercurius – communication; financial gain; guide of souls to the underworld; messages; thieves; travellers; trickery
Neptune – freshwater; sea
Pluto – underworld

Roman goddesses
Clementia – forgiveness leniency; mercy; penance
Fortuna – chance; fortune; lot in life
Invidia – envy; jealousy; retribution
Juturna – fountains; springs; wells
Mana Genita – infant mortality
Morta – death
Parcae – (Morta, Decima; Nona - similar to the 3 Fates) controlled the thread of life; destiny
Salus – safety; well-being
Tempestas – storms; sudden weather changes

Gaelic used in Beathan The Brigante
athair – father
braccae – trousers
Ceigan Ròmanach! – Roman Turds!
Ciamar a tha sibh? – How are you?
Cò sibhse? – Who are you?
Fàilte! – Welcome!
Feasgar Math – Good Afternoon
Madainn Mhath – Good Morning
mathàir – mother
mo charaid – my friend
mo chairdean – my friends
Ròmanach buchar each! – Roman horse shit!

Seall! – Look!
tapadh leat – thank you

Roman/Latin terms used

amphorae – storage jars

Brittunculi – derogatory name attested at Vindolanda Fort meaning 'nasty little Britons'

century – (ideally) 80 soldiers [half-century 40; quarter century 20]; (slaves brought number to more like 100 in total)

cohortes urbanae – urban cohort in Rome; like a police force patrolling in the daytime

contubernium – basic squad/ unit of 8 soldiers

cursus honorum – general career ladder for a Roman citizen to gain high employment/honours

decanus – soldier in charge of a contubernium group of 8 men

dolia – larger storage jars; used for transportation of greater volumes

dulchia piperata – honey cake

eques – special dispatch rider

frigidarium – cold room in the bathhouse

gubernator – captain of a vessel; skipper

judicial legate – *juridicius legatus (Augustorum)* conducted administrative and judicial business in the provinces (e.g. Britannia); responsibility for covering absence of consul in the provinces

lares – household gods; personal to a family

legate – *legatus legionis* officer holding full power over a legion

liburna – small galley; coastal/ fluvial vessel

mansio – official stopping place (available rooms) on a Roman road for use of military/ officials on Roman Empire business; maintained by central government in Rome

medicus – surgeon

millites – second stage recruits

optio – assistant to a centurion; soldier in charge of a half-century

pilum – Roman javelin

posticum – servant entrance in a Roman villa

praefectus castrorum – camp commander; third most senior of a legion; generally, from the centurionate (having risen through the ranks)

prefect – commander of a cavalry fort (often from equestrian class)

quaestor – assistant to a consul in Rome; assistant to a governor in a province

signifer – standard bearer who carried the Roman standard for a unit . In mounted cavalry units, a standard could be named a vexillum. In an infantry legion, a standard was named a signum.

speculatores – scouts in the Roman army

strigil – wooden blade used to scrape off oil used to cleanse the body in the bathhouse

taberna – single room booth/ storage room/ or shop (pl. tabernae)

tribunus laticlavius – 'broad striped' tribune; second in command of a legion (generally of senatorial class)

turma – basic cavalry unit of 30/32 horsemen

vexillation – a unit of soldiers gathered for a specific purpose; generally attached to a legion complement but in addition to it.

vigiles – night guard force in Rome; sometimes fire fighters

Fort interior terminology

aedes – area set aside for shrines; niches to pay homage to the gods; place for safe storage of standards; place used for pit dug to safely store the unit/ cohort/ legion strongbox (cash reserves). Tended to be at the rear of the headquarters building with sufficient height for standards which might be 15 feet high.

intervallum – empty area inside and below fort/camp walls; wide enough for stray enemy missiles to avoid barracks/ tents; used as a road around the inside perimeter; possibly place for walking horses not getting outside exercise

porta decumana – rear gate of the fortress/ fort/ camp

porta praetoria – front (main) gate in the fortress/ fort/ camp

porta principalis – side gates of the fortress/ fort/ camp (sinistra/right and dextra/ left)

praetorium – accommodation for most high-ranking officer (pl. praetoria)

principia – headquarters building; administration block

tabernae– booths/ storage rooms; single-room shops; (sing. taberna)

valetudinarium – hospital block

via decumana – road from rear gate into fort

via praetoria – road leading from main gate (front) to main buildings

via principalis – road between side gates running in front of main buildings (principia and praetorium)

via quintana – road running behind main buildings

Legions Mentioned in Bethan the Brigante
Legio II Adiutrix
Legio IX
Legio XX

First Cohort Tungrians at Vindolanda Fort
Ala Petriana- mounted forces at Corstopitum/ Coria Fort

Historical Context

Written evidence of what actually happened in northern Britannia, around the time that General Gnaeus Iulius Agricola was recalled to Rome c. AD 85, is very vague. The words of the Ancient Roman writer *Cornelius Tacitus* include some general details about the campaigns of General Agricola. In Tacitus' 'On the life and character of Julius Agricola' (*De vita et moribus Iulii Agricolae*), there is a brief mention about Agricola's recall to Rome which translates to something like 'Agricola held the whole of Britannia in his palm…but it was let go'

What is available to study from Tacitus is not his original, but a later copy, which may explain some inconsistencies. Sections of Tacitus' writing are missing, the particulars of which might well make a historian sigh with delight. Complete verification of any of Tacitus' mentions is problematic, with regard to the specifics about military engagement in Caledonia.

According to Tacitus, one major pitched-battle – *Mons Graupius* – was fought on Caledonian soil. Tacitus stated that this took place late in the campaign season, which was generally from April to September/October. However, no Ancient Roman against Caledon Allies battle site has ever been identified north of the central belt area of Scotland (Clyde/Forth line). Possibilities, for the place of battle, range from sites in Fife all the way to the north-east Moray coast near Elgin. There are some historians who are not convinced there even was a battle, so – till proof is found – the site remains elusive.

According to Tacitus, after the successful battle, Agricola moved on to the territory of the *Boresti* where he took some hostages and ordered the prefect of the fleet to sail all around Britannia. Then, Agricola marched slowly southwards inspiring fear in the territory he had recently invaded and placed his infantry and cavalry in winter quarters. Details are not specified for this by Tacitus, or any other Roman writer. No area named *Boresti* has ever been identified (not verifiable on the map 'co-ordinates' of the geographer Ptolemaeus), and the locations of the winter quarters can only be guessed at.

Tacitus wrote that Agricola was recalled to Rome (late A.D. 84 or early A.D. 85) and that Agricola was awarded with triumphal decorations and nominated for a statue to be erected in his name. This would have been the highest military honours given to someone who was not an emperor. Again, the facts are not known. No statue has ever been found.

However, Tacitus also makes comment that Agricola re-entered Rome unobtrusively at night. This would likely have been unusual behaviour for someone who had done a good job for the Roman Empire. Tacitus hints that Agricola's supporters thought some form of triumphal march into Rome was merited, but it could never eclipse any formal triumphant re-entry of Emperor Domitian after the 'triumphs' led by the emperor (e.g. Germania).

Tacitus hints that Emperor Domitian offered a province (perhaps Africa) but Agricola declined the post and never held another civil or military position of authority. He retired to his estates in Gallia Narbonensis and remained there (according to Tacitus) till he died in AD 93. There is some conjecture, again briefly touched on by ancient writers, that Agricola's death may not have been from purely natural causes. Though, proof of any interference by Emperor Domitian, or anyone else, has yet to be found.

Since the written historical record is virtually non-existent, it falls to the keen historian to take into account the archaeological record. The study of archaeological remains is a vibrant and organic process and, day after day, new discoveries are made across Britain.

Visible evidence on the ground to the north of the Forth/Clyde line in Scotland is scant. However, the general progress of Agricola's northern campaigns is evident in the trail of forts, fortlets, and watchtowers on the Gask Ridge, and in the 'Glen blocker' forts attributed to the Flavian era. The large fortress at Inchtuthil in Perthshire, probably built by Agricola, is highly important with regard to Flavian occupation. And, even less permanent, temporary marching camps lead all the way from just south of the city of Aberdeen all the way north-eastwards to the Moray coast.

Till new exploration is conducted at some of the sites – where limited archaeological digs took place during centuries prior to the present– what Agricola did in north-east Scotland can only be speculated on.

From evidence found at Inchtuthil Roman Fortress in Perthshire, it is assumed that this huge Roman supply fortress was officially abandoned, after a partial dismantling process, though it had only been in use for, at best, a handful of years. Coin evidence attests it to being inhabited till around AD 86, but proving its use after that is not conclusive. Inchtuthil was an immensely important and strategic installation when built. It was perfectly positioned for Roman expansion and settlement of northern Caledonia. It was well placed for advances into the Caledon mountains using the nearby mountain passes. The River Dee (TAVA according to Ptolemy) was a main supplies route, and there was easy access from the Inchtuthil plateau out to the north-eastern plains leading all the way to the Moray coast.

Inchtuthil Fortress is an incredibly informative site in Roman archaeology. When excavated in the late 1950s and 1960s, it allowed for the best interpretation of a fortress/fort ground plan anywhere across the Roman Empire. The fields it is buried under had never been more than 'top-cropped' and few buildings of any kind had been constructed across its extensive ground area.

Inchtuthil Fortress remains incredible for another find – that of the pit deliberately dug into the floor of the very large workhouse area. There are many examples across the Roman Empire of forts being dismantled before abandonment. That process included burying materials that could not be carted away for future use, or were regarded as refuse. During the 1960s excavation at Inchtuthil, when the pit was opened up in the workhouse, the revelations were astonishing. Nearly ten tons of iron in the form of multiple sized nails, approximately 850,000 of them were uncovered. From the smallest pin, to the very large ones used for fort wall or gate construction, they were almost all completely new. They had been packed into the pit, along with a few other items like wheel rims, and covered over by six feet of earth. The process denied the local Iron Age tribes the use of the iron which was to them like gold is to other societies. There is no clear reason why so many valuable nails were not carted south for use elsewhere. It's possible that either most, or some of the nails, were fashioned at the huge smithing-hearth at Inchtuthil, which was big enough for more than one smith to use at a time. So many nails would have been extremely heavy and would have taken quite some time and effort to cart away. It has been mooted that the garrison at the fortress was seriously undermanned and the burial was the most expedient way to deal with the products. It's not known if the pit was dug and filled while the wall timbers of the workshop were still in situ, or if the pit was dug after the workshop timbers were pulled down and burned.

If Agricola was recalled to Rome in early A.D. 85, then his successor, or some other senior officer, possibly maintained the fortress at Inchtuthil for a short time afterwards before the complete withdrawal of Roman troops from northern Scotland. This withdrawal is estimated, from coin evidence, to have been around AD 86.

The Roman presence continued south of the central belt of Scotland and in the borders area, for some years after the withdrawal from the north – substantial evidence for this found at forts like Trimontium, near Melrose.

Author's Note

The five novels in this series follow the adventures of my fictitious Garrigill Clan who originate in the Hillfort of Garrigill, in northern Brigantia. At the end of Book 1, *The Beltane Choice*, a baby is born to the main characters Nara and Lorcan, a child they name, Beathan – which means *life*. As the series progresses, time marches forwards and by the end of Book 3 *After Whorl: Donning Double Cloaks* Beathan has reached the age of almost thirteen.

Historically speaking, it's thought that infant and childhood mortality rates were much higher than present ones. Beathan thrives during his first seven years at Garrigill Hillfort, and then the next five years are spent on the move as a refugee, avoiding the Roman invasions of the north. I feel sure that such a life would have matured a young boy faster than a child of today, so Beathan is already warrior trained by the time he is twelve. At the end of Book 3 *After Whorl: Donning Double Cloak,* he is in the rear of the battle lines at Beinn na Ciche. Being captured after the battle, by some of General Agricola's soldiers, is not due to lack of maturity but is down to bad luck – his goddess has not favoured him

Book 5 was conceived as the continuing story of Beathan, and in part that of Agricola. Though, I felt that the general's story needed to end before the half way point of the book, leaving the rest for a further maturing of Beathan. Since Nara (Beathan's mother) believes in Book 1 *The Beltane Choice* that her son is destined to be a warrior leader, I needed to find credible ideas for events that led to Bethan fulfilling that prophecy.

However, since the general concept of my whole series has been to build a credible picture of what real life may have been like during that era of turmoil, to make Beathan into some form of modern teenage superhero didn't work for me. And I didn't think that would work for my loyal readers, either. I do hope my readers love how Beathan matures into a believable young warrior of his time, shaped by his experiences and events around him.

The writing of Books 1-4 was driven by my need to create a believable world using the archaeological and historical evidence at my fingertips. Book 5 is also wrapped around as accurate a picture as I can portray, using the archaeology gleaned from my continuous research, but I have particularly loved the entirely fictional aspects too.

I quite liked the idea of making Beathan's stay in Rome a lot longer, selfishly to incorporate more of the incredibly fascinating details that I've learned about ancient Rome, but that didn't get Beathan home to Brigantia quickly enough. I had the most desperate urge to make him be a famous Brigante as a seventeen year old. Why? In part, because my research into the incredible site named

Vindolanda, Northumberland, England gleaned details about the nine different forts. It's thought that the earliest wooden fort, possibly built by a Tungrian unit around AD 85, was replaced fairly quickly and by AD 90. Reasons for stripping down the timbers and building new sometimes were because the incoming new garrison built to their own specifications and needs, but fire has also been an attributable factor in the need to rebuild wooden installations.

I have no evidence that tells me that the earliest Vindolanda fort was destroyed by fire, during an attack by insurgents in the area, but it seemed to me to be highly…possible.

I have also stretched 'known' evidence in portraying my character named Verecundus at Vindolanda. Historically, there is tablet evidence that one of the early forts at Vindolanda was commanded by Verecundus, but my portrayal of how he died is pure fiction. Similarly, how the standard bearer Flavinus met his death near Corstopitum is unknown, and my version entirely invented.

Any mistakes I've made in the writing of the series, regarding the use of military terms or engagement situations during battle between Roman and Iron Age Celts, are unintentional. In my defence, when I began the writing of the series around 2011, I had not read as extensively about Romano/British history as I have now in 2020. I have learned an immense amount, and intend to continue to learn about the Roman Empire, and especially about its conquest of Britain.

Author's Note – Names

I'm often asked how, or why, I have chosen my character names. I generally have a good reason, at the time of writing, for choosing a name that reflects the traits the character displays (Though sometimes I can't remember afterwards why I have chosen a particular one!). I tend to use online sites for baby names, or Gaelic names. This can be a problem when a similar name is shown to mean something slightly different depending on the site chosen. However, since I'm writing fiction, the name becomes what I want it to mean in my story. Here are the meanings of some of the character names as found on the internet, and as I choose them to mean.

Aonghas (ang-us) – one, choice
Beathan (bay-n) – life
Brennus (bren-us) – king, prince or raven
Cailean (kay-len) – young dog, or child
Cathal (ka-hal) – war, ruler
Crispus (crisp-oos) – curly
Derwi (dew-i) – friend
Enya (enn-ya) – fire
Gillean (gill-ayn) – servant
Lorcan (lor-can) – little/ fierce one
Mearna (mer-na) – beloved and tender
Niamh (knee-v) – bright or radiant
Secundus (seck-oon-doos) – second born; favourable; lucky
Senan (sen-ann) – brightness, little wise one
Seumas (shame-us) – one who supplants
Tertius (ter-ti-oos) – third
Torquil (tor-quill) – sacrificial cauldron
Torrin (tor-in) – thunder, little hills

Additional Characters (mentioned) some who also appear in other Celtic Fervour Saga Series novels:

Calgacus (kal-ga-coos) – swordsman
Callan (kall-ann) – battle, or rock
Cian (key-ann) – ancient
Farrahll (far-ll) – descendant of Fearghal
Fiadh (fee-at) – little deer
Lentulus (len-tool -oos) – unhasty, slow

Genuine historical characters: (dates are estimates)

Agricola, Gnaeus Iulius – (agricolae– farmer); *Governor of Britannia and Commander of the Britannic Legions AD c. 77-85*
Barrus (or Barrius) – name attested at Trimontium Fort
Cerialis, Quintus Petillius C. R. – (of corn, or meal (?)); Governor of Britannia and Commander of the Legions AD 71-74
Domitian, Titus Flavianus – Roman Emperor AD 81-96
Flavinus – name attested on a funerary stone. A 25-year-old standard bearer of the Turma of Candidus buried at Corbridge /Corstopitum.
Liberalis, Gaius Salvius – (freedom; dignified; honourable); Roman Senator; Juridicius Augustorum Britannia 78-81; Pro-consul Macedonia-c.82/83; Arval Brethren
Lucullus Sallustius (Governor of Britannia sometime soon after Agricola and before AD 93)
Nigrinus Marcus Cornelius – Roman senator
G.O.T.T.L. Priscus Javolenus – Roman senator (possible juridicus - senior judge in Britannia c. AD 84)
Verecundus – (feeling shame; bashful; shy; modest) , attested as a Fort Commander at Vindolanda Fort, late Flavian era

The following are all names associated with the actual historical forts I've mentioned in Britannia. There are brief mentions of the names in funerary altars, or on written tablets, (though the time period covered by the novel may not equate).

Ovidus (Optio at Vinovia Fort)
Quirinus (Prefect of Corstopitum Supply Fortress);
Rubrius (of Cohort IV at Trimontium)
Spectatus (Centurion at Vinovia fort)

About the Author

Nancy Jardine's passion for all aspects of history continues, the Ancient Roman invasion of northern Britain having become a deep study. Those barbarians (according to the Romans) who lived beyond the Roman Empire's boundaries left secrets that have still to be unravelled. Thankfully, there are hundreds of archaeological projects being undertaken and it's so welcome that the findings are shared with the general public very quickly. Since she became a devotee of the academia.org site Nancy now has far more academic archaeological papers to read than she can cope with! It's worth mentioning here that there are so many theories about what Roman Britain was like but…we don't really know and that's part of the fun, and the slog to find out.

When not researching, or engaged in various writing and marketing tasks, Nancy is a fair-weather gardener. The 'castle' country of Aberdeenshire, Scotland, is a fabulous place to live—there are thousands of years of history on the doorstep which she delights in. This can be through physical visits, when possible, and also via the internet.

A member of an Aberdeenshire Crafters group, she takes the opportunity to sign and sell paperback versions of her novels at various local venues. She relishes the meetings with new readers and with customers who have become regular buyers of her work. This direct contact is also a fabulous way to gain bookings for the author presentations she gives to various groups across Aberdeenshire. Some smaller groups prefer to learn about her novels, though many larger groups book her for professional presentations on Roman Scotland.

Since retiring from primary teaching in 2011, she now has five historical novels published; one historical 'teen' time travel and three contemporary mysteries – two of which have ancestral based plots. Two of her short stories feature in two different published anthologies. She's currently taking a break from writing about the Roman Scotland era and is working on a family saga which begins in Victorian Scotland.

Nancy is a member of the Historical Novel Society; The Romantic Novelists Association; The Scottish Association of Writers, The Federation of Writers Scotland and the Alliance of Independent Authors. A quick 'google' search will take you to many other places she is associated with via the internet.

Novels by Nancy Jardine

Historical Fiction
Celtic Fervour Series
Book 1 *The Beltane Choice*
Book 2 *After Whorl: Bran Reborn*
Book 3 *After Whorl: Donning Double Cloaks*
Book 4 *Agricola's Bane*
Book 5 *Beathan The Brigante*

Contemporary Novels
Ancestral/ family tree based Mystery/Thrillers:
Monogamy Twist
Topaz Eyes
Romantic Comedy Mystery
Take Me Now

Time Travel Historical Adventure
Set in Roman Scotland AD 210, *The Taexali Game* is suitable from an early teens through adult readership.

Anthologies- contributions by Nancy Jardine to:
Crooked Cat Tales (short story about characters from Topaz Eyes)
Doorways To The Past: (short story about Ruoridh of Garrigill and Feargus of Monymusk- Celtic Fervour Saga Series)

Buy in e-book and print from **Amazon (Type Nancy Jardine to make a search on Amazon).** Paperback versions of all novels are available to order from bookstores.

Nominations

After Whorl: Bran Reborn, Book 2 of the Celtic Fervour Series, was accepted for THE WALTER SCOTT PRIZE FOR HISTORICAL FICTION 2014.

The Taexali Game, a time travel novel set in Roman 'Aberdeenshire' AD 210 achieved Second Place for Best Self-Published Book in the SCOTTISH ASSOCIATION OF WRITERS – Barbara Hammond Competition 2017. It achieved an *indieBRAG* Medallion status, January 2018.

Topaz Eyes, an ancestral based mystery thriller, was a Finalist for THE PEOPLE'S BOOK PRIZE FICTION 2014

Books in the *Celtic Fervour Series* have Discovered Diamond Status and other Book Club awards.

Ocelot Press

Thank you for reading this Ocelot Press book. If you enjoyed it, we'd greatly appreciate it if you could take a moment to write a short review on the website where you bought the book e.g. Amazon, and/or on Goodreads, You can email the author and/ or recommend the book to a friend. Sharing your thoughts helps other readers to choose good books, and authors to keep writing.

You might like to try books by other Ocelot Press authors. We cover a range of genres, with a focus on historical fiction (including historical mystery and paranormal), romance and fantasy. To find out more, please don't hesitate to connect with us on:

Website: https://ocelotpress.wordpress.com
Email: ocelotpress@gmail.com
Twitter: @OcelotPress
Facebook: https://www.facebook.com/OcelotPress/

Lightning Source UK Ltd.
Milton Keynes UK
UKHW021848300921
391375UK00012B/291

9 781916 003880